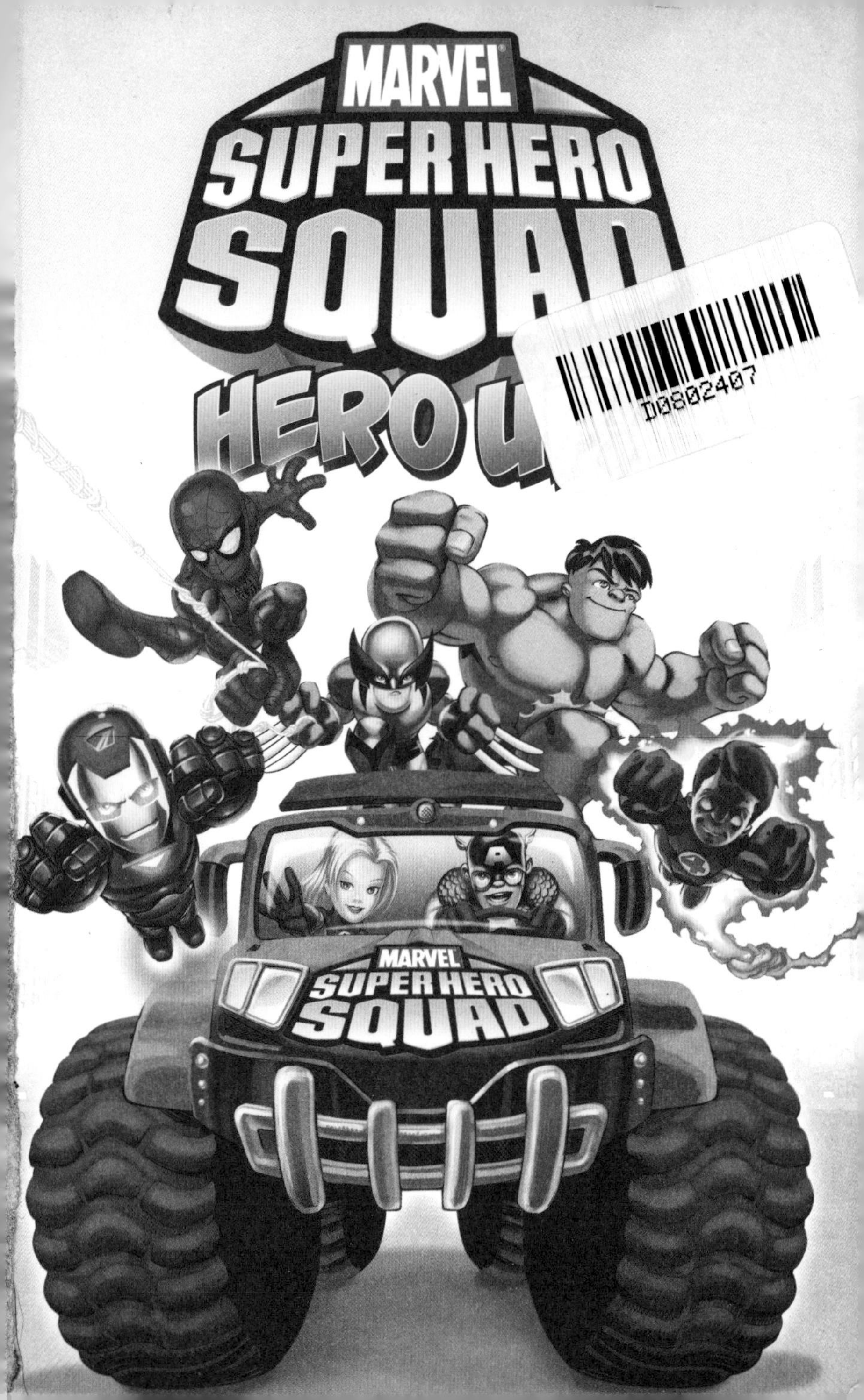
MARVEL
SUPER HERO
SQUAD
HERO
MARVEL
SUPER HERO
SQUAD

MARVEL SUPER HERO SQUAD

HERO UP!

PAUL TOBIN - SCRIPTS AND IDEAS
MARCELO DICHIARA, TODD NAUCK, DARIO BRIZUELA - ART
CHRIS SOTOMAYOR - COLORS
BLAMBOT'S NATE PIEKOS - LETTERS
DICHIARA & SOTOMAYOR - COVER ART
NATHAN COSBY - EDITOR

SUPER SPECIAL THANKS TO COURTNEY LANE,
CHRIS FONDACARO, TOM MARVELLI, PAT MCGRATH,
MARK PANICCIA, RUWAN JAYATILLEKE,
TIM DILLON AND MIKE PASCIULLO

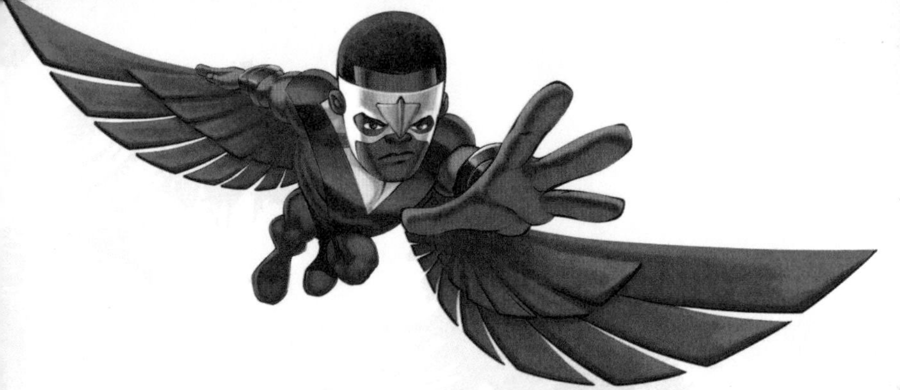

COLLECTION EDITOR: CORY LEVINE
ASSISTANT EDITORS: ALEX STARBUCK & JOHN DENNING
EDITORS, SPECIAL PROJECTS: JENNIFER GRÜNWALD & MARK D. BEAZLEY
SENIOR EDITOR, SPECIAL PROJECTS: JEFF YOUNGQUIST
SENIOR VICE PRESIDENT OF SALES: DAVID GABRIEL
COVER DESIGN: DAYLE CHESLER
INTERIOR DESIGN: NANCY LEE

EDITOR IN CHIEF: JOE QUESADA
PUBLISHER: DAN BUCKLEY
EXECUTIVE PRODUCER: ALAN FINE

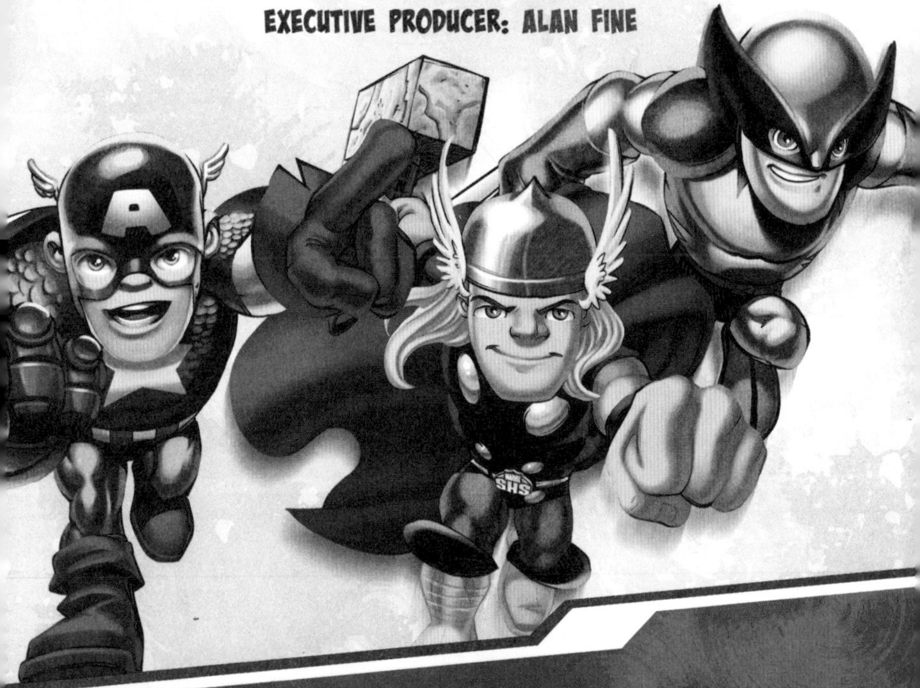

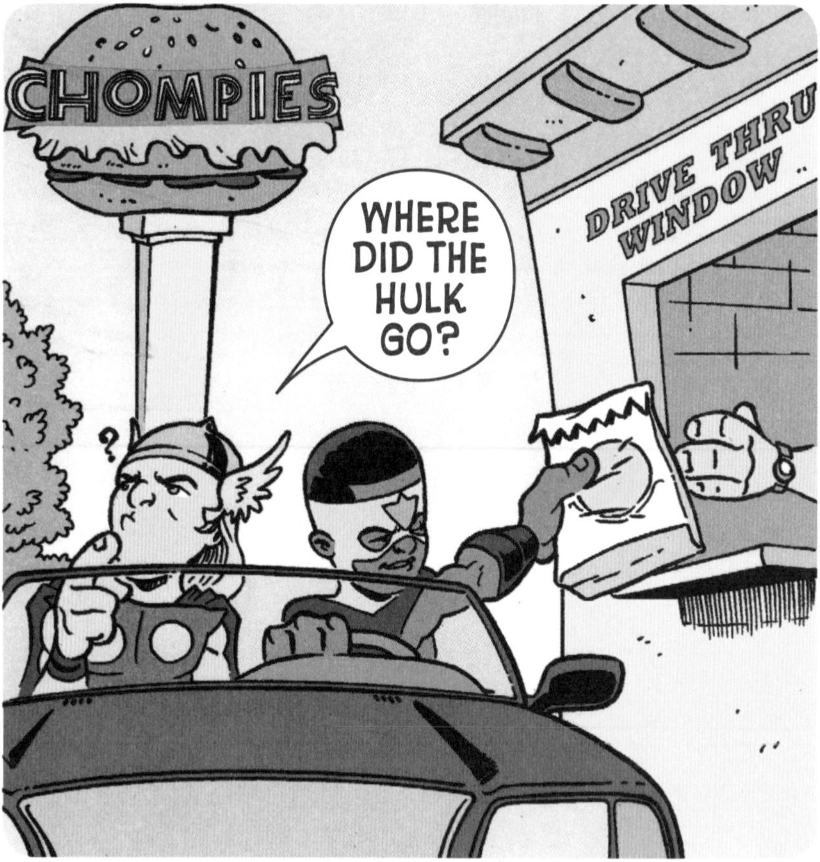
CHOMPIES
DRIVE THRU WINDOW
WHERE DID THE HULK GO?
?

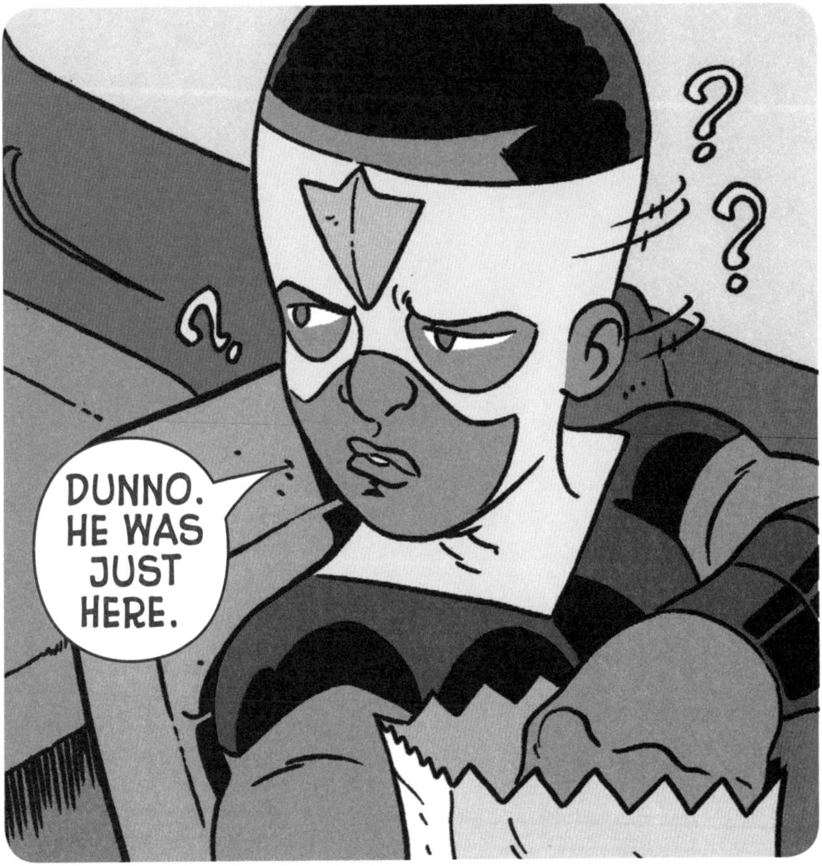
DUNNO. HE WAS JUST HERE.

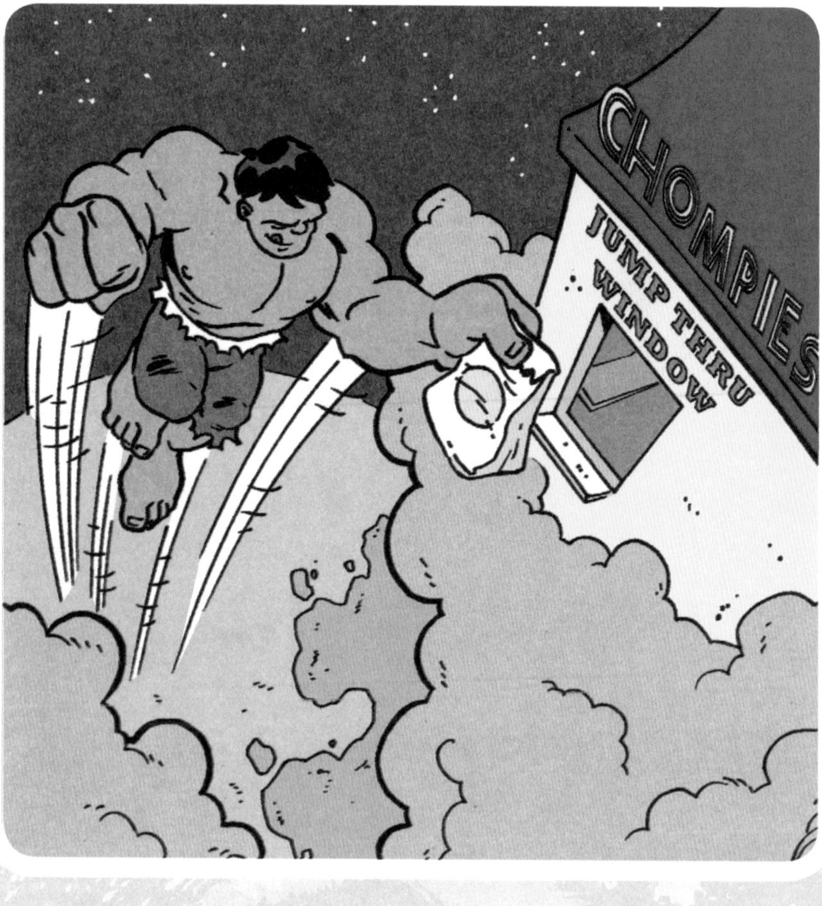
CHOMPIES
JUMP THRU WINDOW

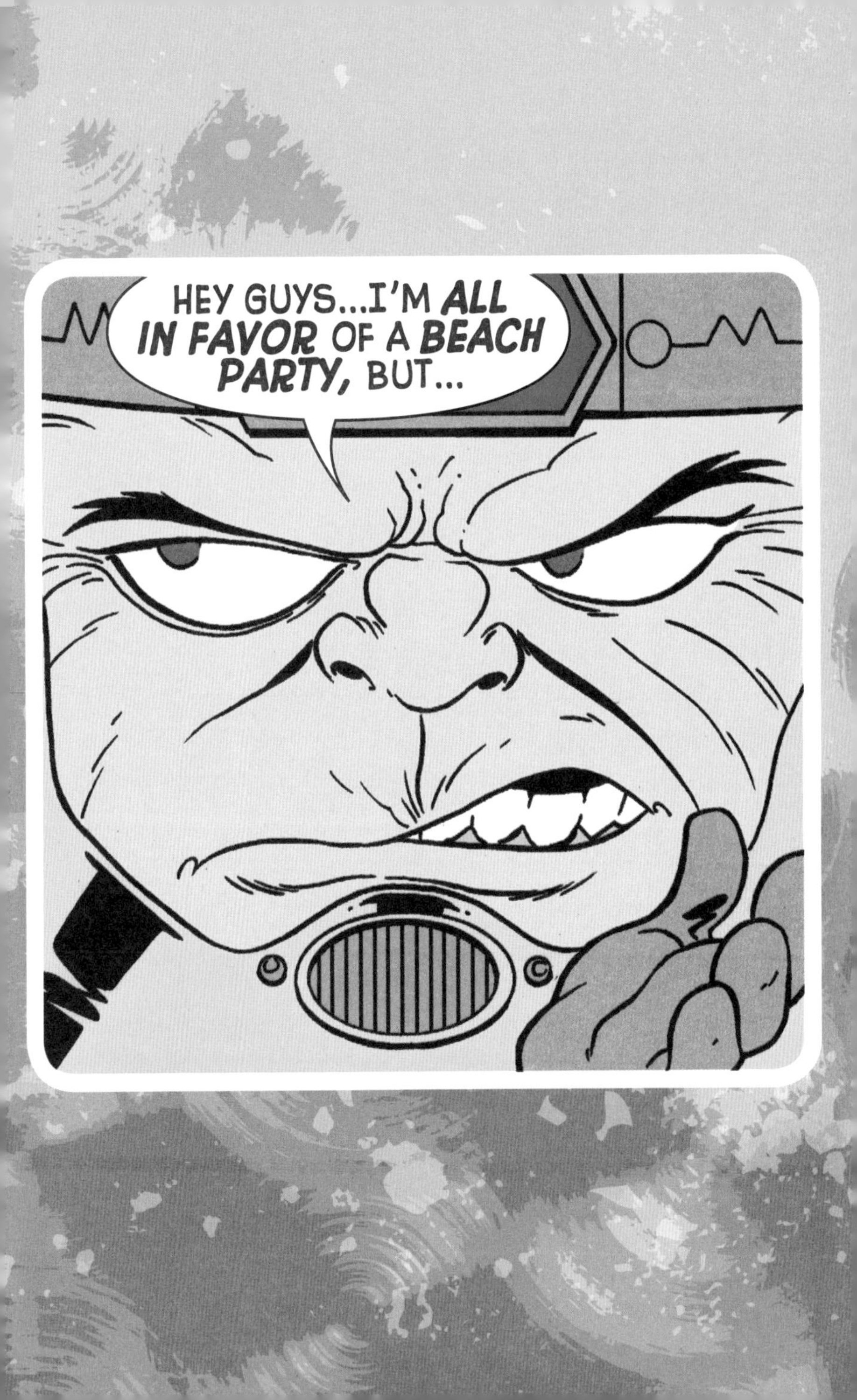
HEY GUYS...I'M ALL IN FAVOR OF A BEACH PARTY, BUT...

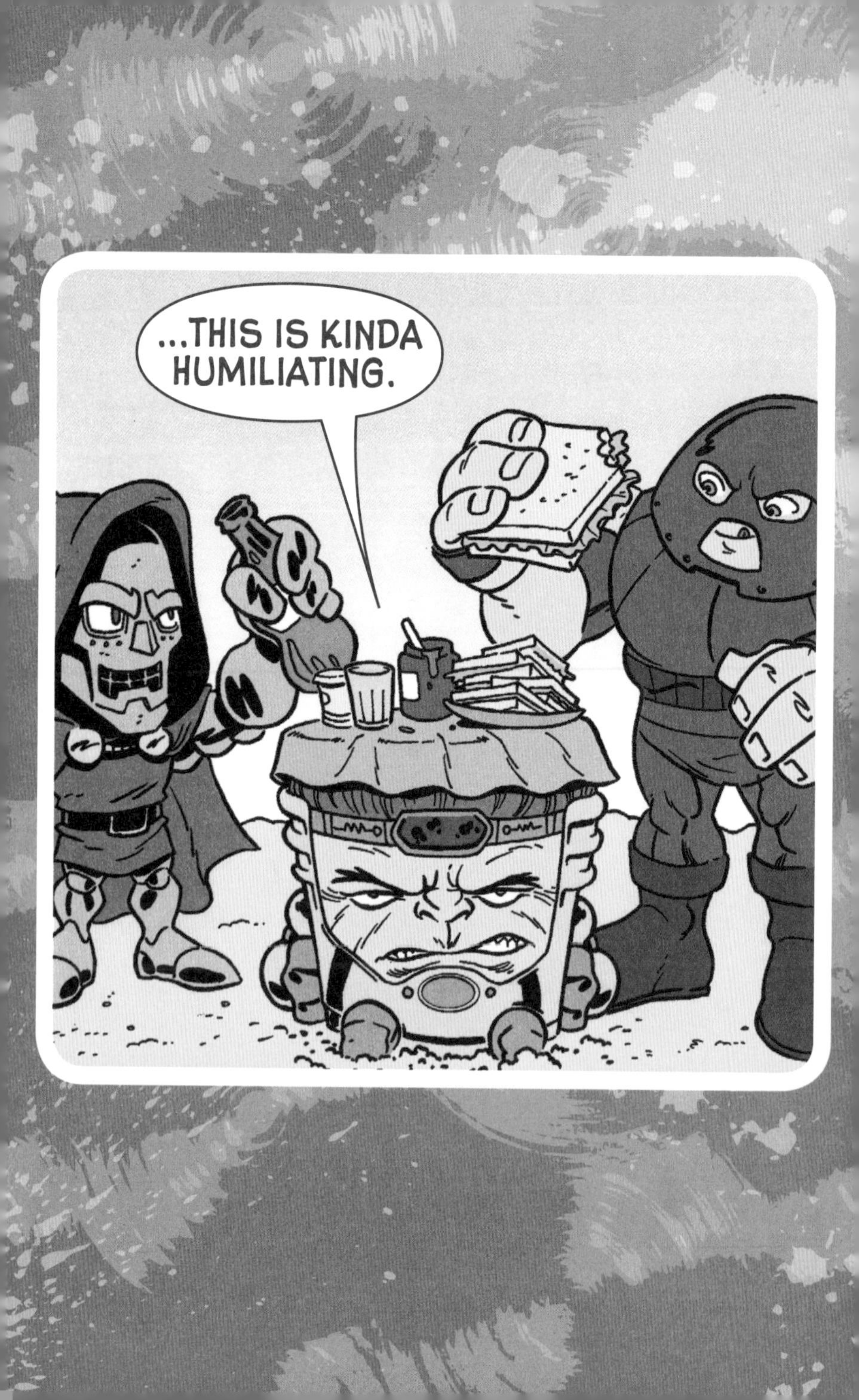
...THIS IS KINDA HUMILIATING.

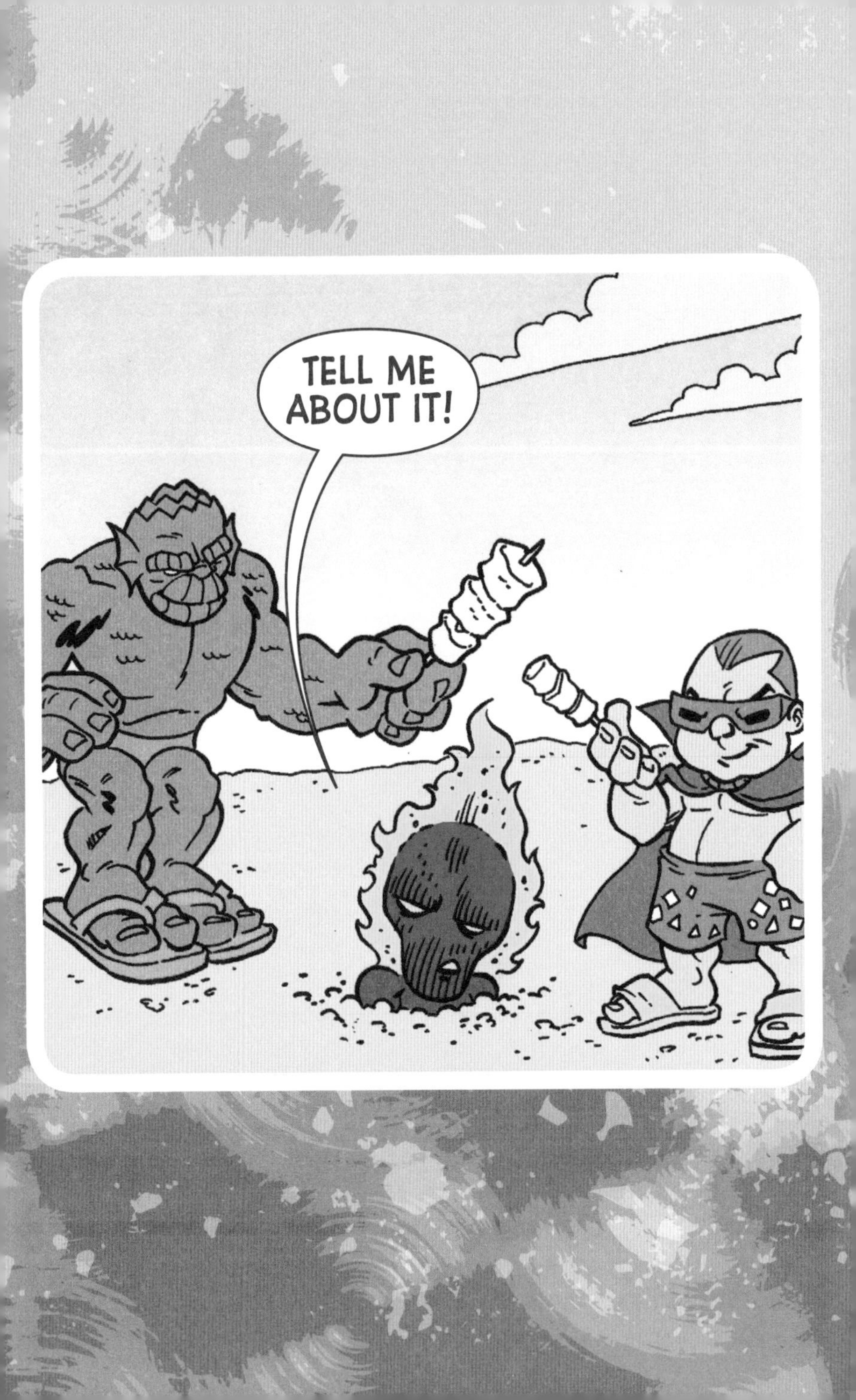
TELL ME ABOUT IT!

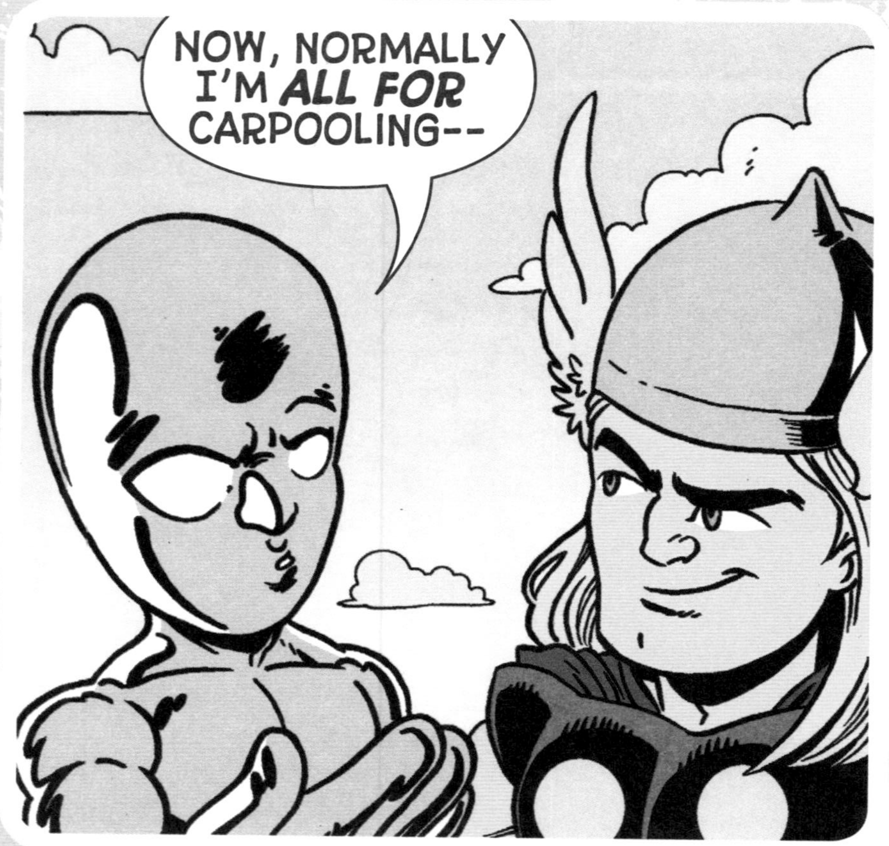
NOW, NORMALLY I'M ALL FOR CARPOOLING--

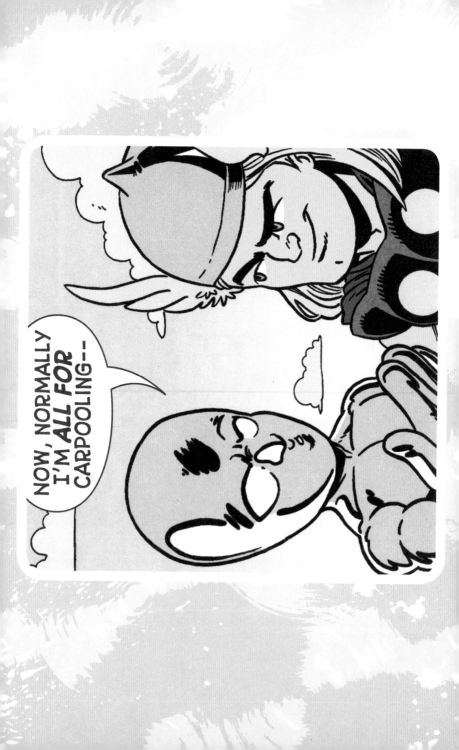

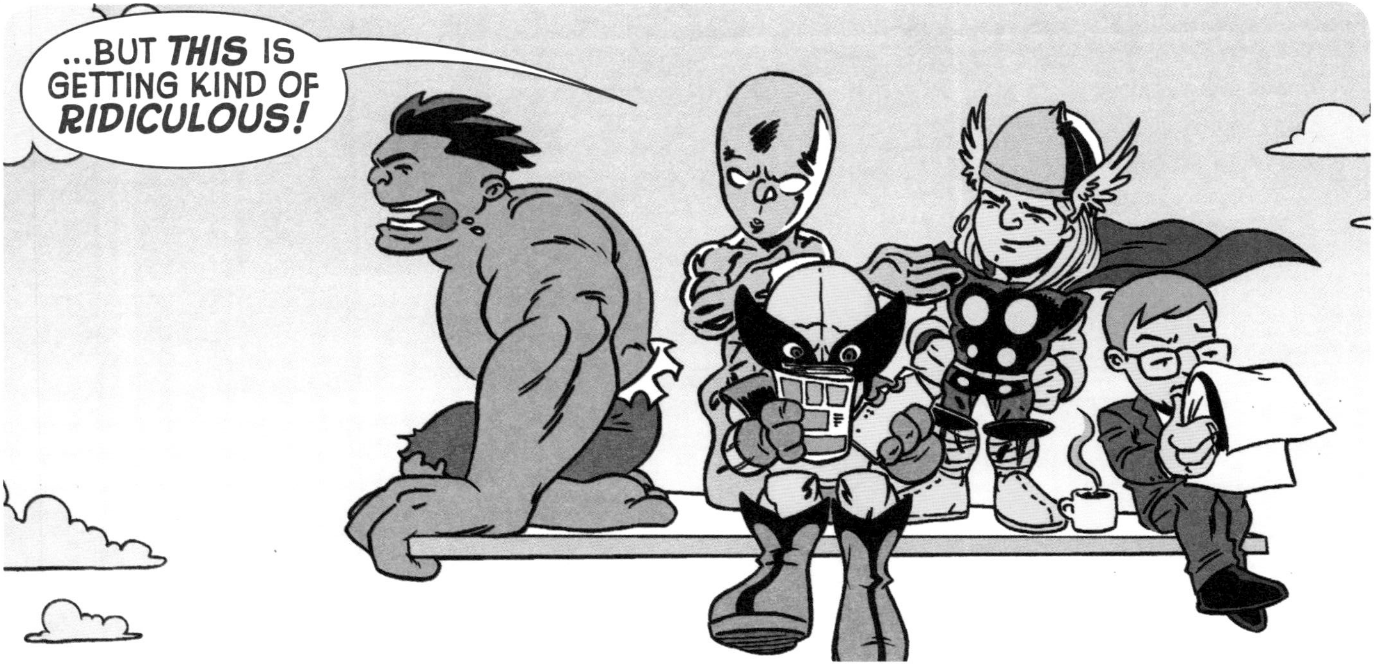
...BUT THIS IS GETTING KIND OF RIDICULOUS!

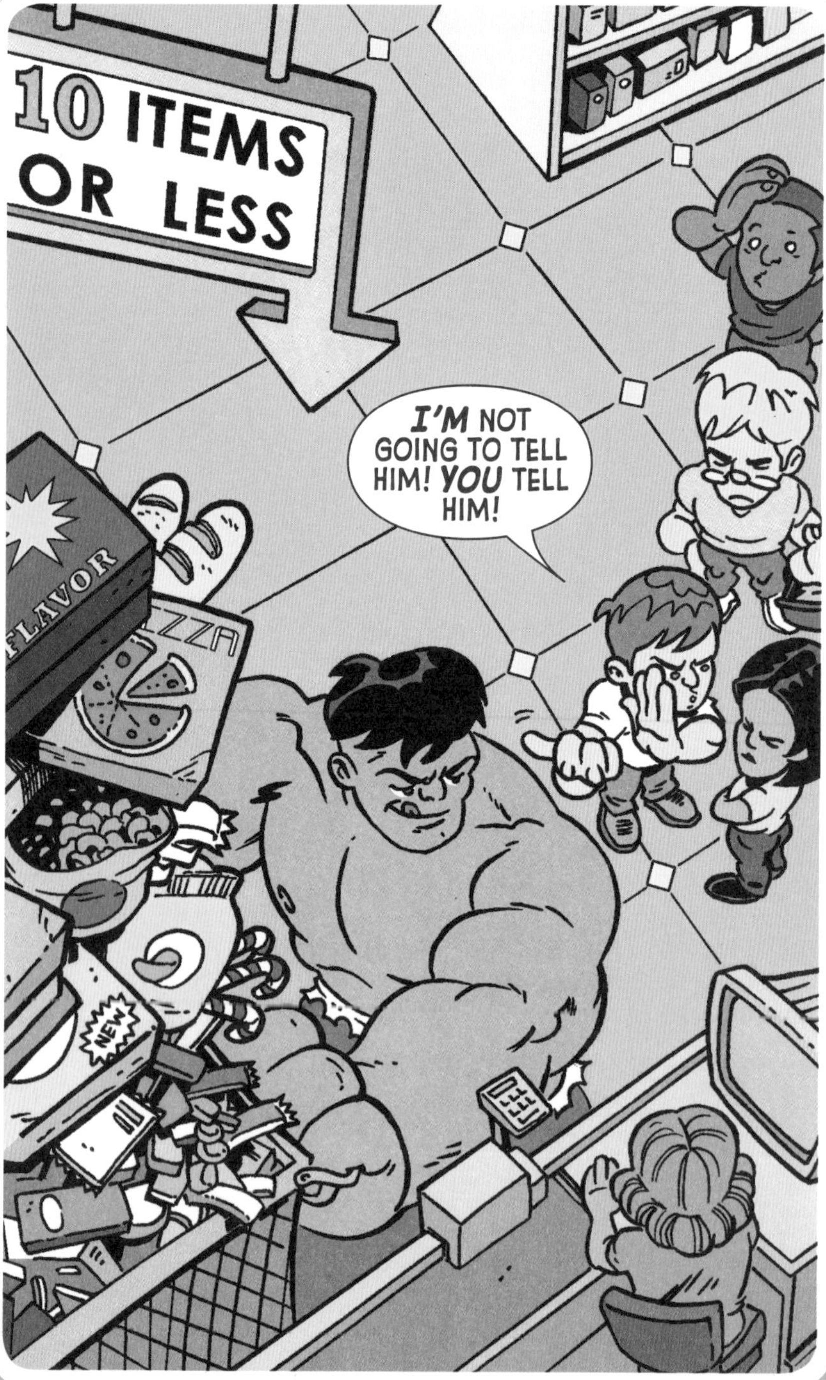
10 ITEMS OR LESS
I'M NOT GOING TO TELL HIM! YOU TELL HIM!
FLAVOR
NEW

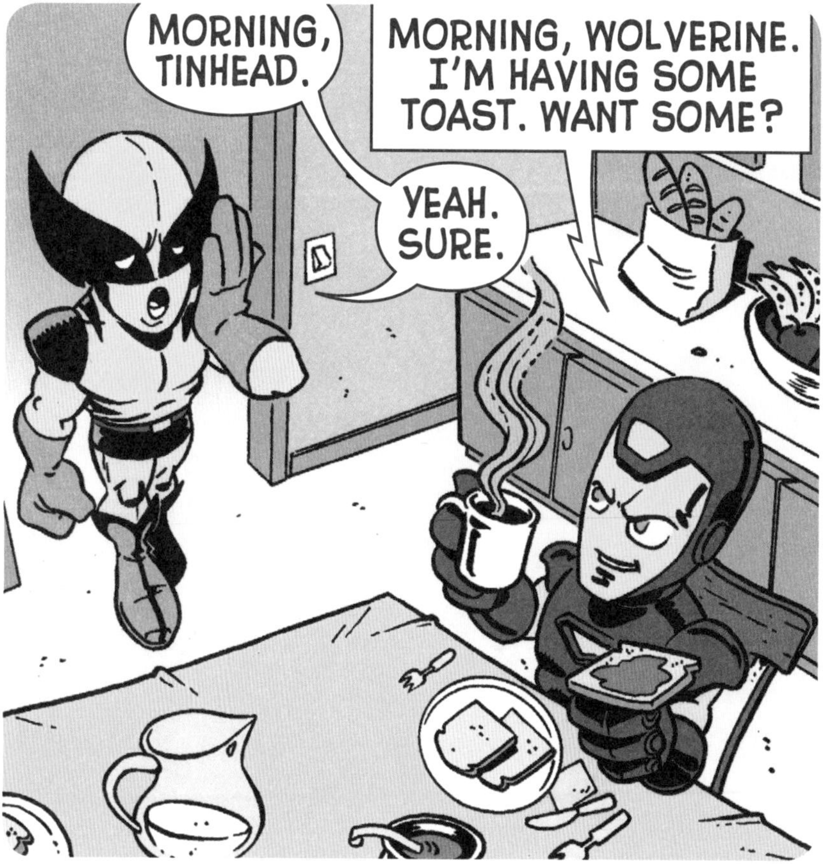
MORNING, TINHEAD.
MORNING, WOLVERINE. I'M HAVING SOME TOAST. WANT SOME?
YEAH. SURE.

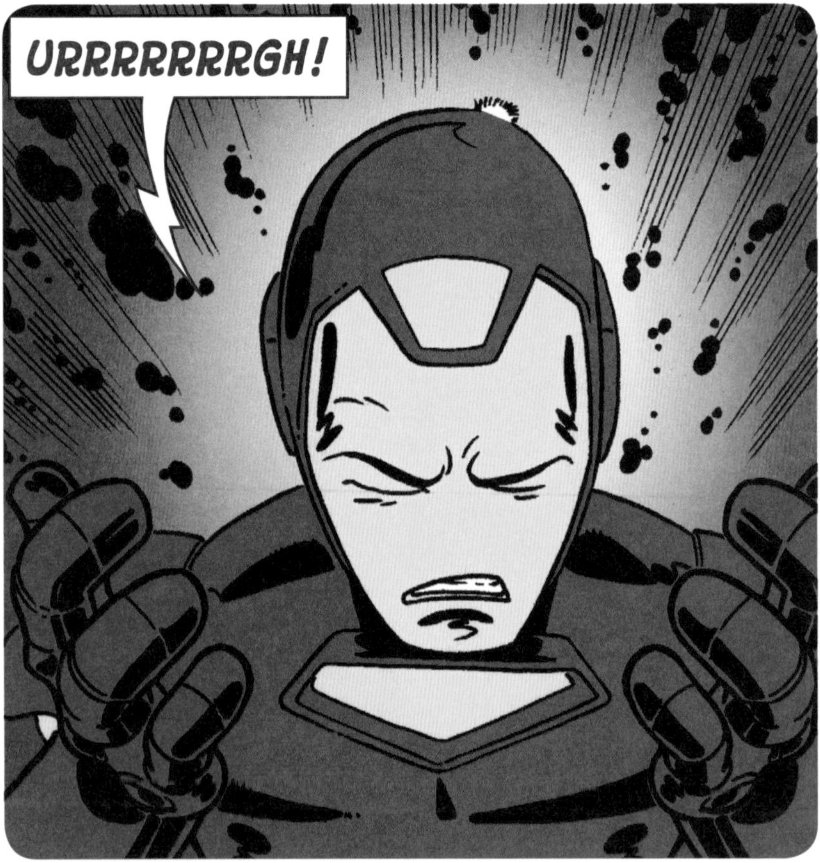
URRRRRRRGH!

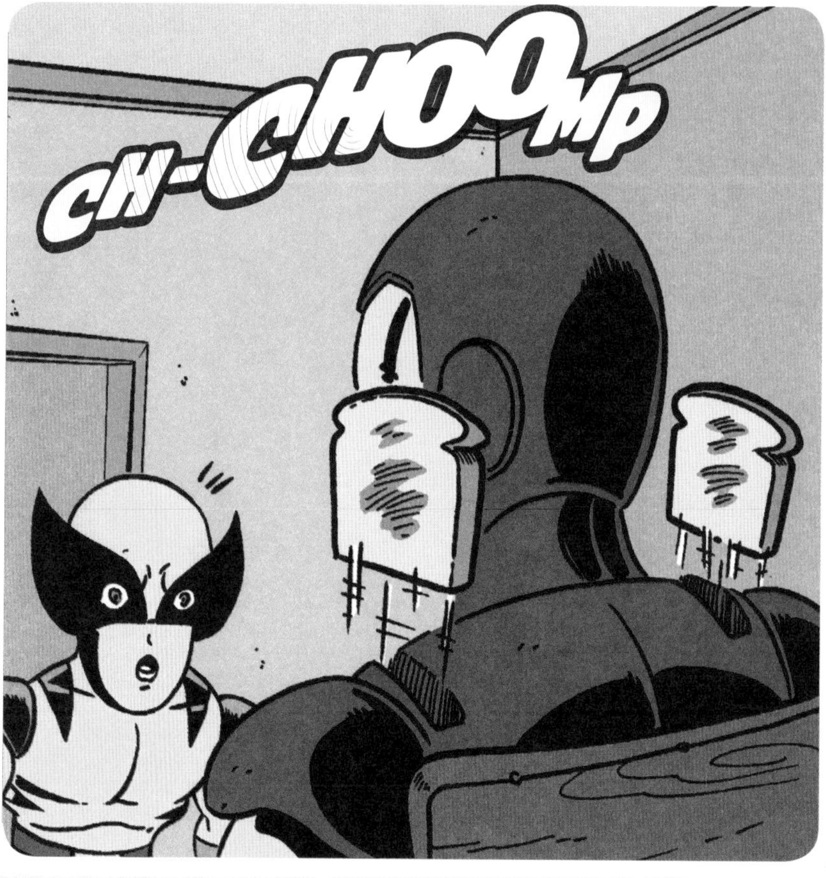
CH-CHOOMP

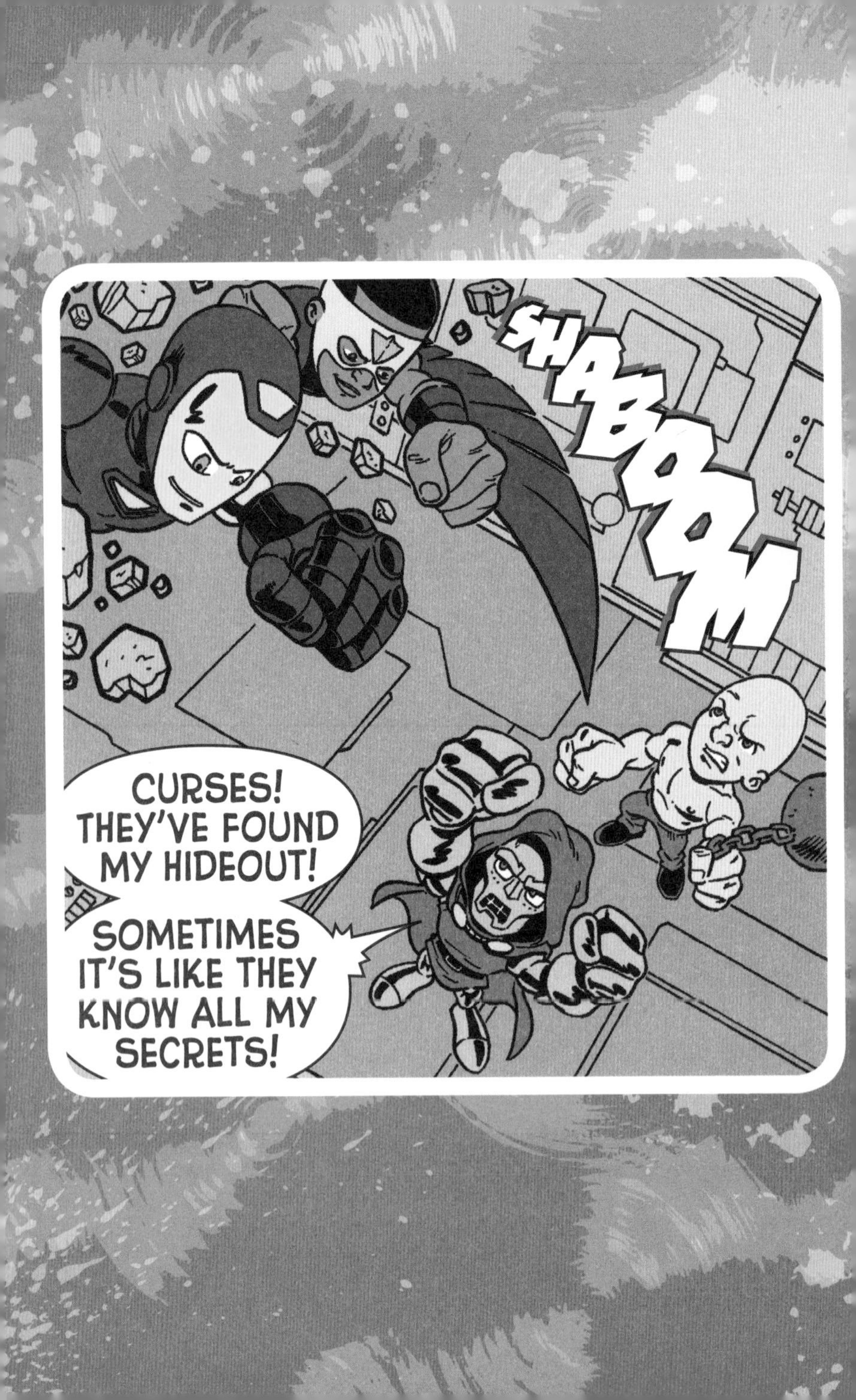
SHABOOM
CURSES! THEY'VE FOUND MY HIDEOUT!
SOMETIMES IT'S LIKE THEY KNOW ALL MY SECRETS!

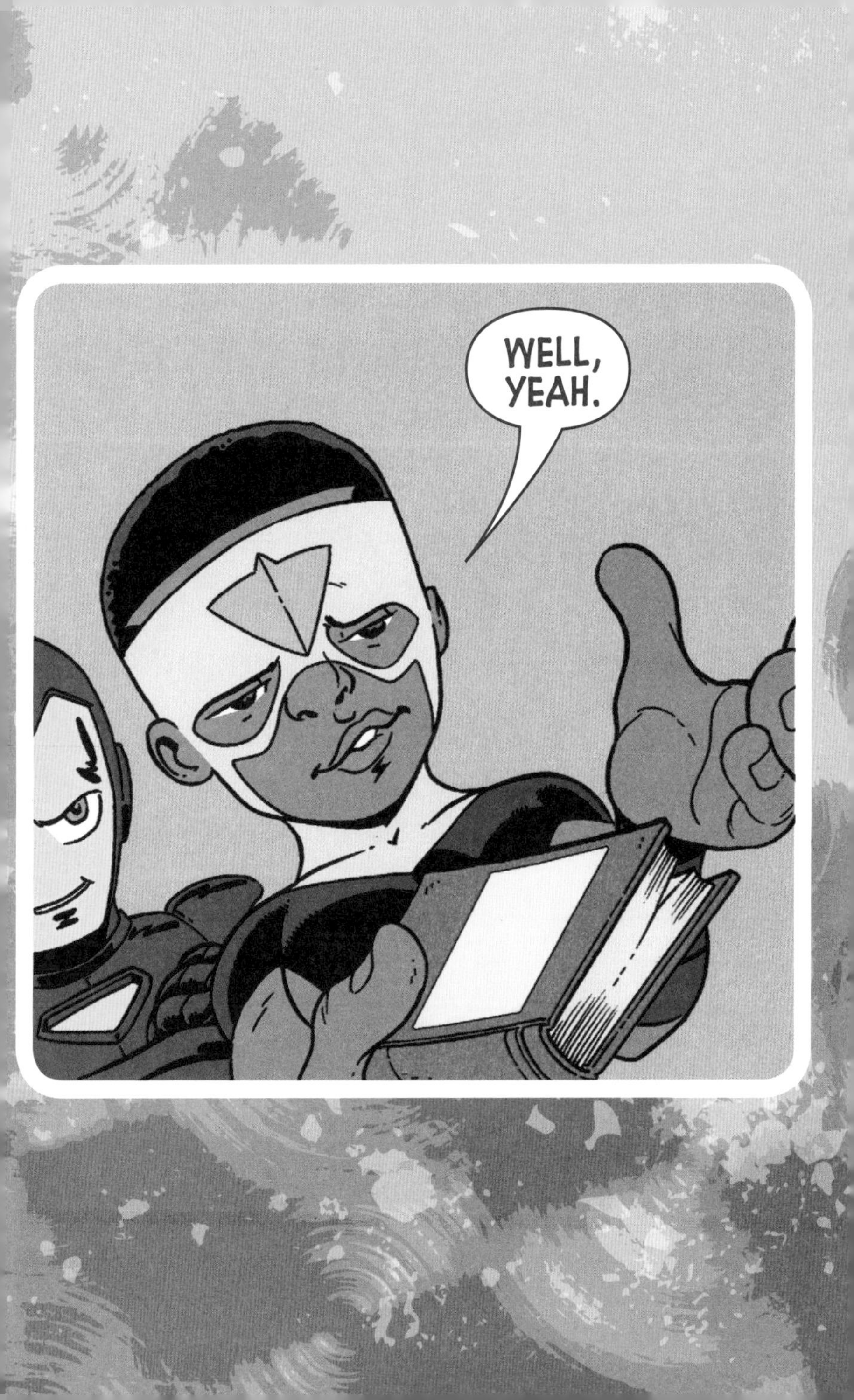
WELL, YEAH.

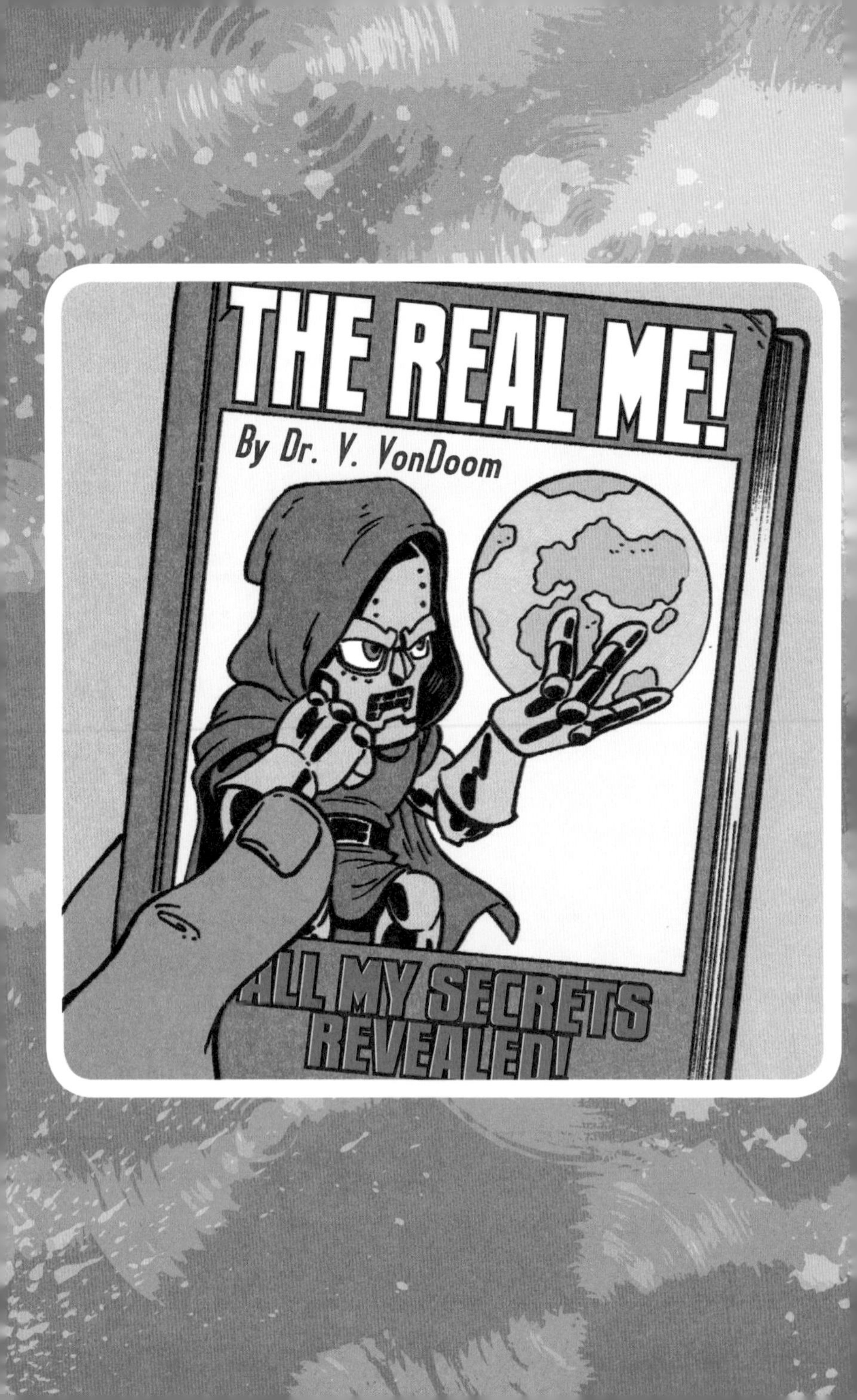
THE REAL ME!
By Dr. V. VonDoom
ALL MY SECRETS REVEALED!

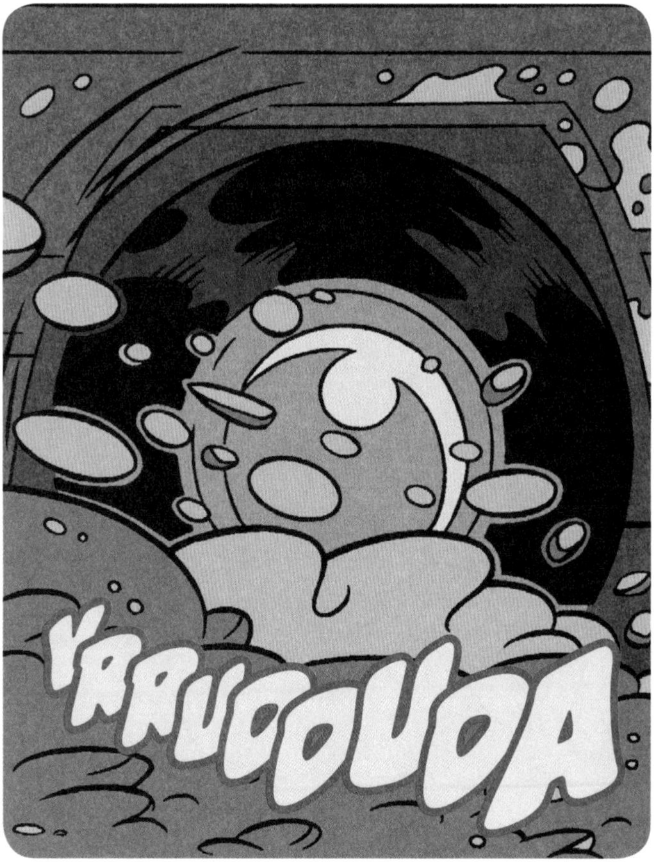
YARUCOUDA

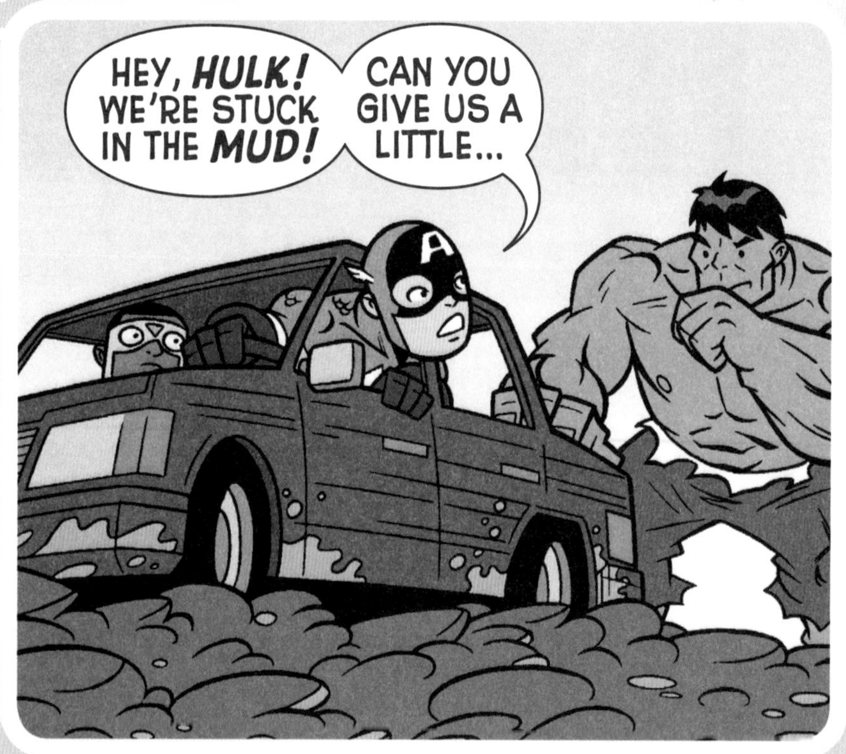
HEY, HULK! WE'RE STUCK IN THE MUD!
CAN YOU GIVE US A LITTLE...

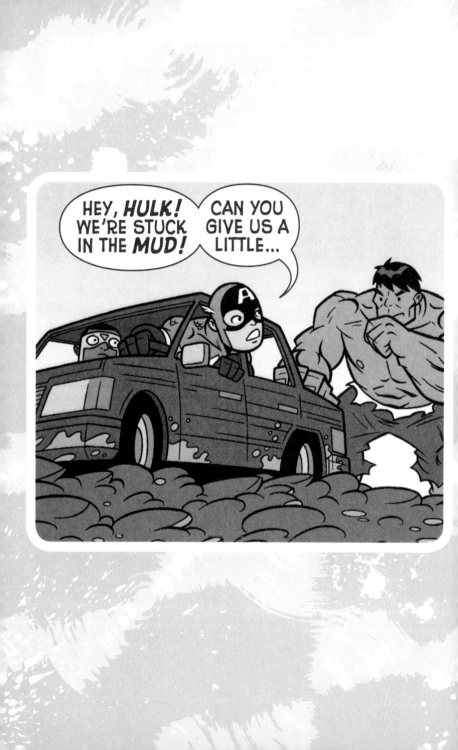

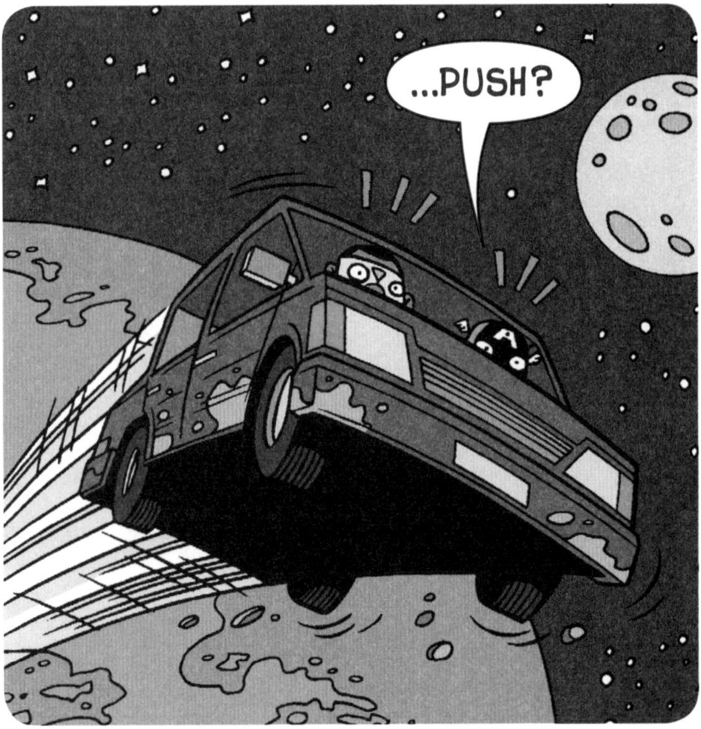
...PUSH?

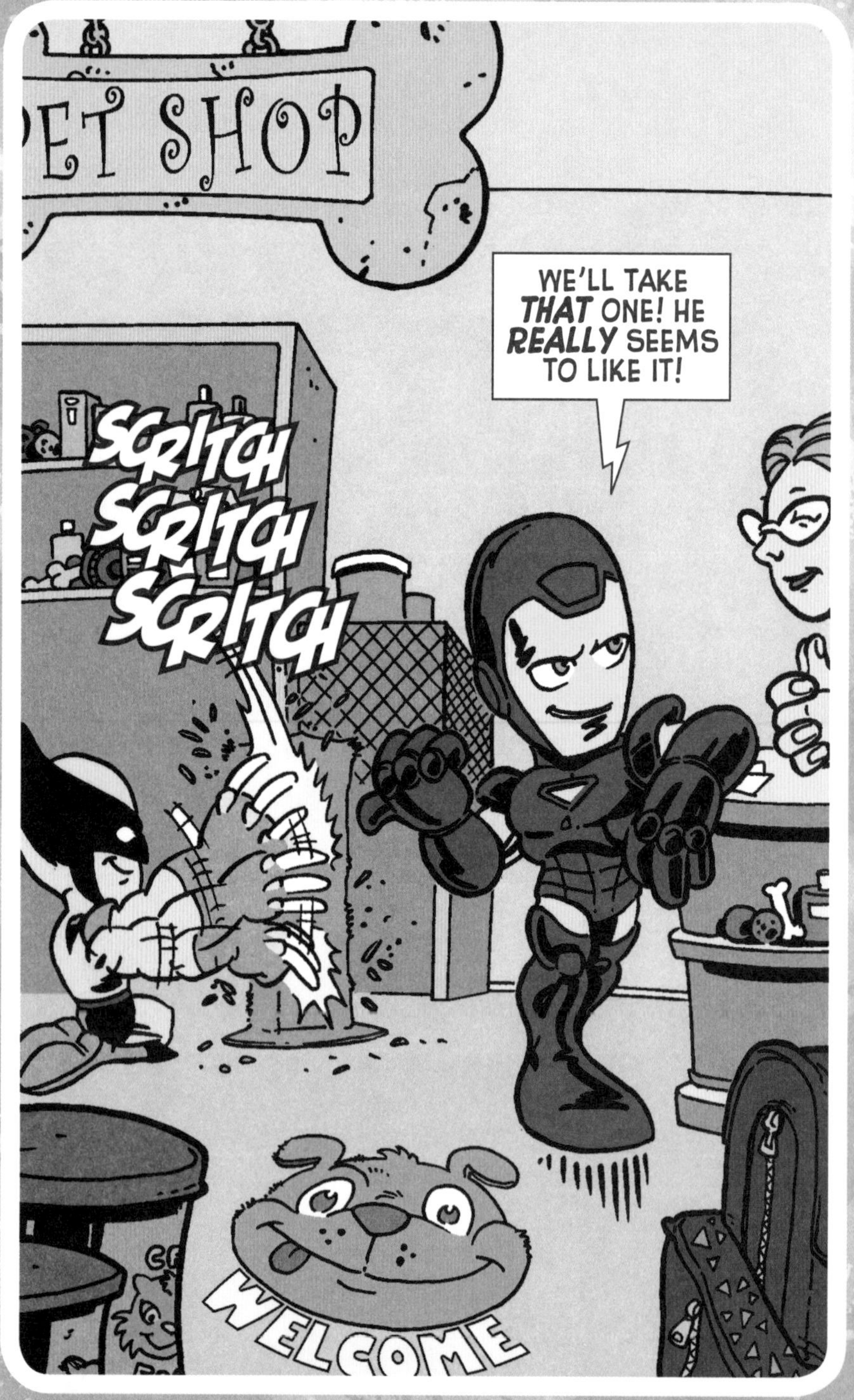
PET SHOP
WE'LL TAKE *THAT* ONE! HE *REALLY* SEEMS TO LIKE IT!
SCRITCH SCRITCH SCRITCH
WELCOME

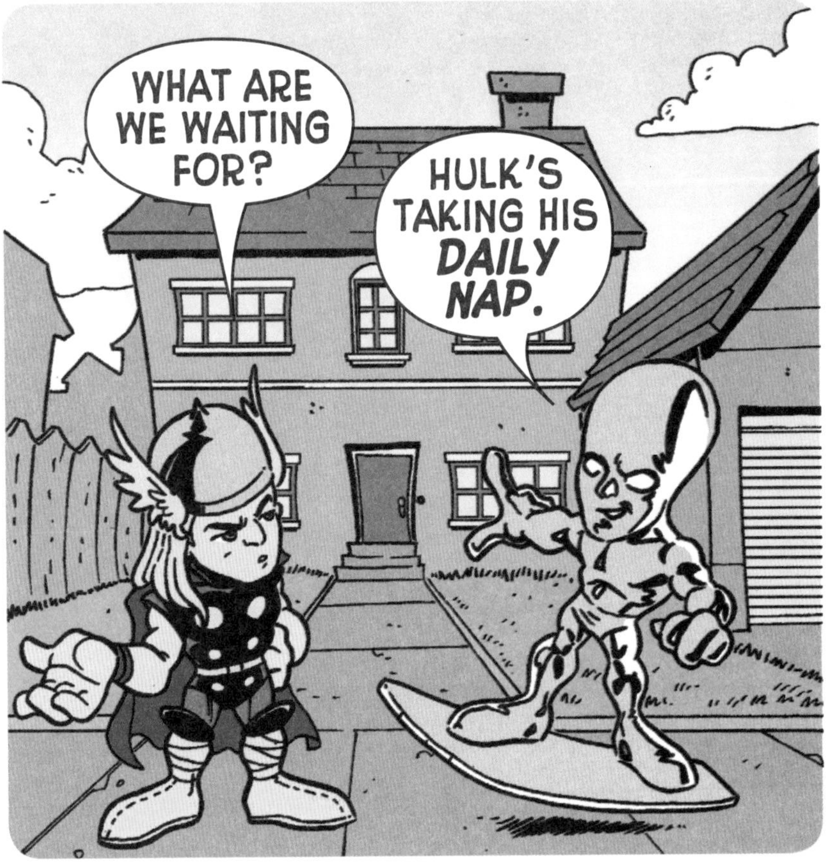
WHAT ARE WE WAITING FOR?
HULK'S TAKING HIS *DAILY NAP.*

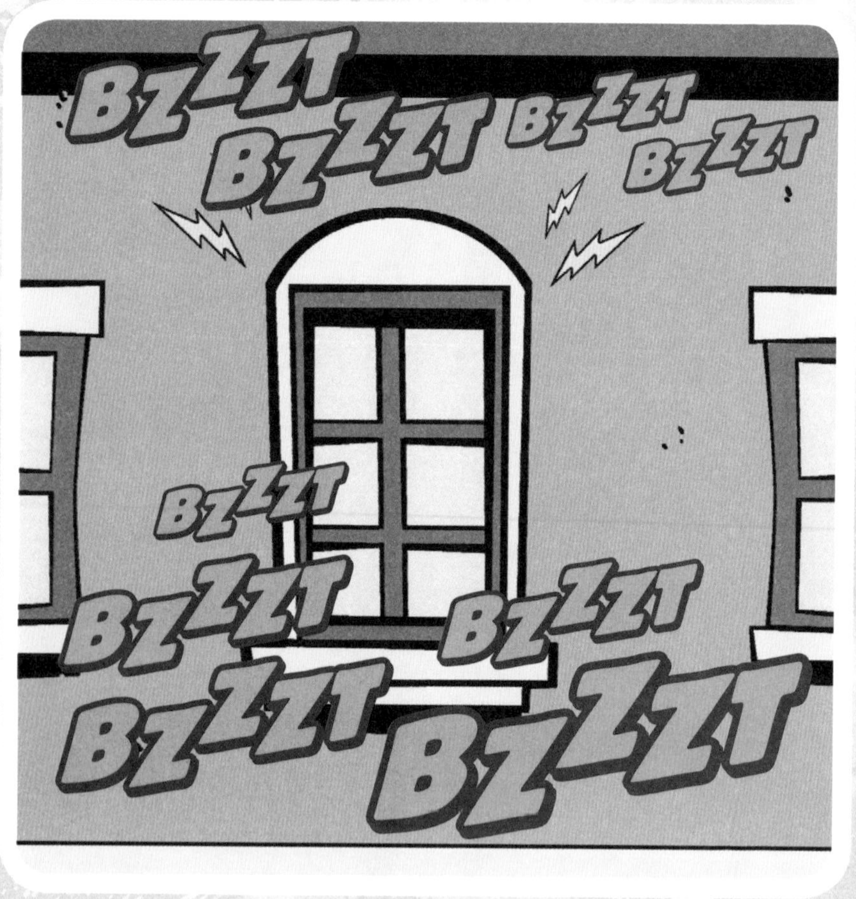
BZZZT
BZZZT
BZZZT
BZZZT
BZZZT
BZZZT
BZZZT
BZZZT
BZZZT

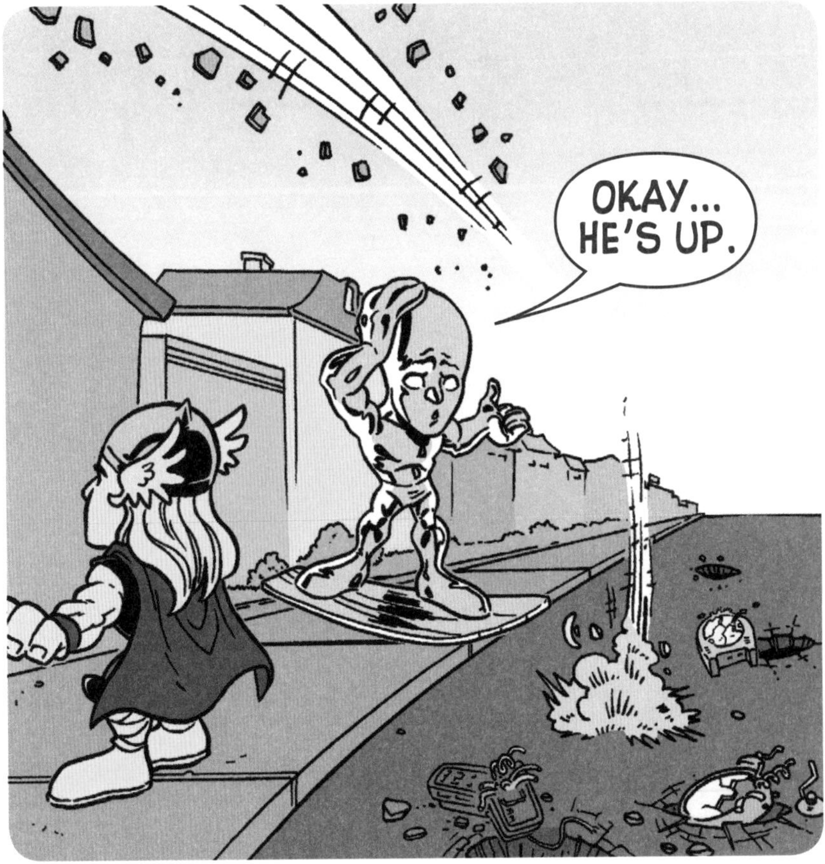
OKAY... HE'S UP.

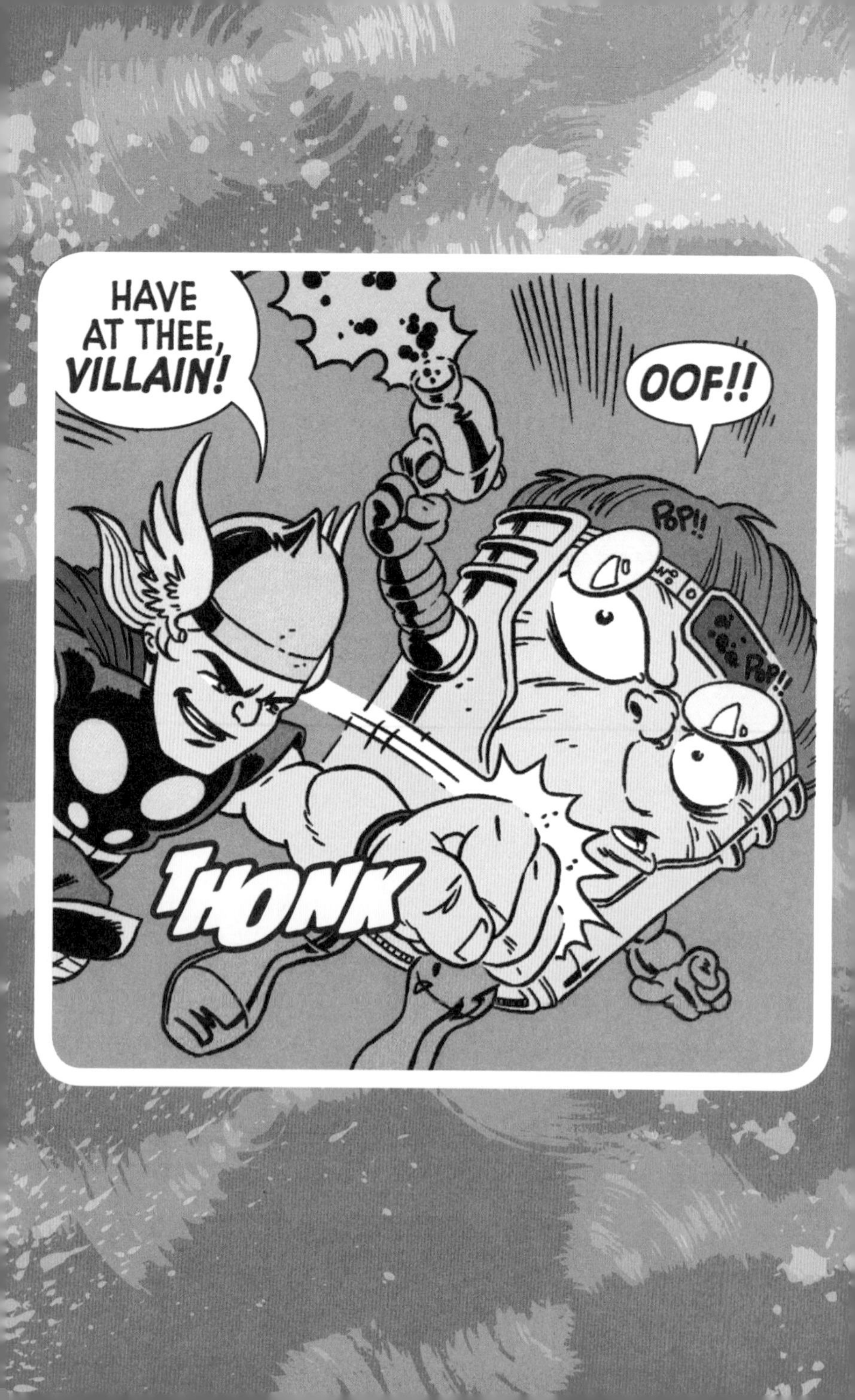
HAVE AT THEE, VILLAIN!
OOF!!
POP!!
POP!!
THONK

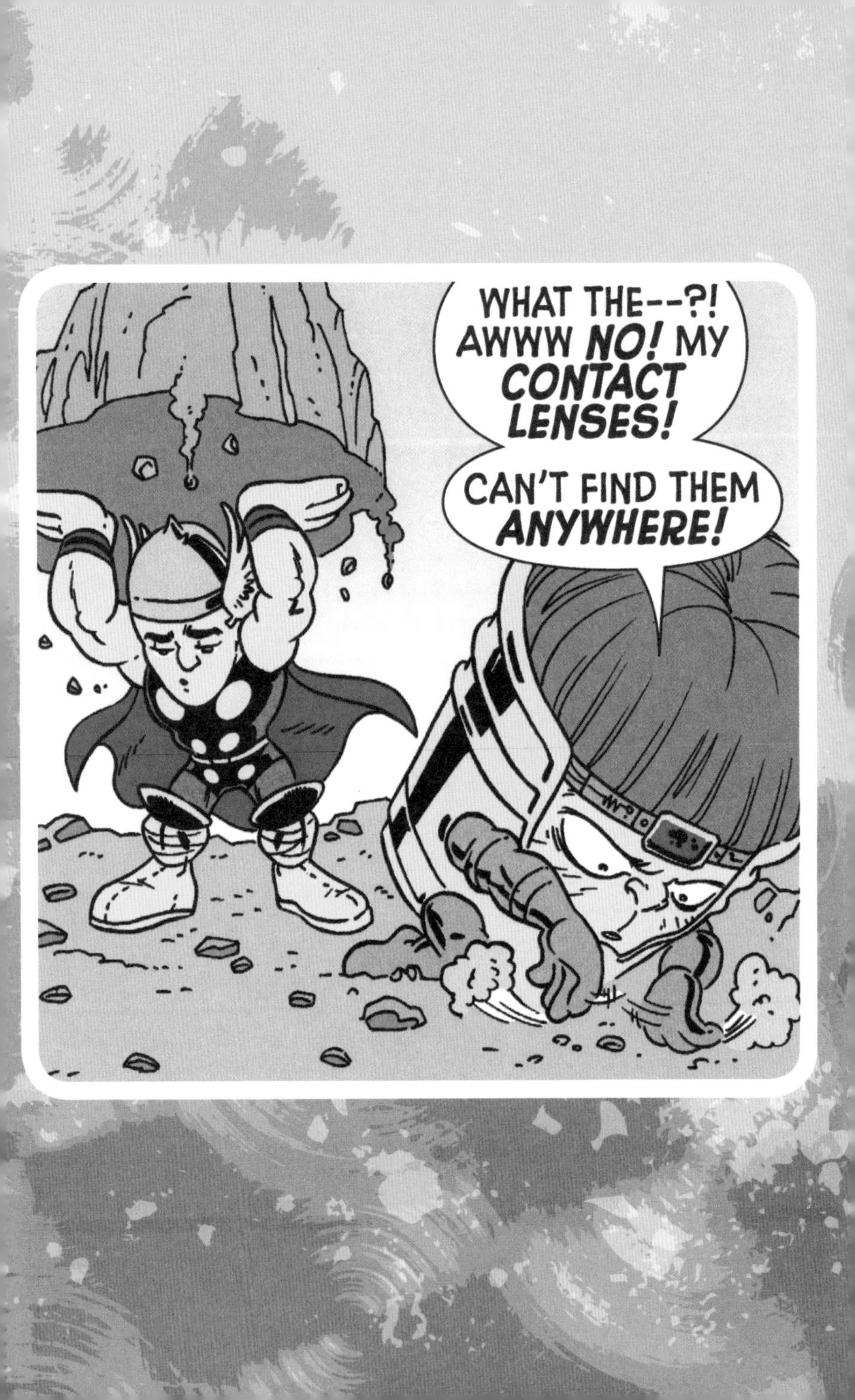
WHAT THE--?! AWWW NO! MY CONTACT LENSES!
CAN'T FIND THEM ANYWHERE!

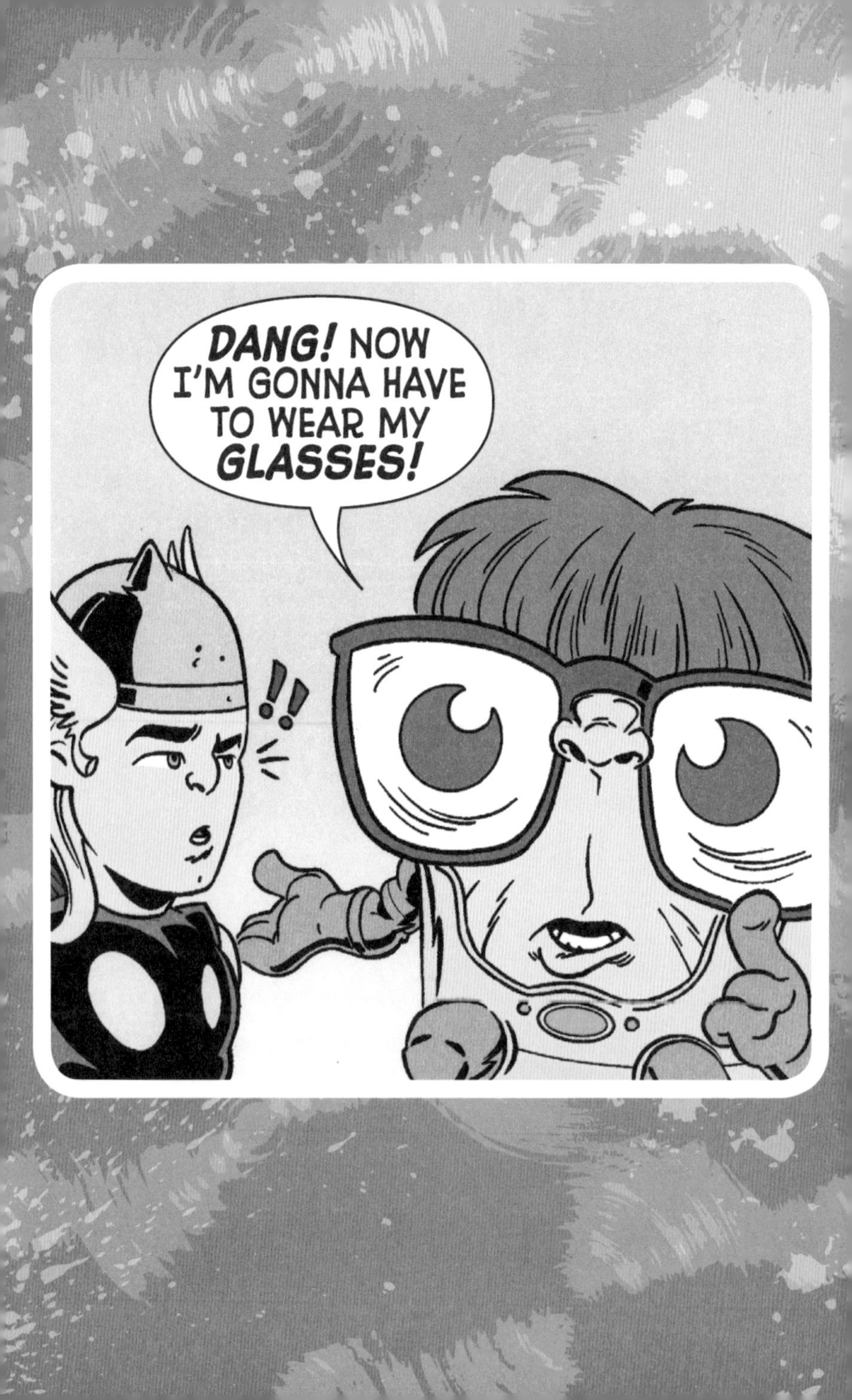
DANG! NOW I'M GONNA HAVE TO WEAR MY GLASSES!
!!

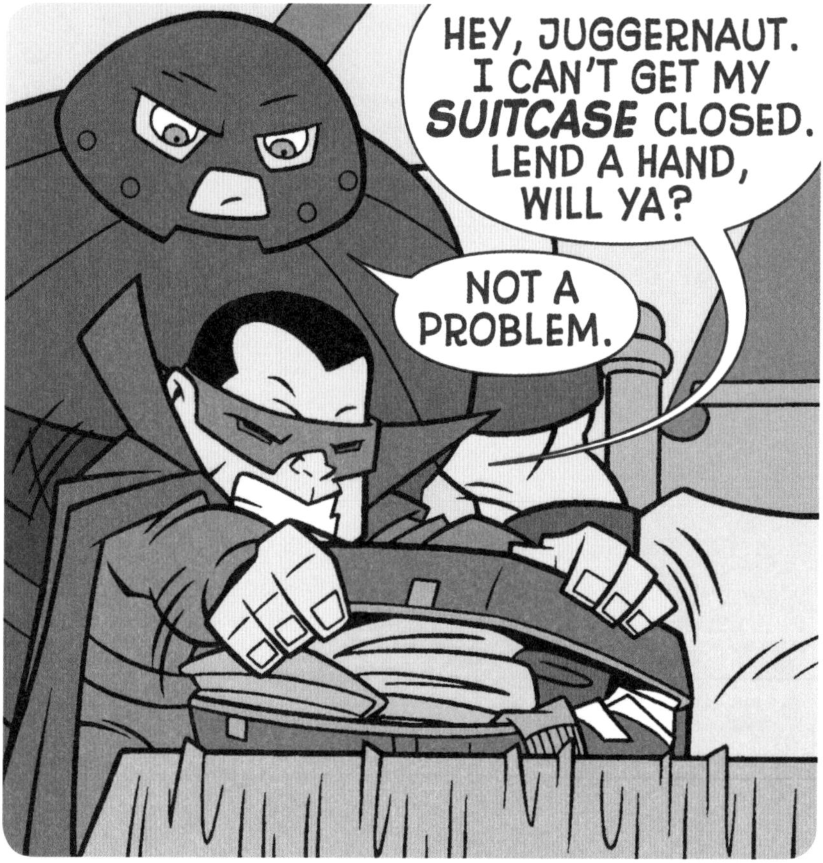
HEY, JUGGERNAUT. I CAN'T GET MY *SUITCASE* CLOSED. LEND A HAND, WILL YA?
NOT A PROBLEM.

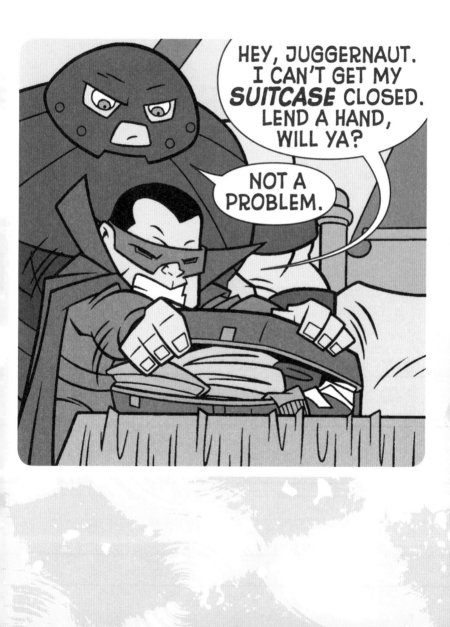

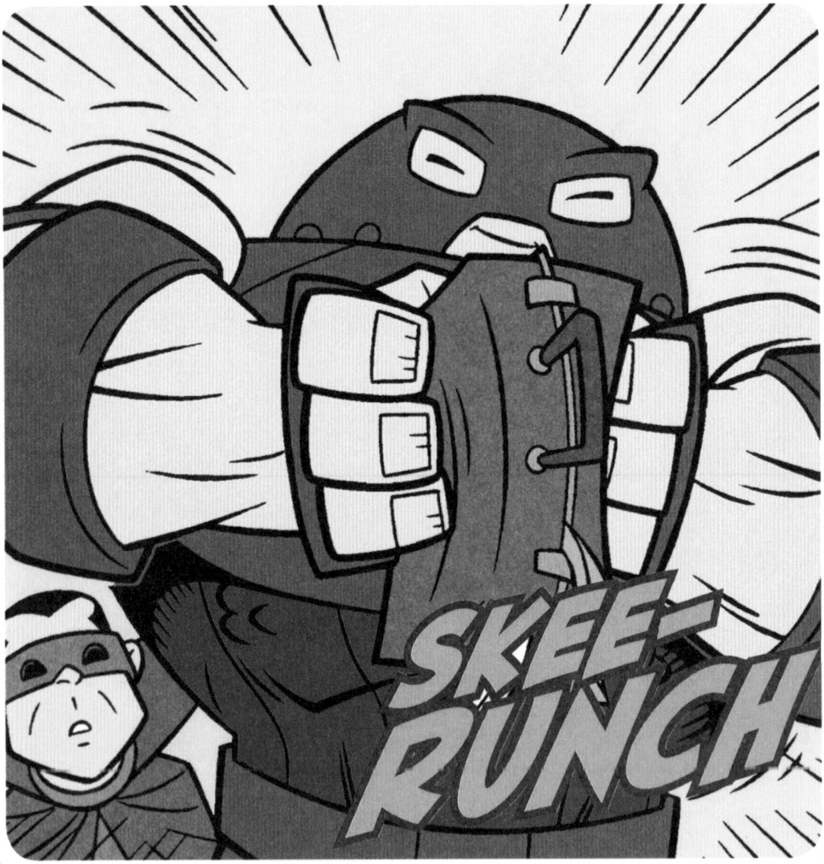
SKEE-RUNCH!

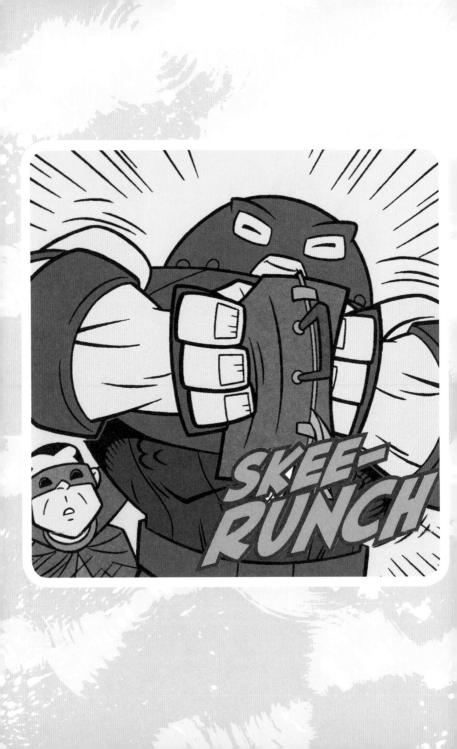

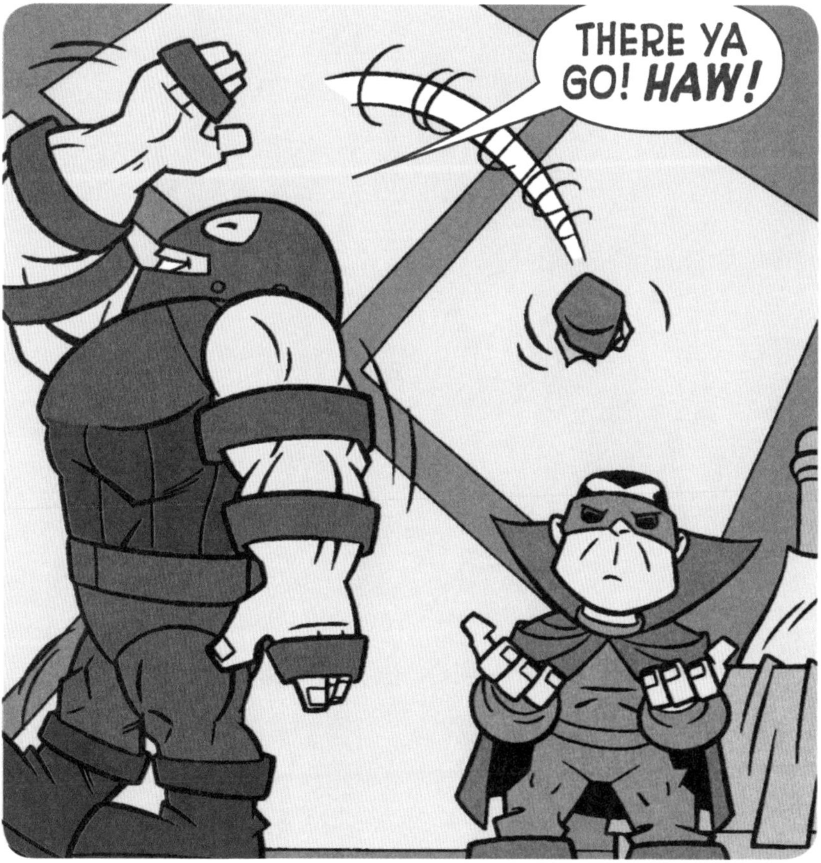
THERE YA GO! HAW!

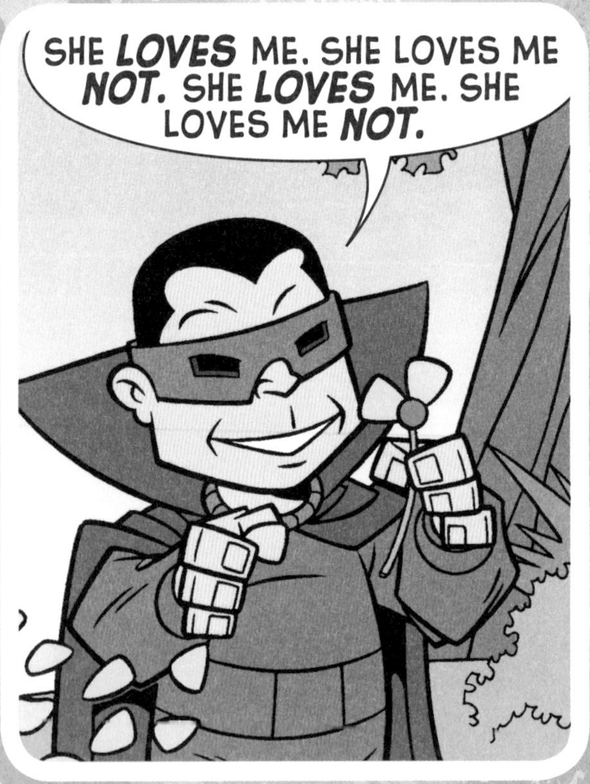
SHE LOVES ME. SHE LOVES ME NOT. SHE LOVES ME. SHE LOVES ME NOT.

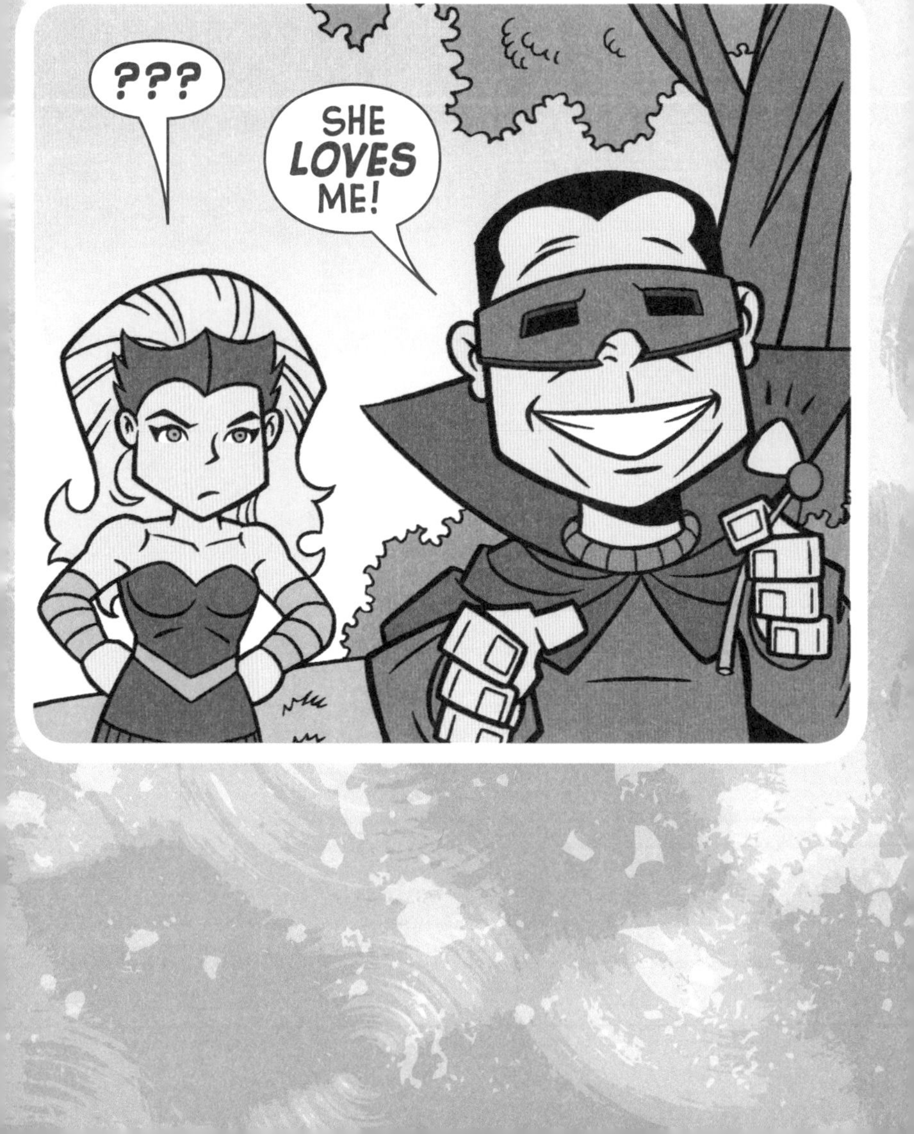
???
SHE LOVES ME!

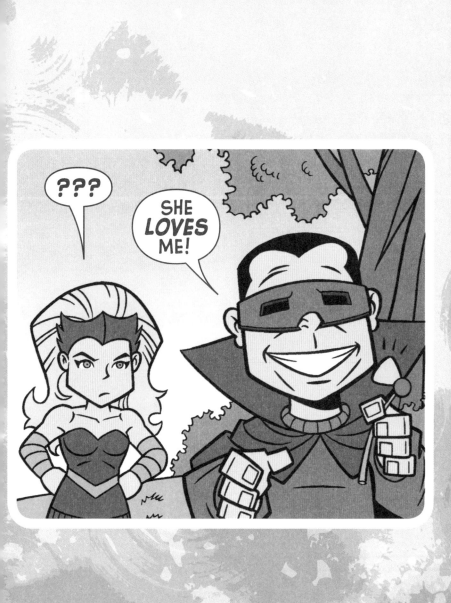

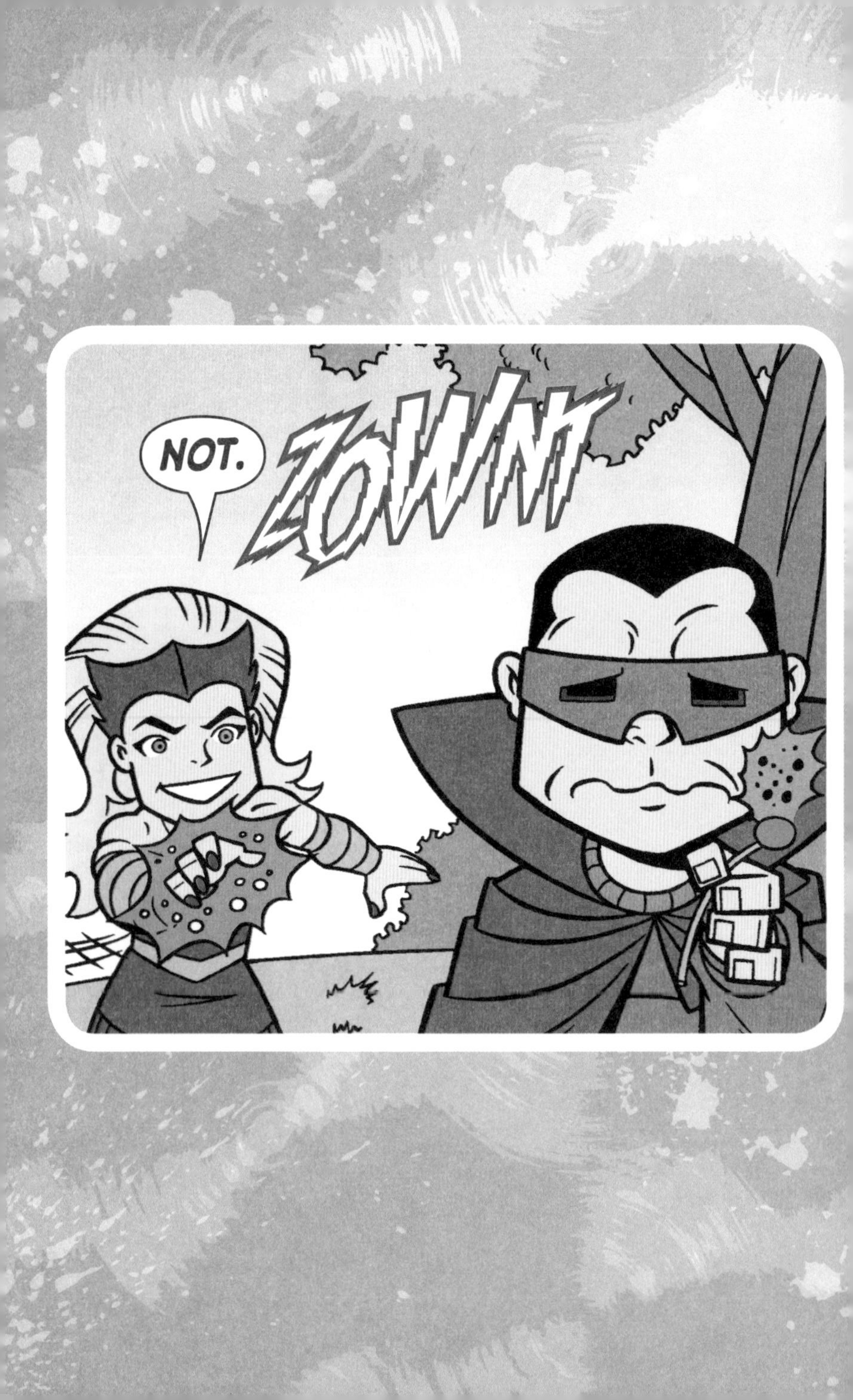
NOT.
ZOWN!

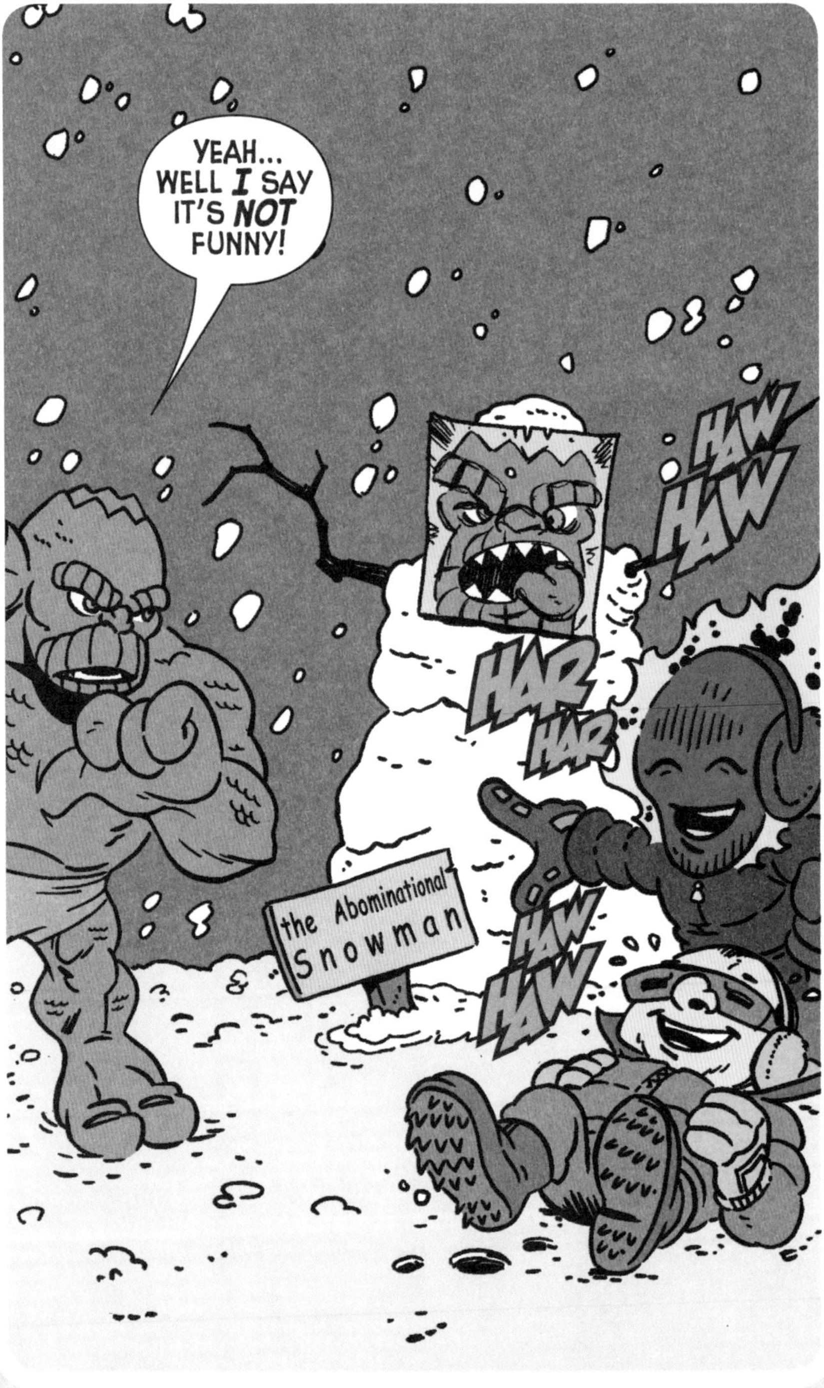
YEAH... WELL I SAY IT'S NOT FUNNY!
HAW HAW
HAR HAR
the Abominational Snowman
HAW HAW

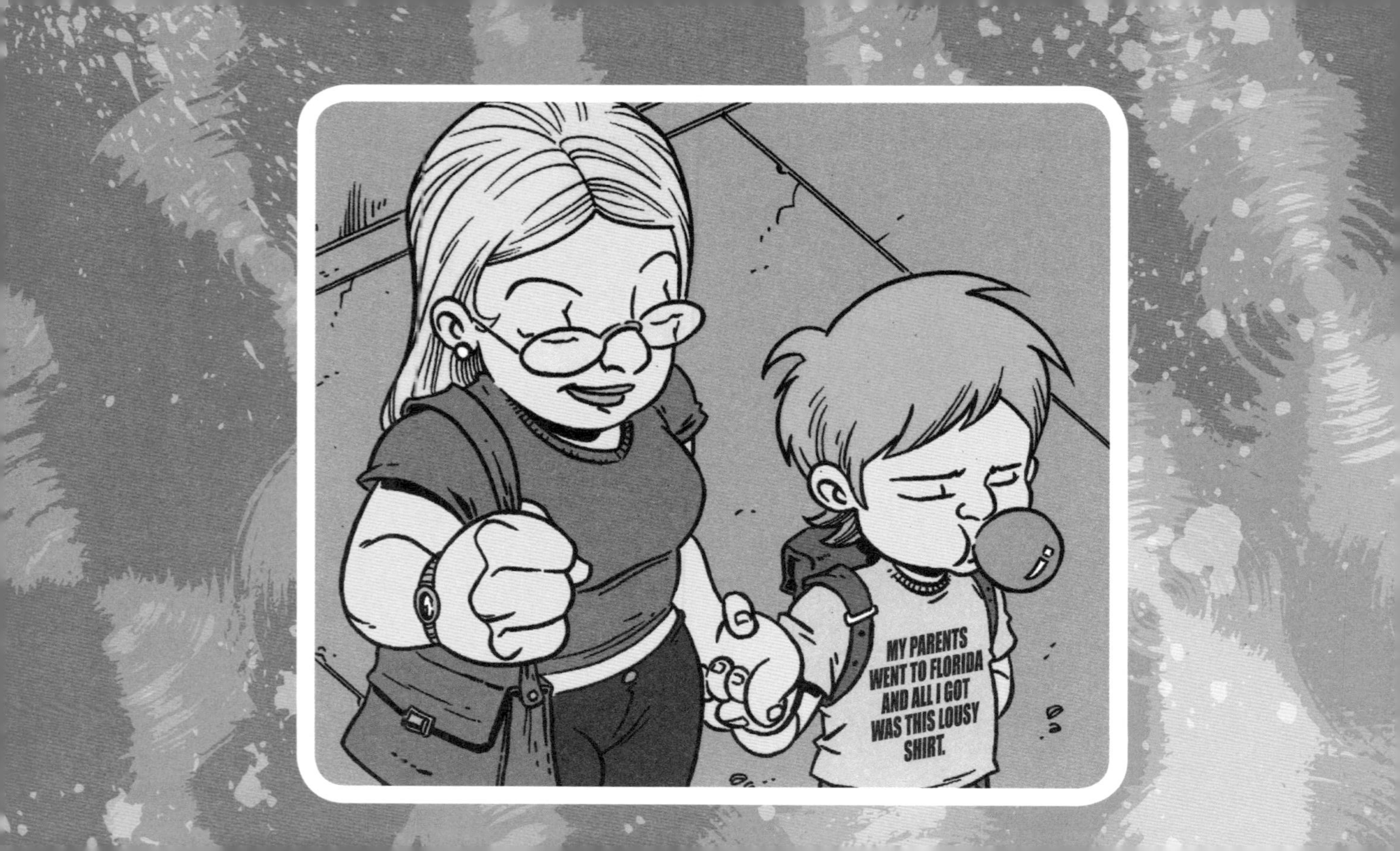
MY PARENTS WENT TO FLORIDA AND ALL I GOT WAS THIS LOUSY SHIRT.

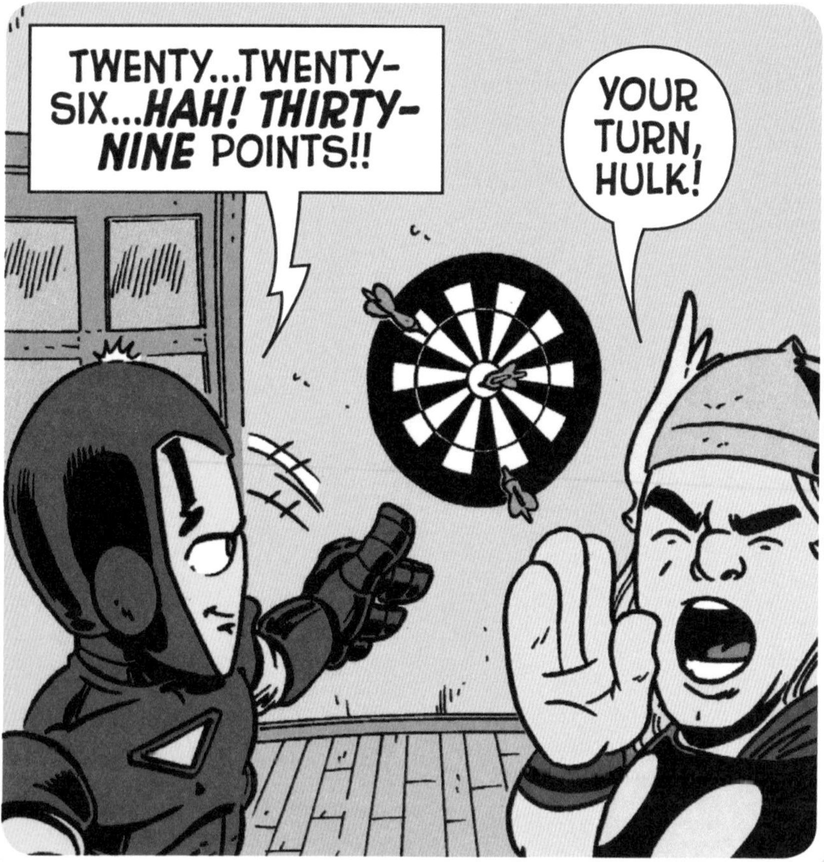
TWENTY...TWENTY-SIX...HAH! THIRTY-NINE POINTS!!
YOUR TURN, HULK!

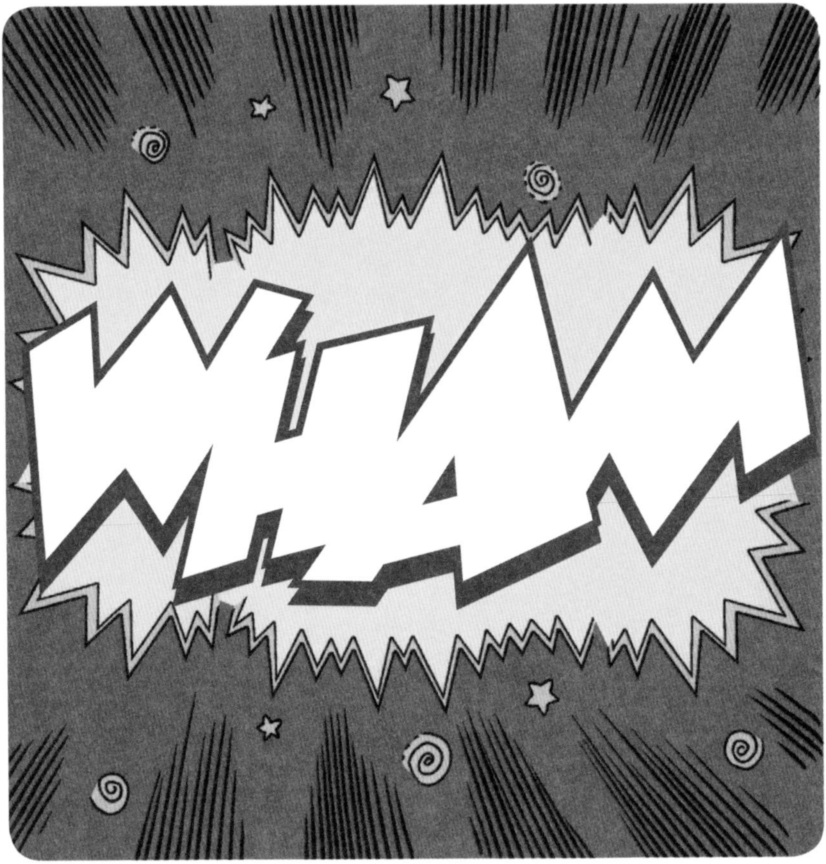
WHAM

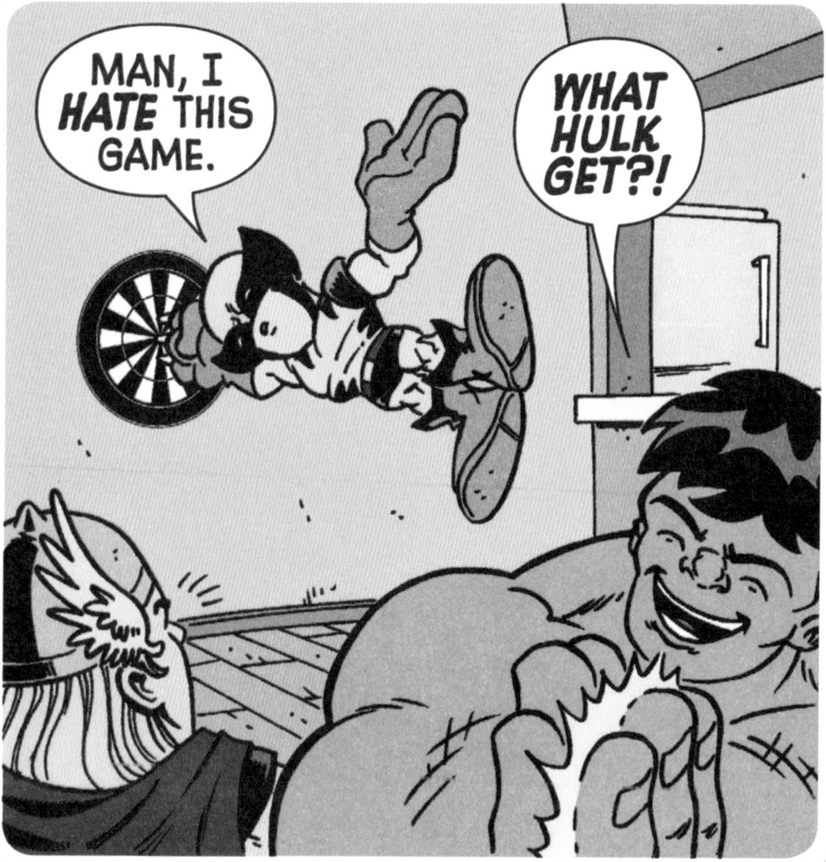
MAN, I *HATE* THIS GAME.
WHAT HULK GET?!

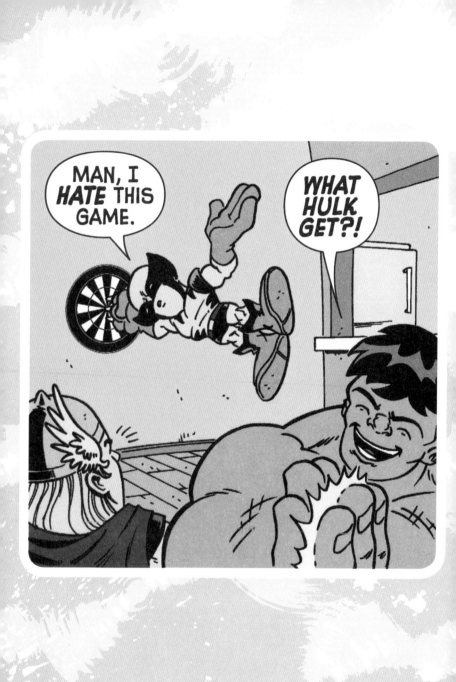

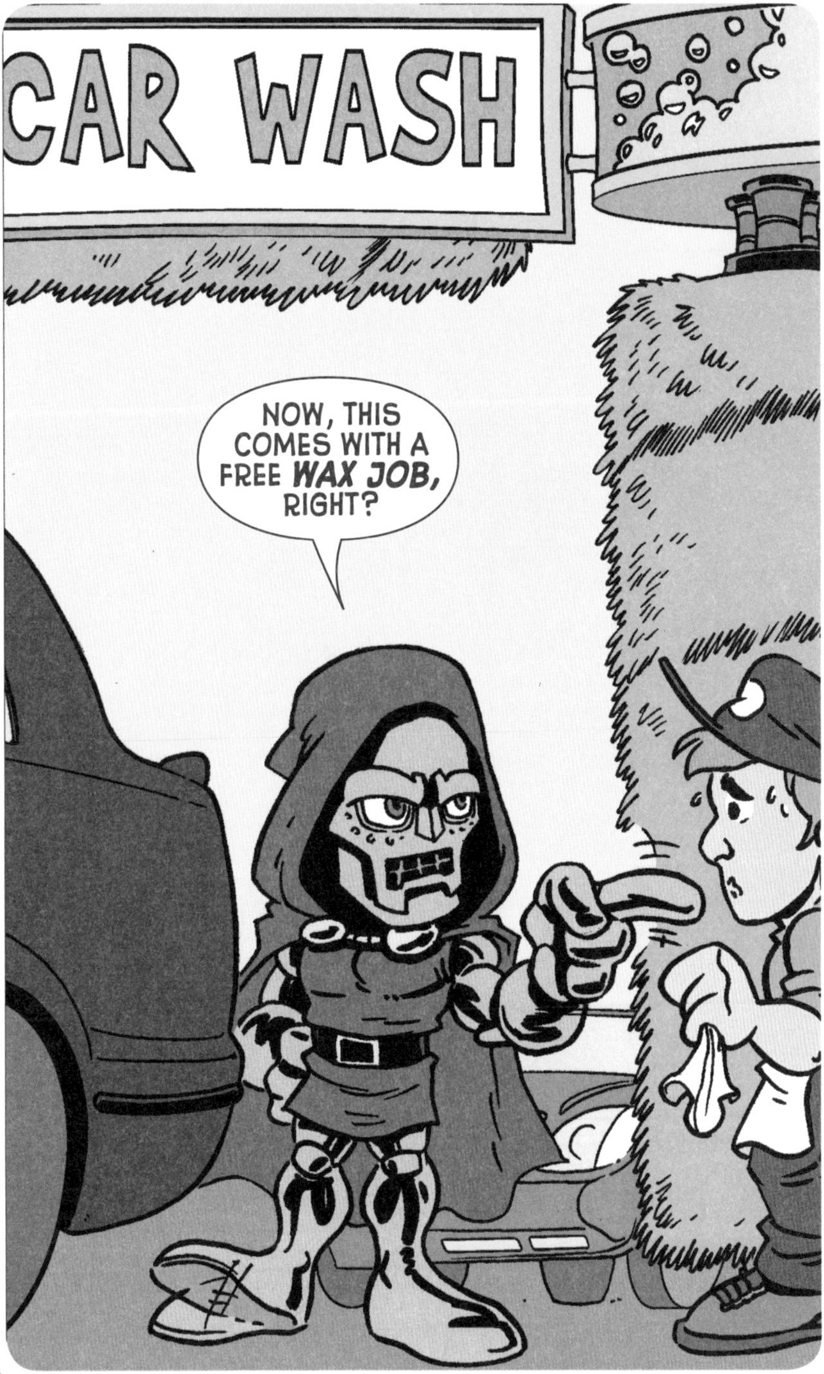
CAR WASH
NOW, THIS COMES WITH A FREE *WAX JOB,* RIGHT?

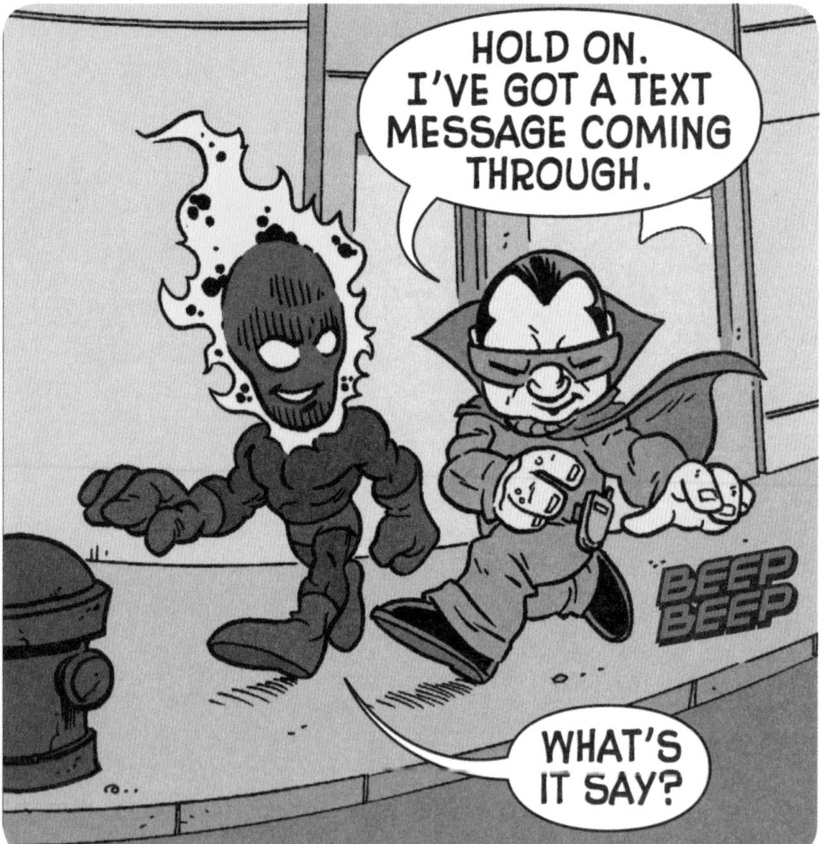
HOLD ON.
I'VE GOT A TEXT
MESSAGE COMING
THROUGH.
BEEP
BEEP
WHAT'S
IT SAY?

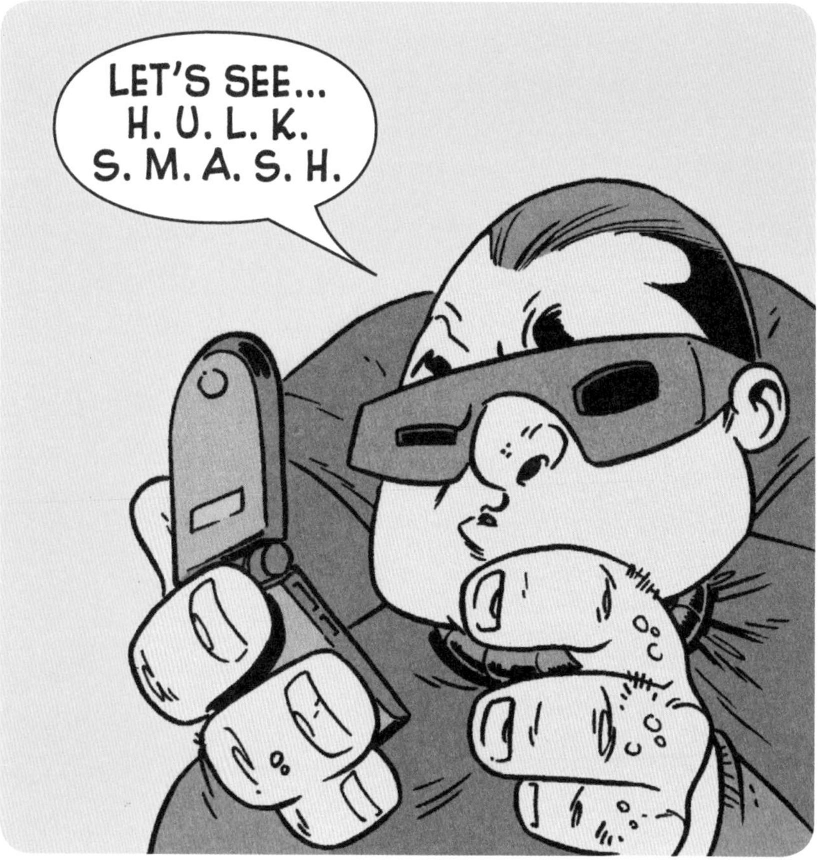
LET'S SEE... H. U. L. K. S. M. A. S. H.

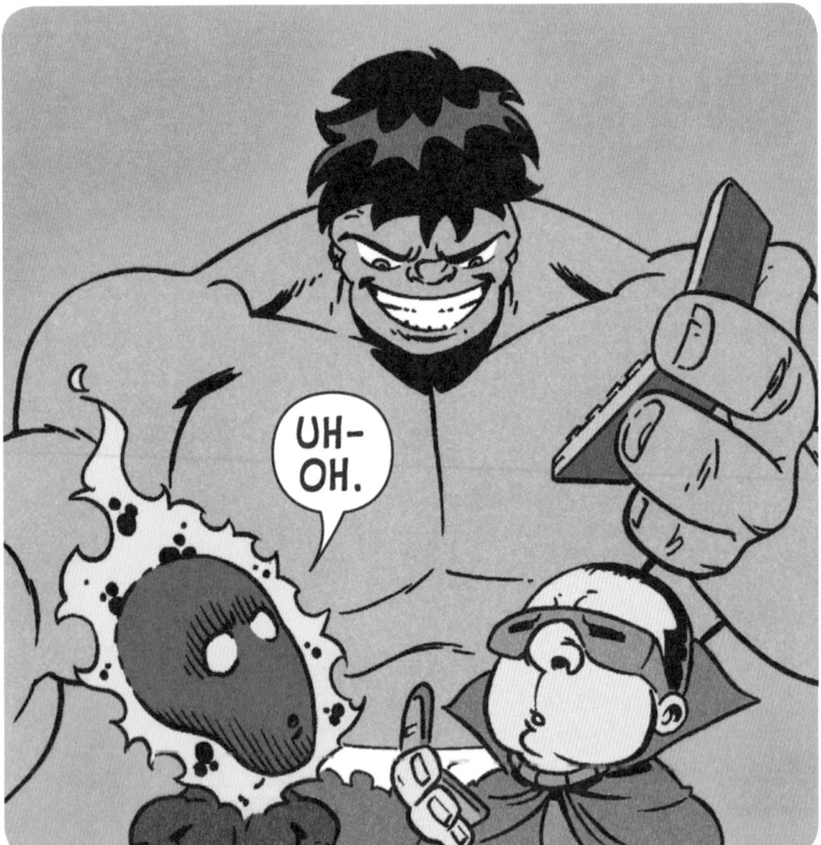
UH-
OH.

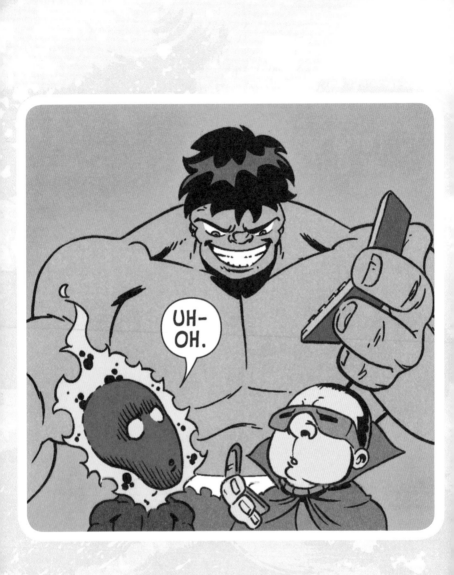

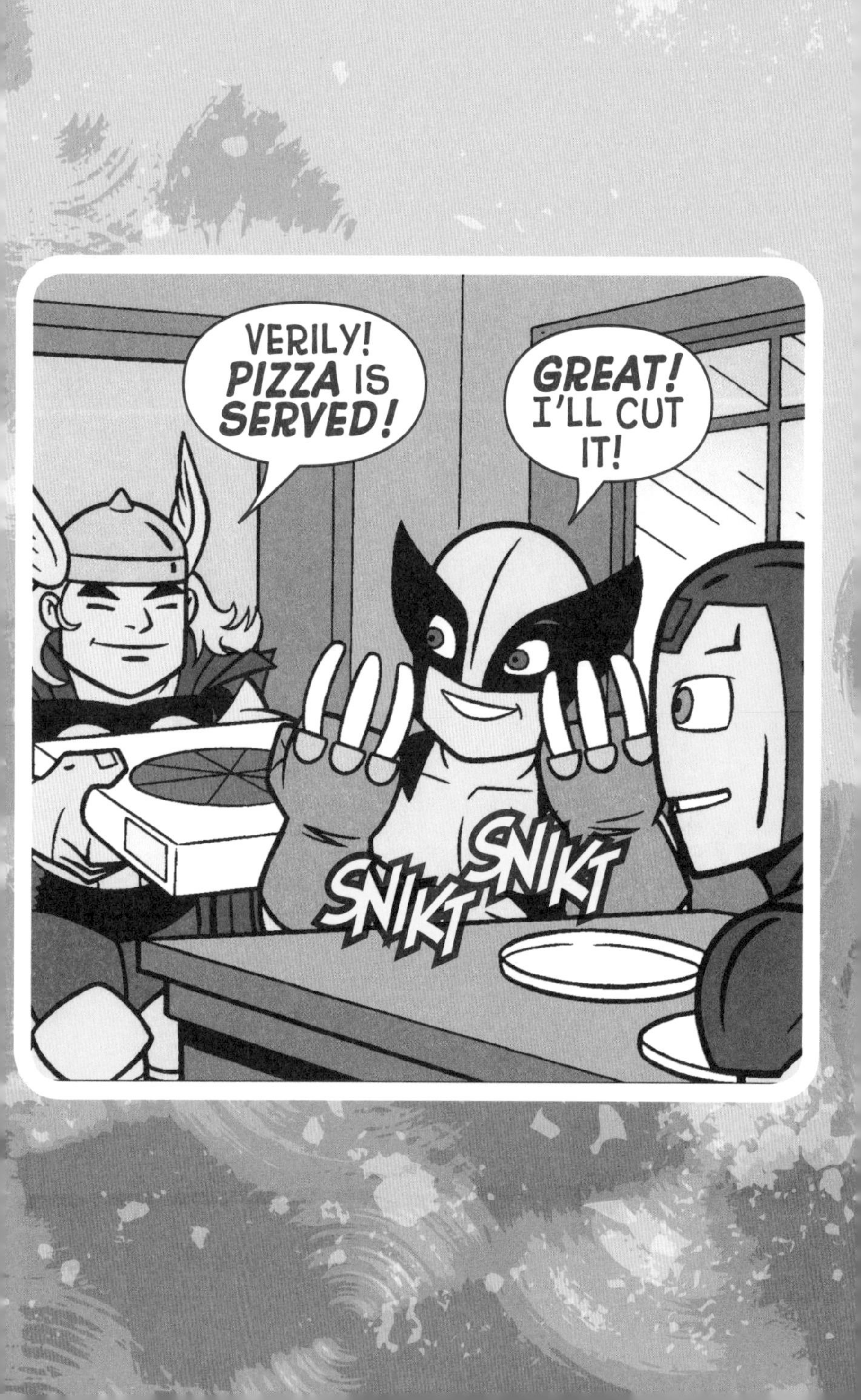
VERILY! PIZZA IS SERVED!
GREAT! I'LL CUT IT!
SNIKT
SNIKT

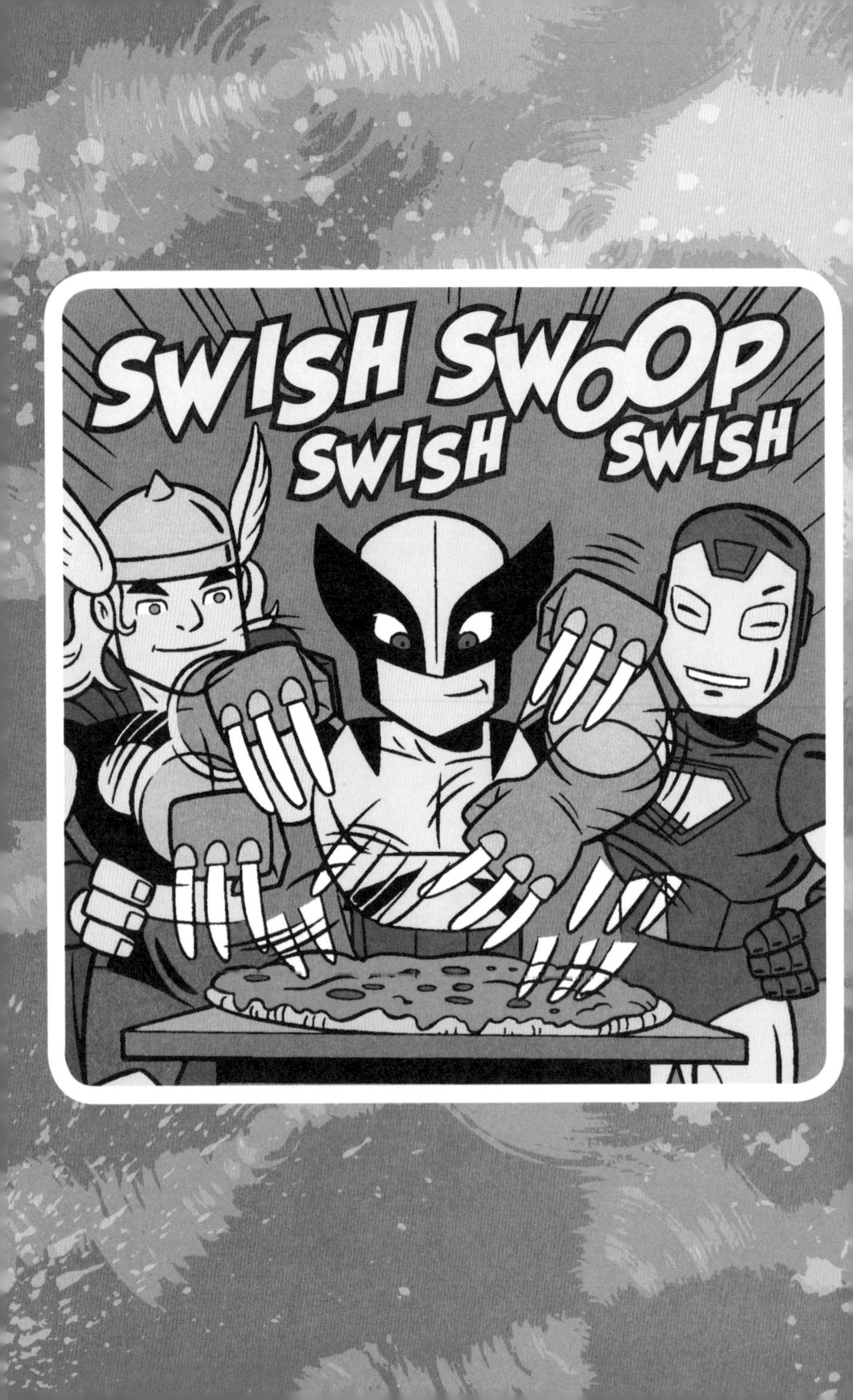
SWISH SWOOP
SWISH
SWISH

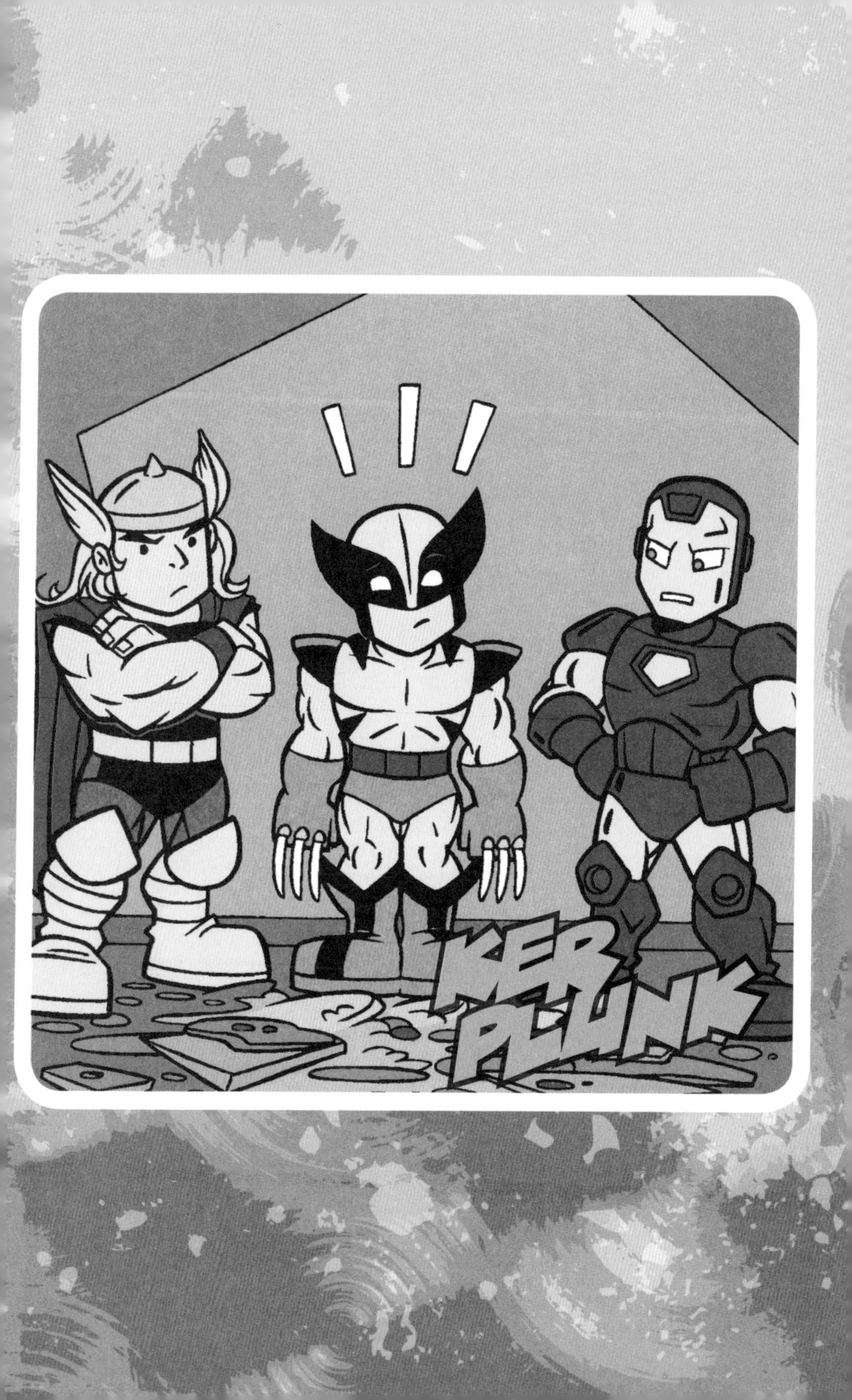
KER PLUNK

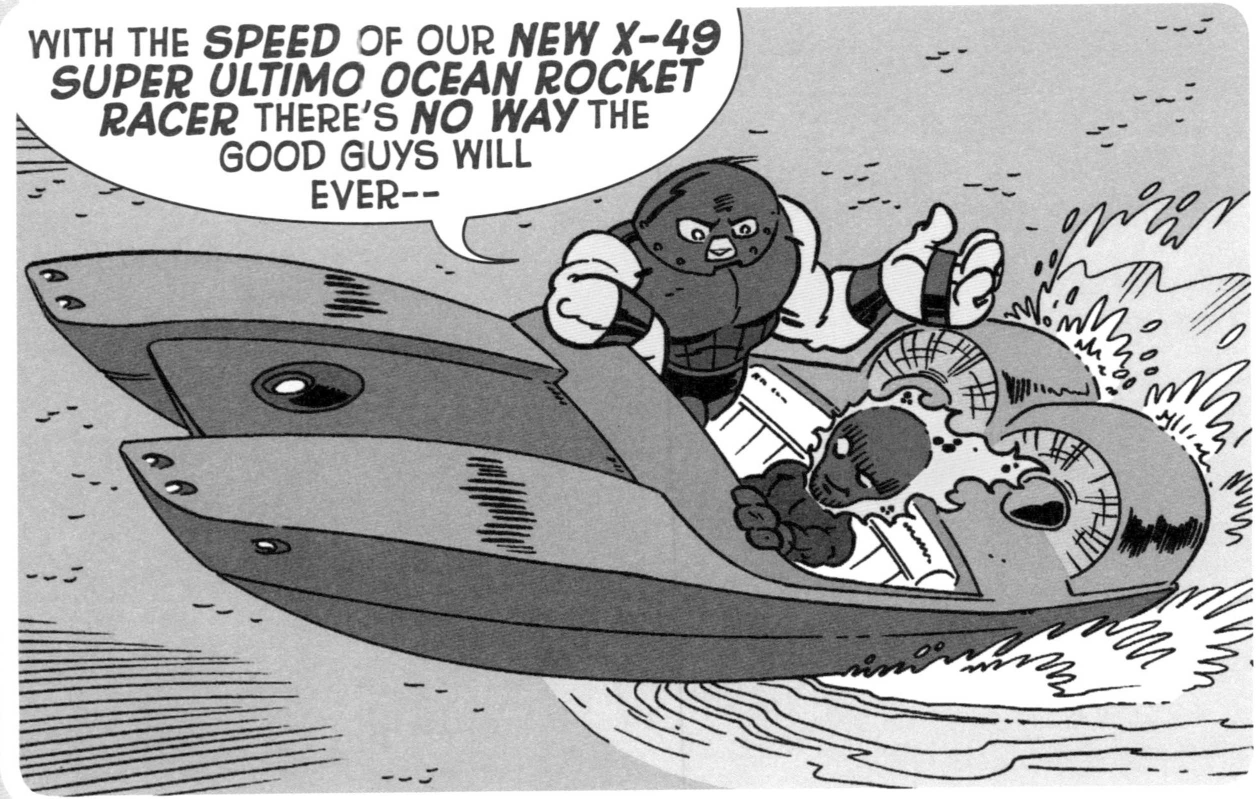
WITH THE SPEED OF OUR NEW X-49 SUPER ULTIMO OCEAN ROCKET RACER THERE'S NO WAY THE GOOD GUYS WILL EVER--

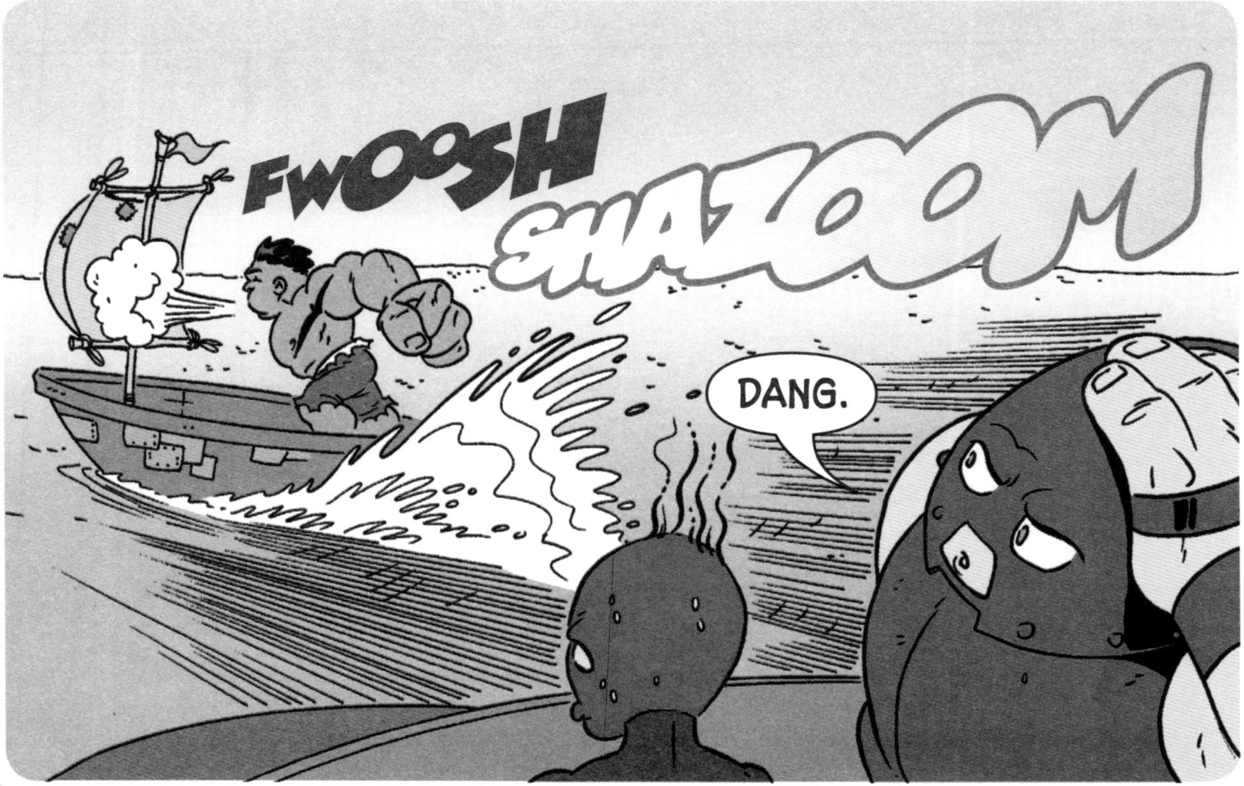
FWOOSH
SHAZOOM
DANG.

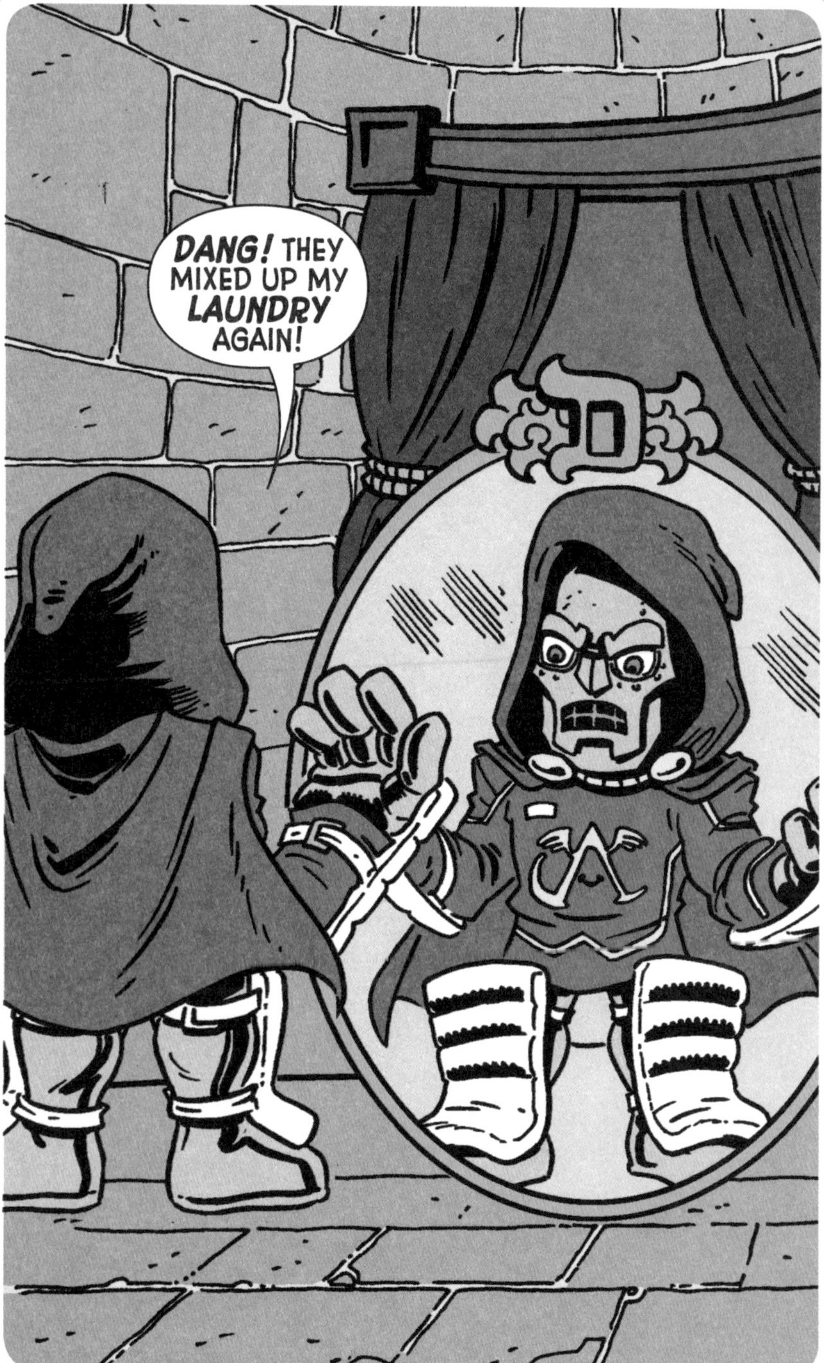
DANG! THEY MIXED UP MY LAUNDRY AGAIN!

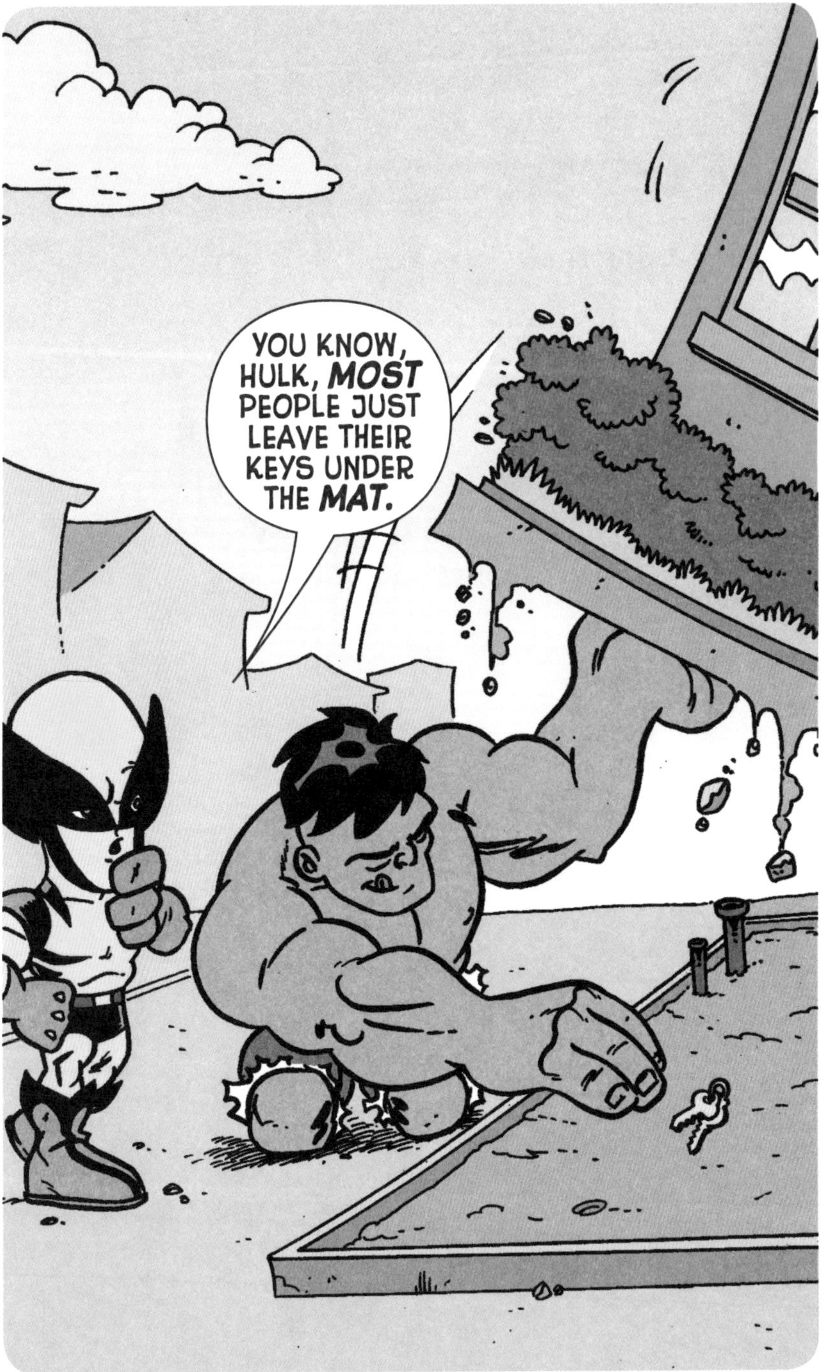
YOU KNOW, HULK, MOST PEOPLE JUST LEAVE THEIR KEYS UNDER THE MAT.

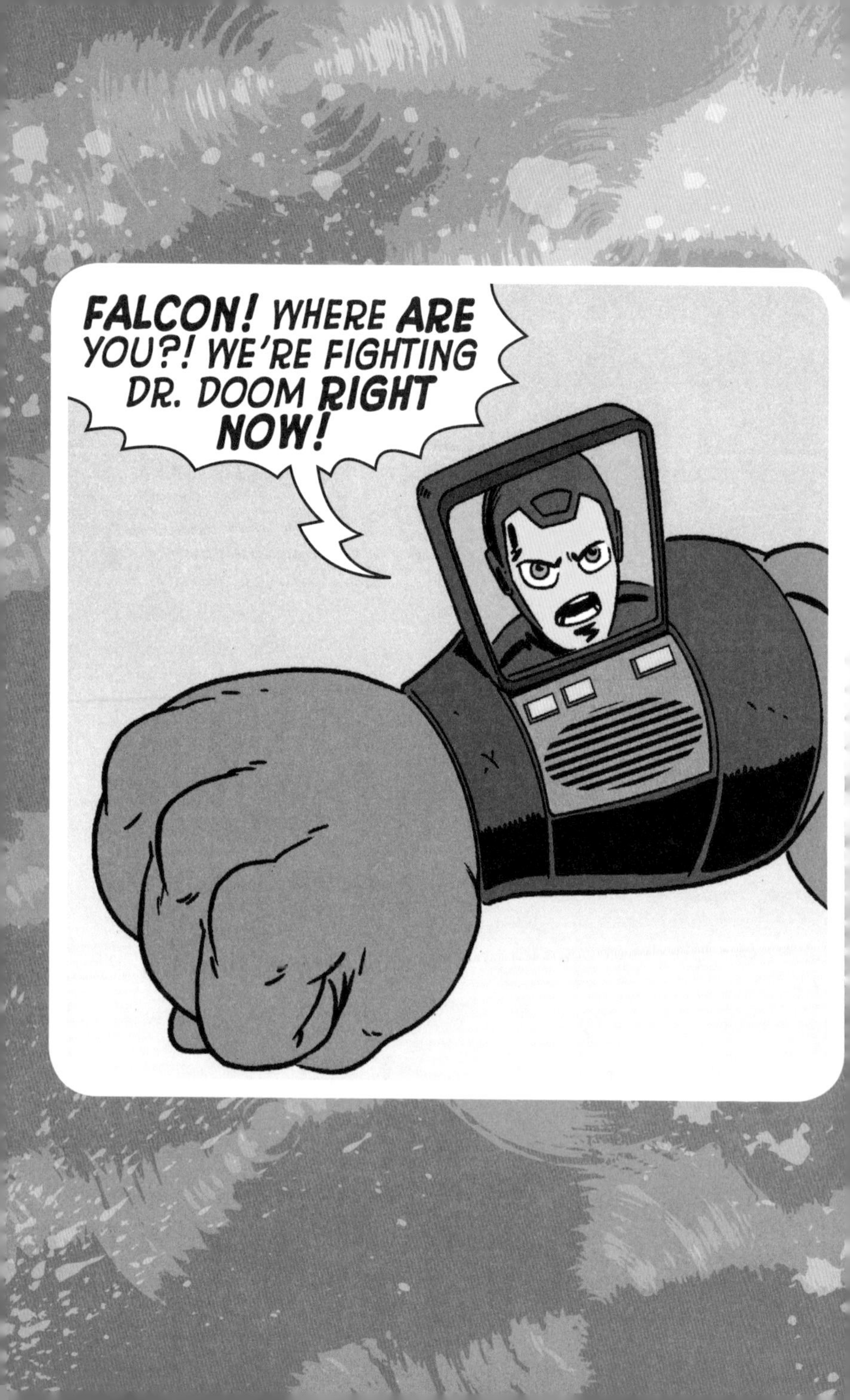
FALCON! WHERE ARE YOU?! WE'RE FIGHTING DR. DOOM RIGHT NOW!

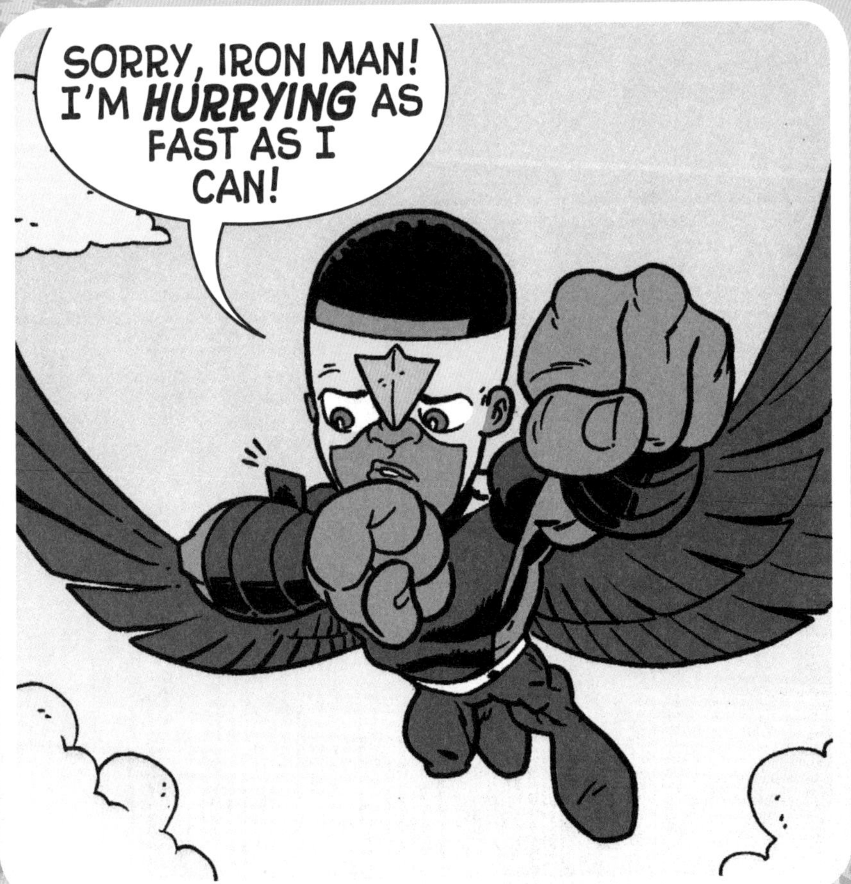
SORRY, IRON MAN! I'M HURRYING AS FAST AS I CAN!

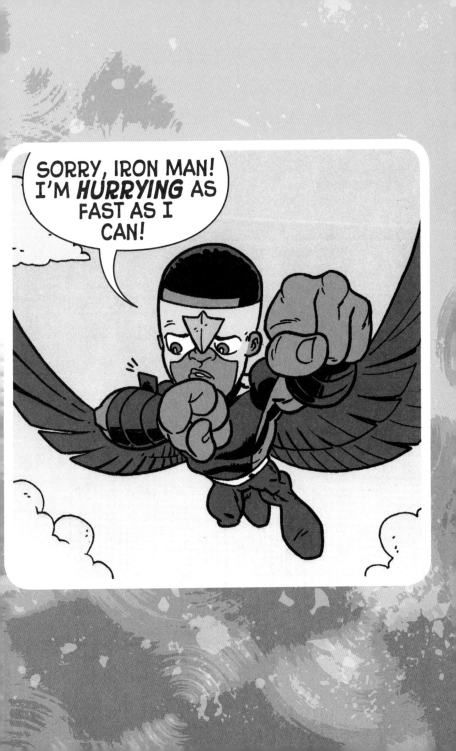

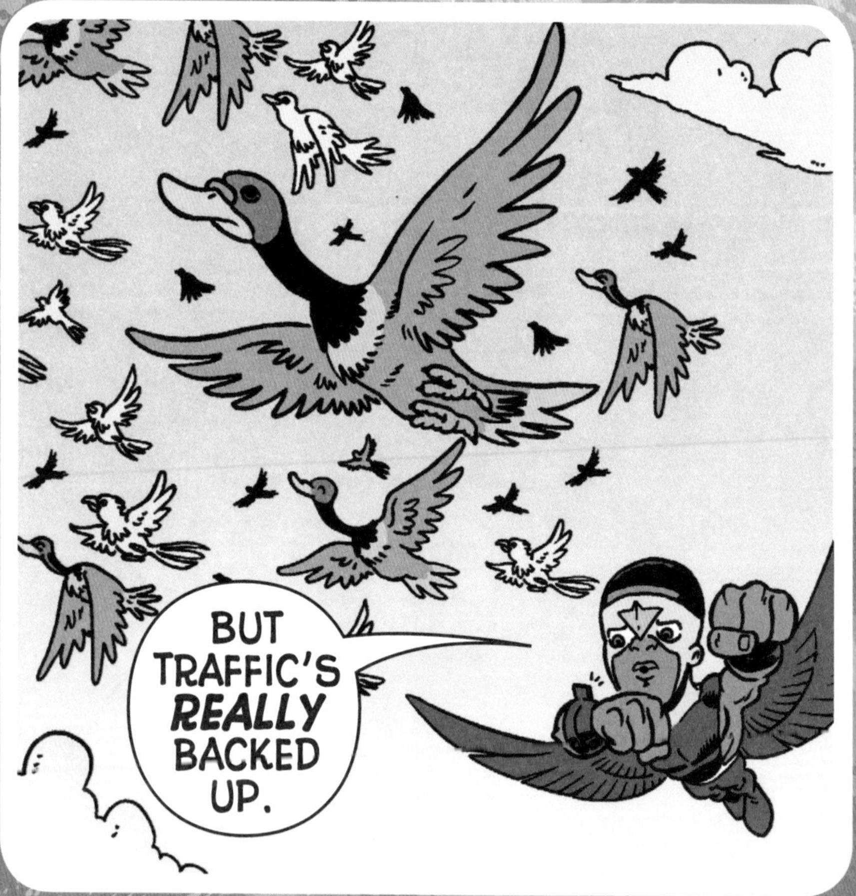
BUT TRAFFIC'S REALLY BACKED UP.

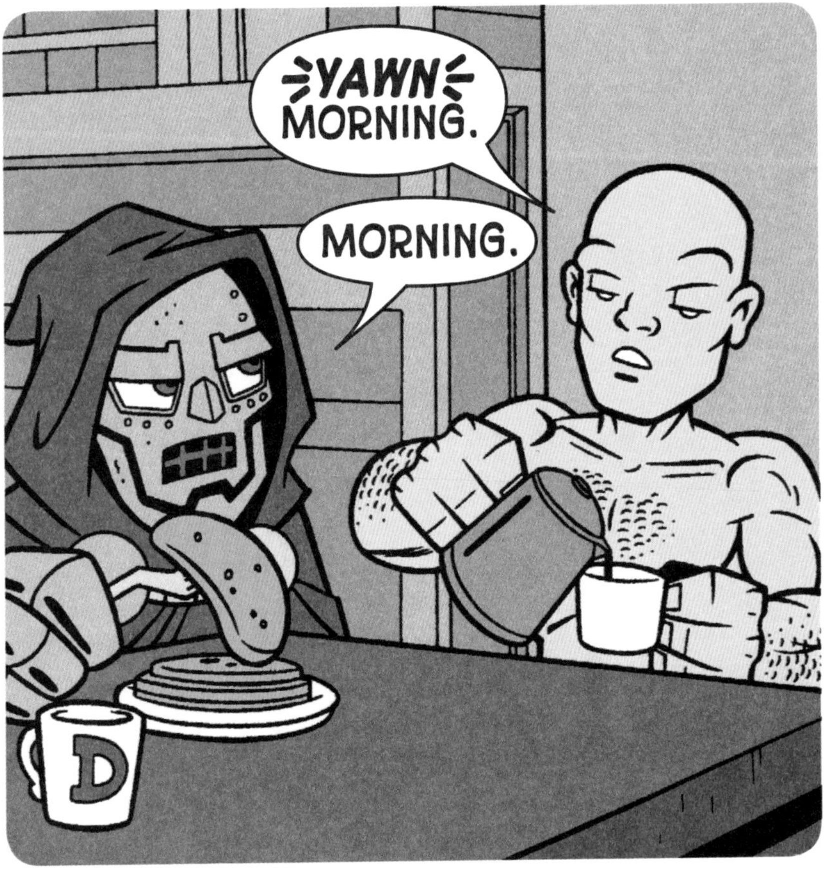
YAWN
MORNING.
MORNING.
D

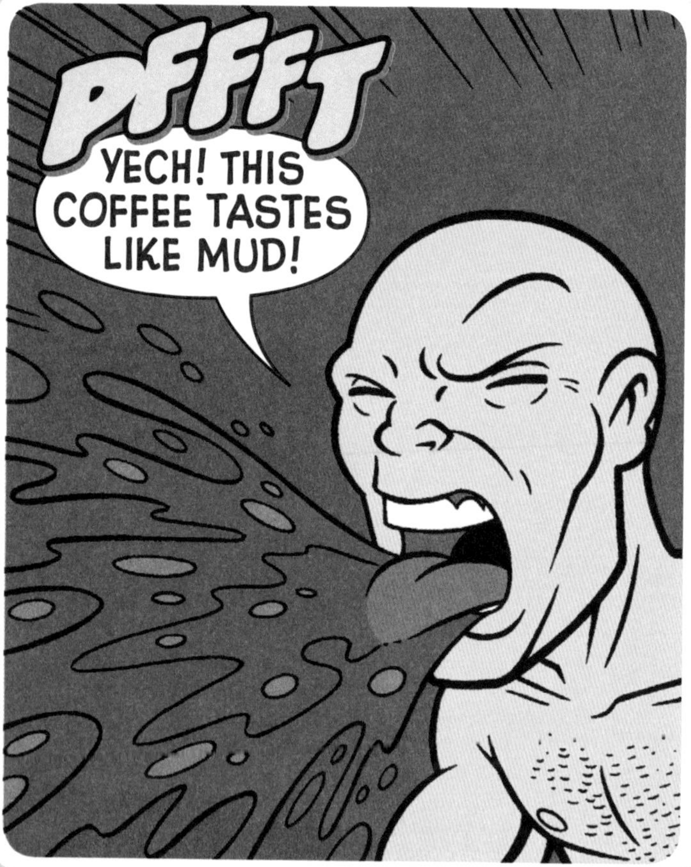
PFFFT
YECH! THIS COFFEE TASTES LIKE MUD!

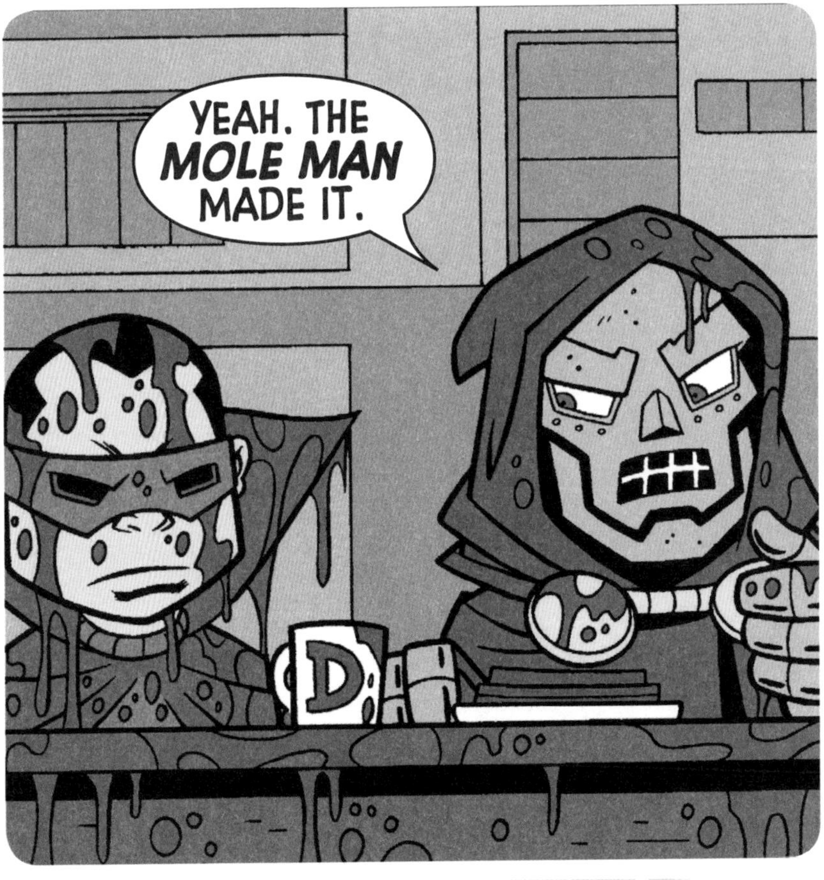
YEAH. THE **MOLE MAN** MADE IT.

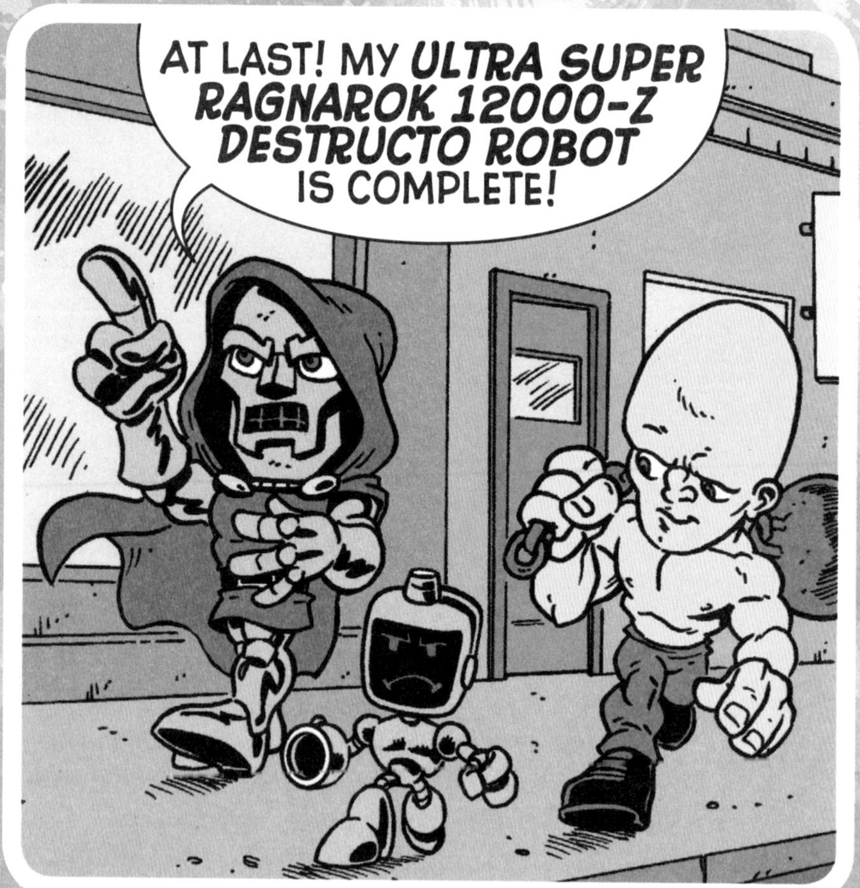
AT LAST! MY ULTRA SUPER RAGNAROK 12000-Z DESTRUCTO ROBOT IS COMPLETE!

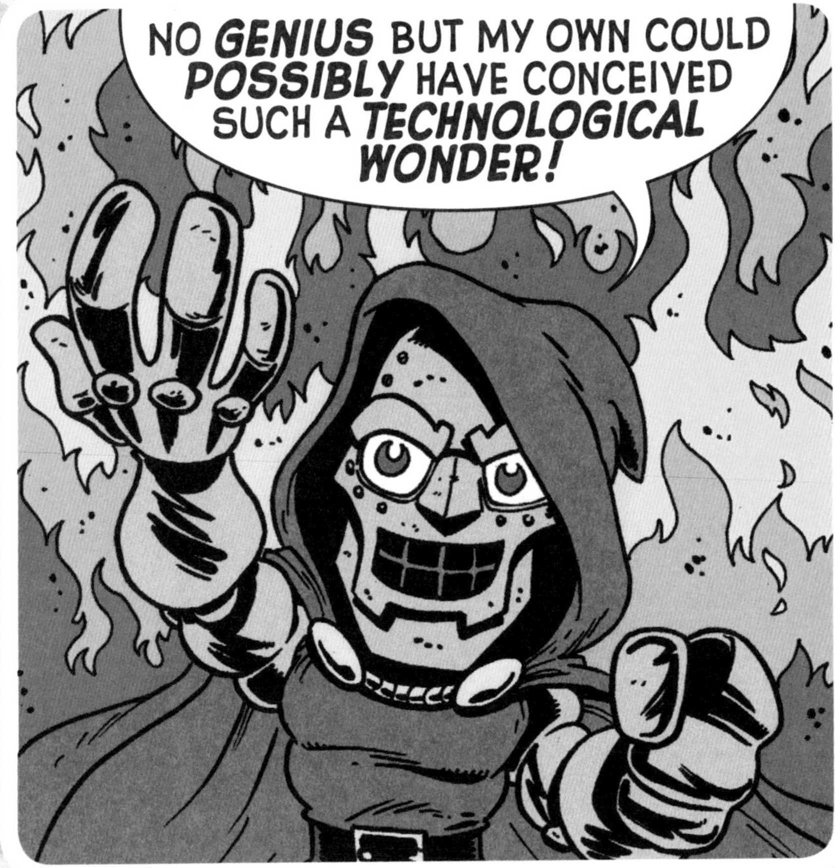
NO GENIUS BUT MY OWN COULD POSSIBLY HAVE CONCEIVED SUCH A TECHNOLOGICAL WONDER!

TOY B-WE
Cuddles the Robot! Now on sale!
Only $ 19.99
Clearance!
NO BRAIN BUT MY...UH.
DANG.

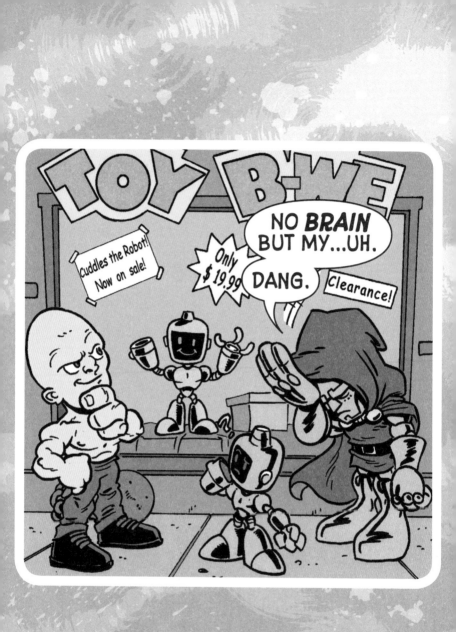

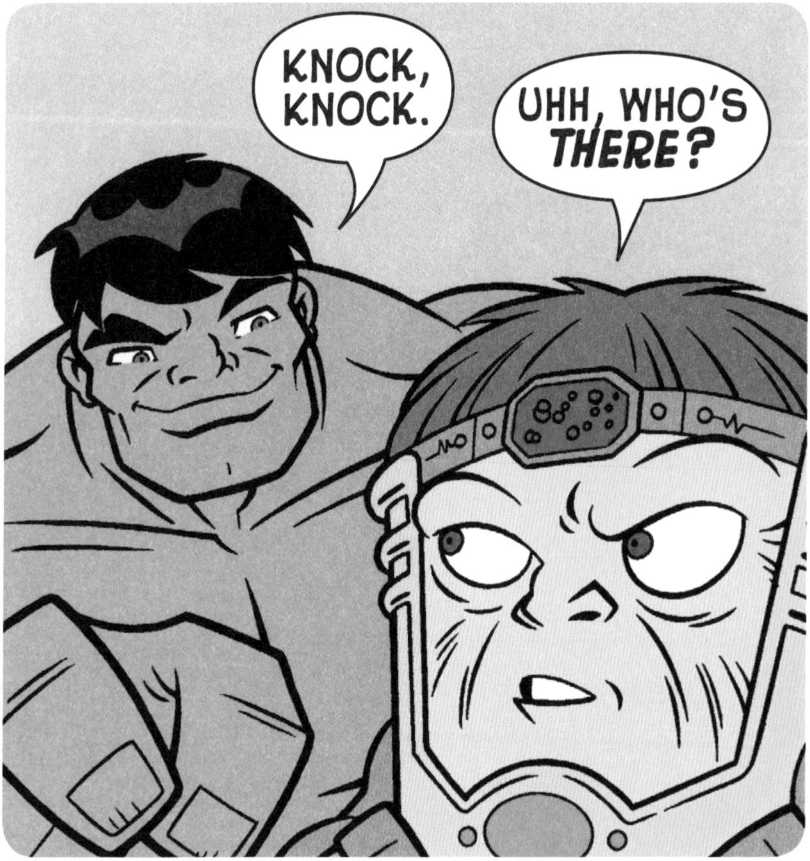
KNOCK, KNOCK.
UHH, WHO'S THERE?

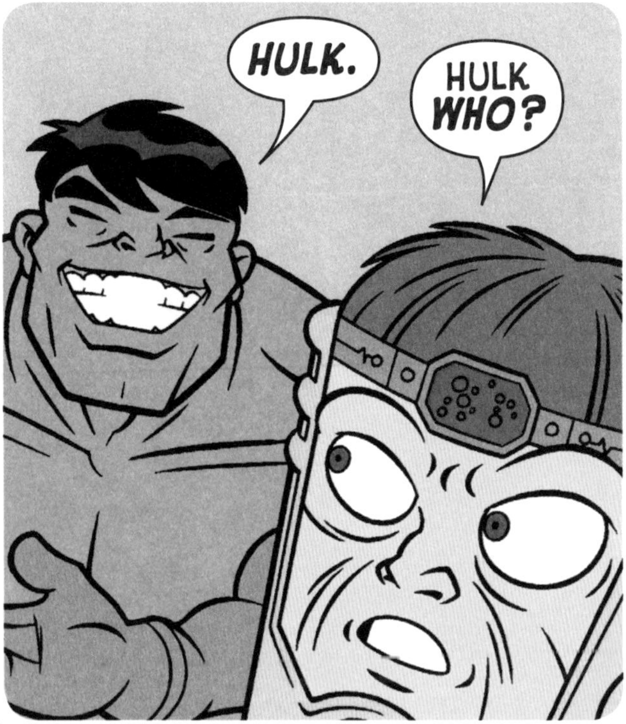
HULK.
HULK WHO?

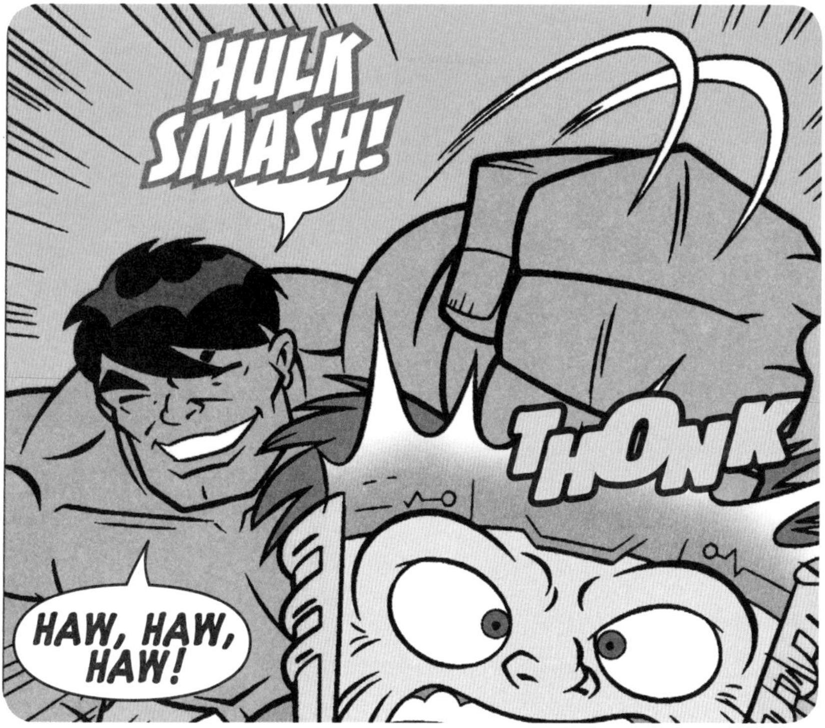
HULK SMASH!
THONK
HAW, HAW, HAW!

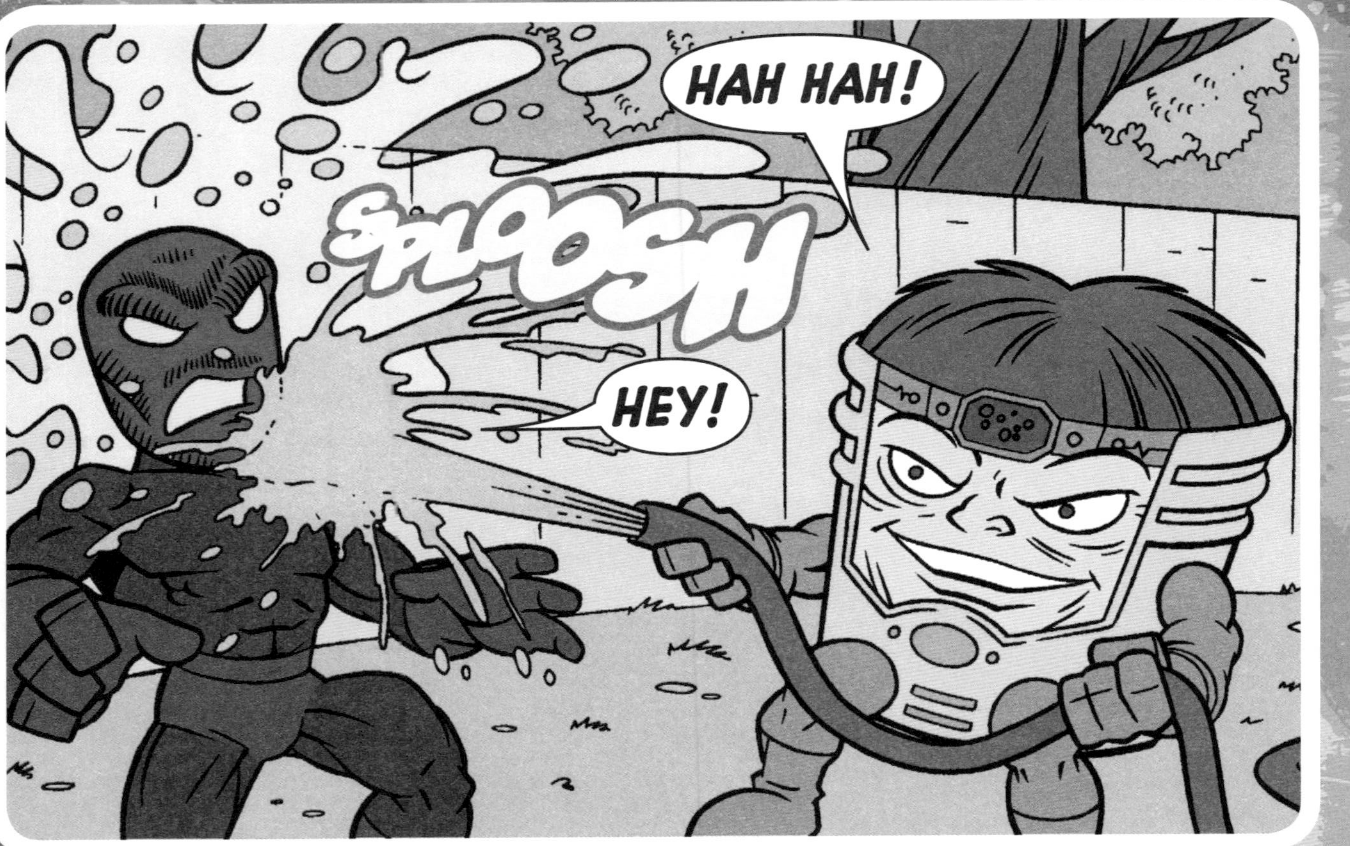
SPLOOSH
HAH HAH!
HEY!

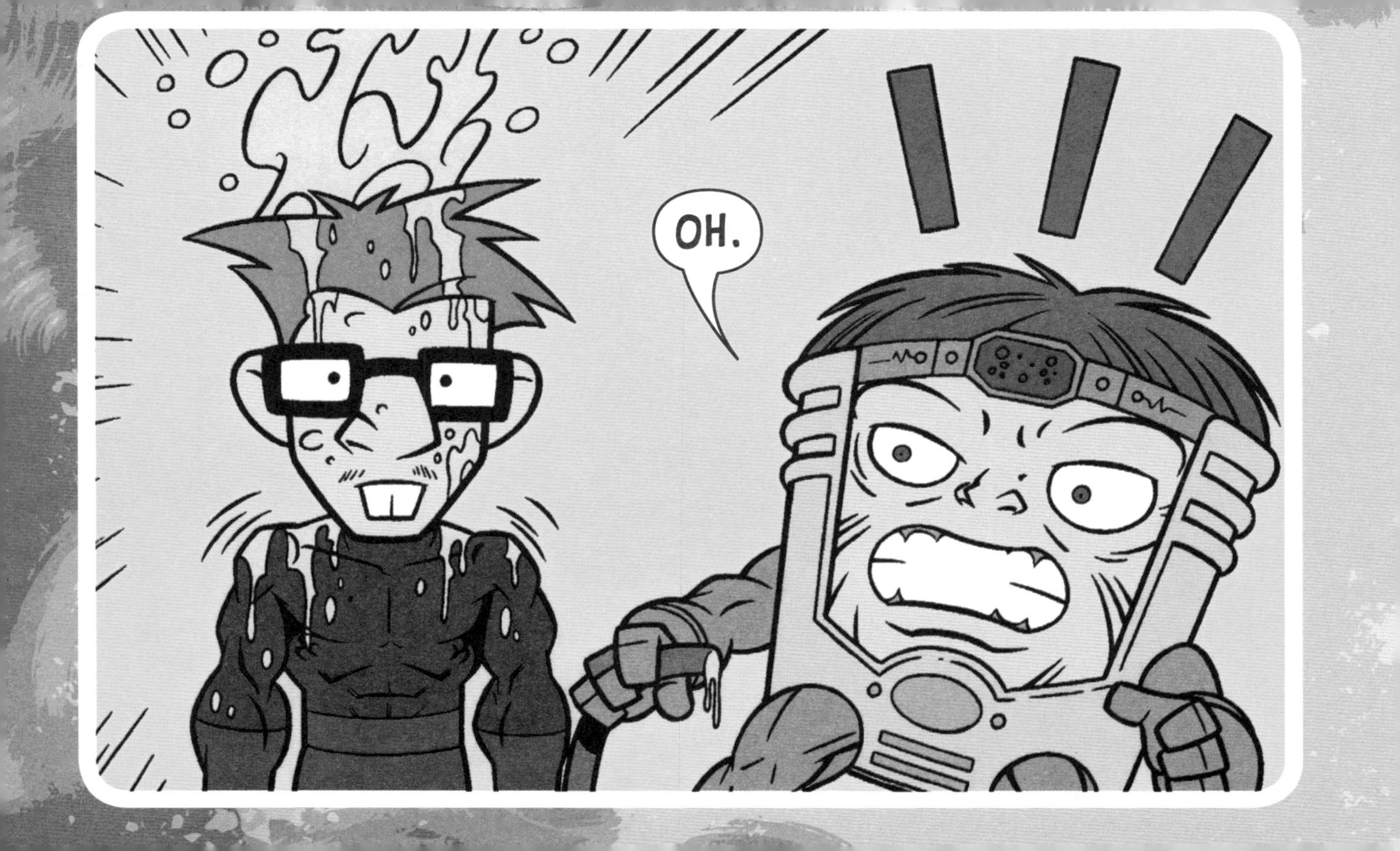
OH.

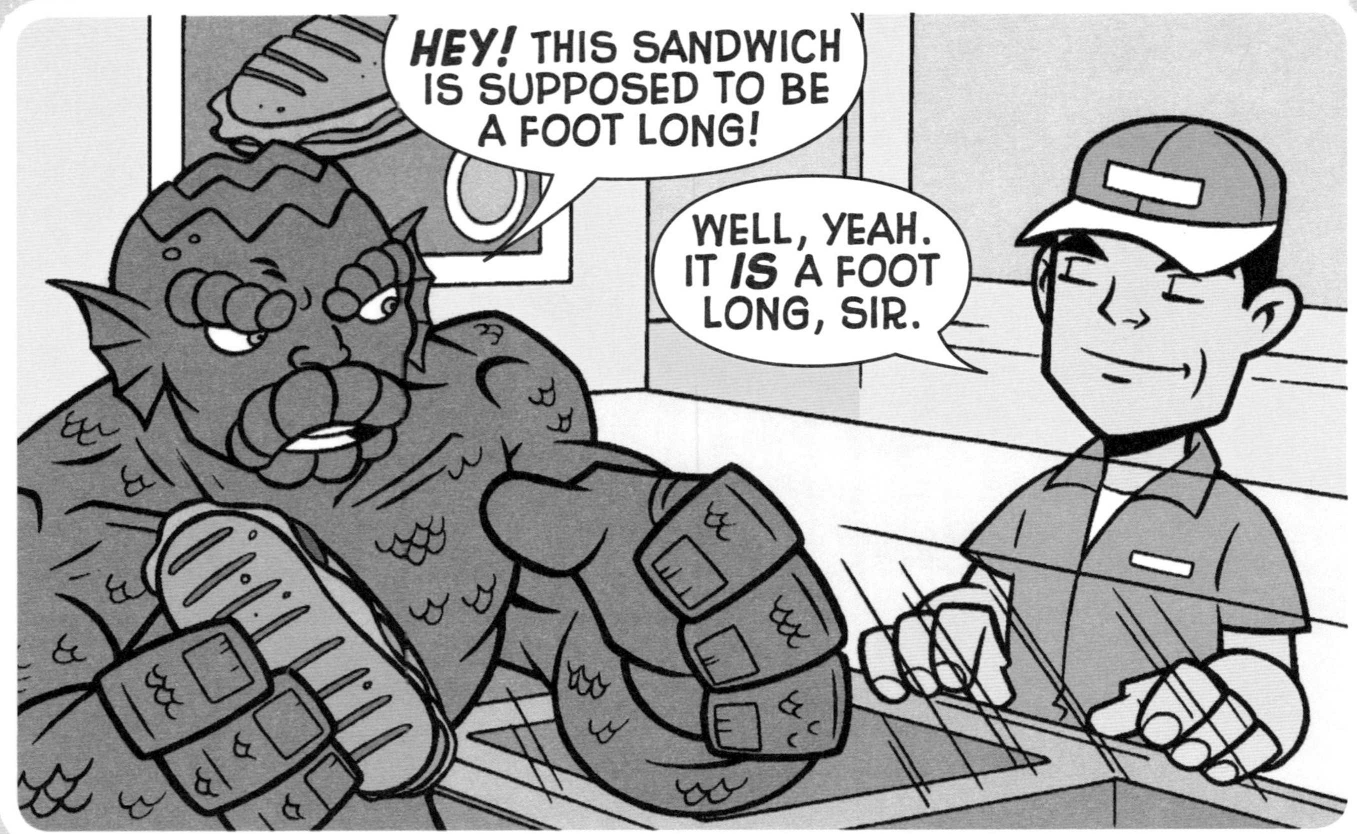
HEY! THIS SANDWICH IS SUPPOSED TO BE A FOOT LONG!
WELL, YEAH. IT ***IS*** A FOOT LONG, SIR.

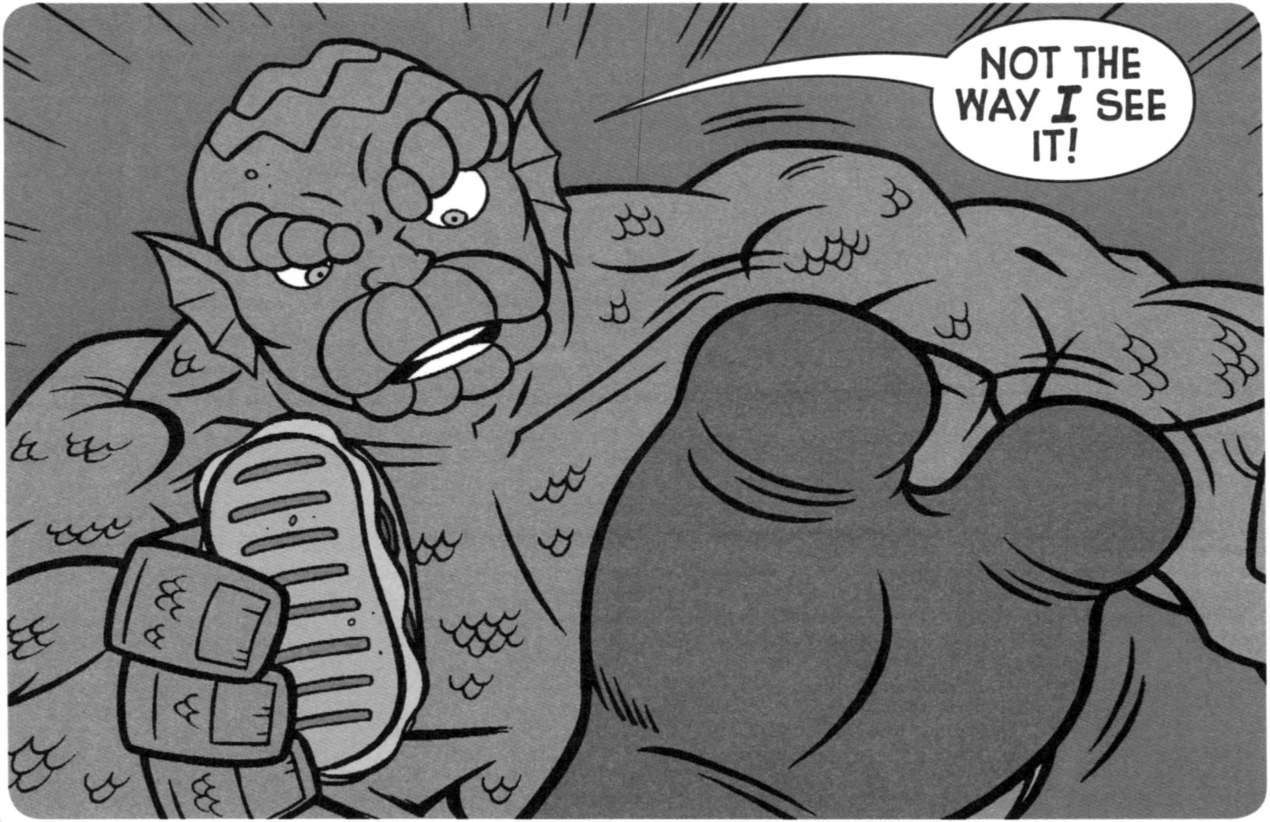
NOT THE WAY I SEE IT!

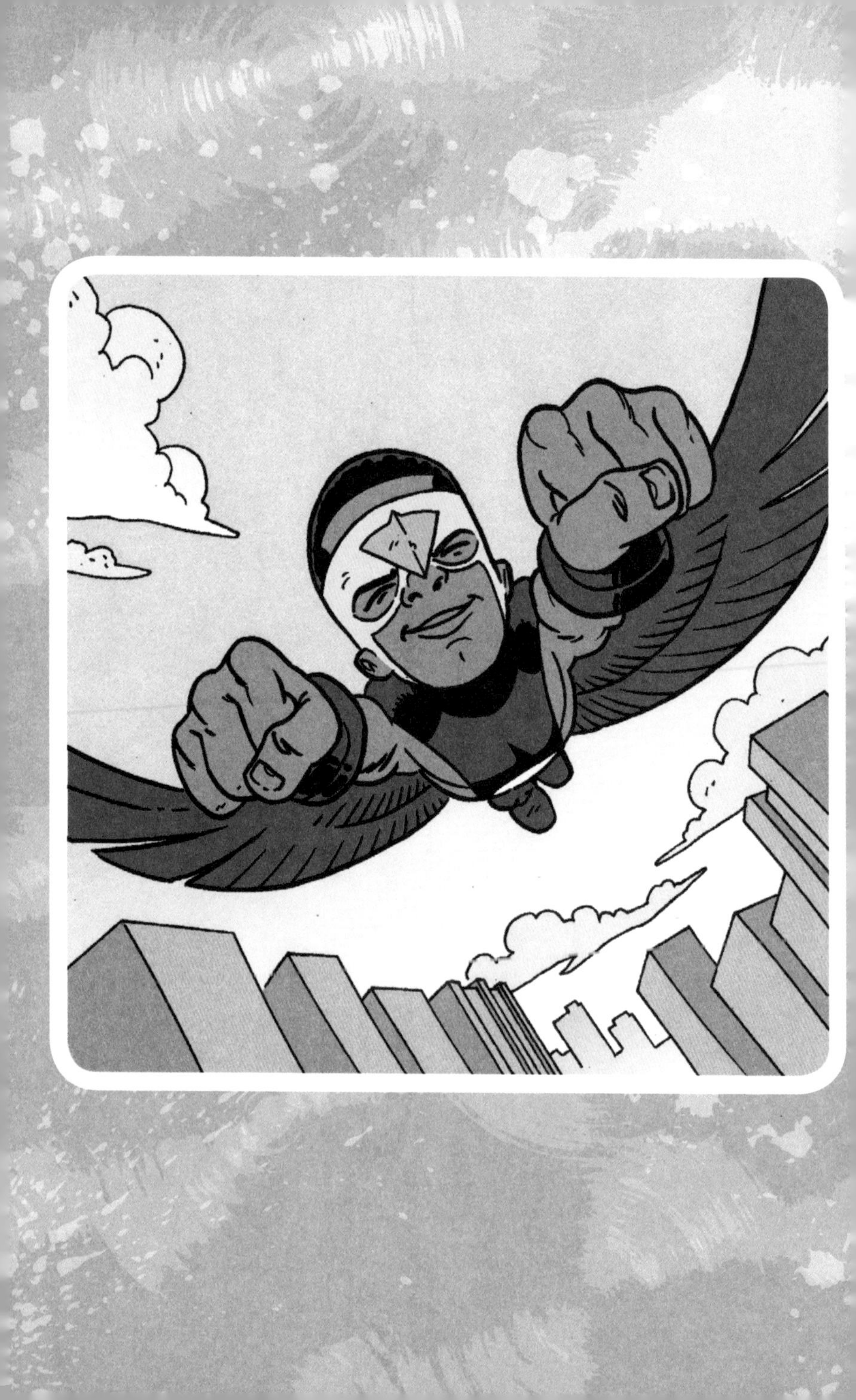

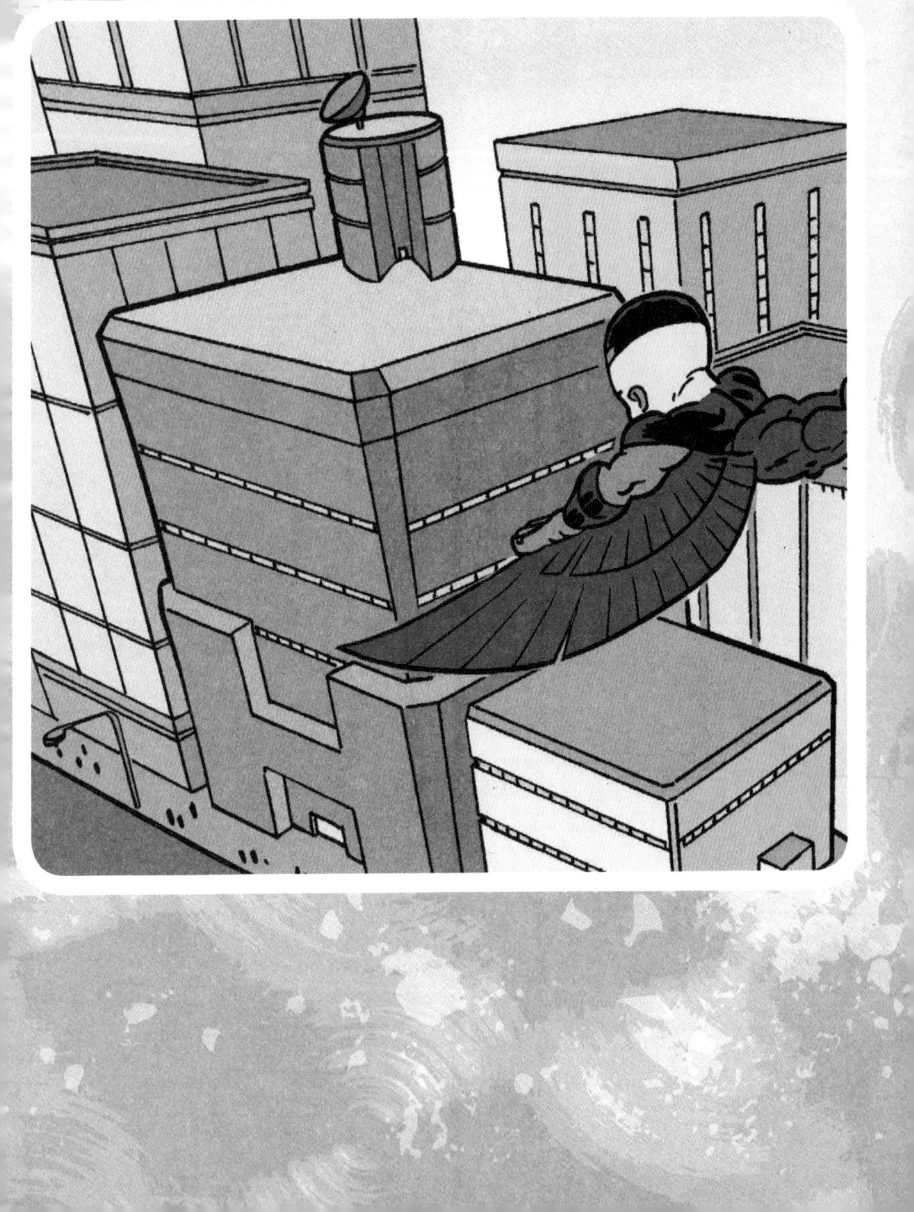

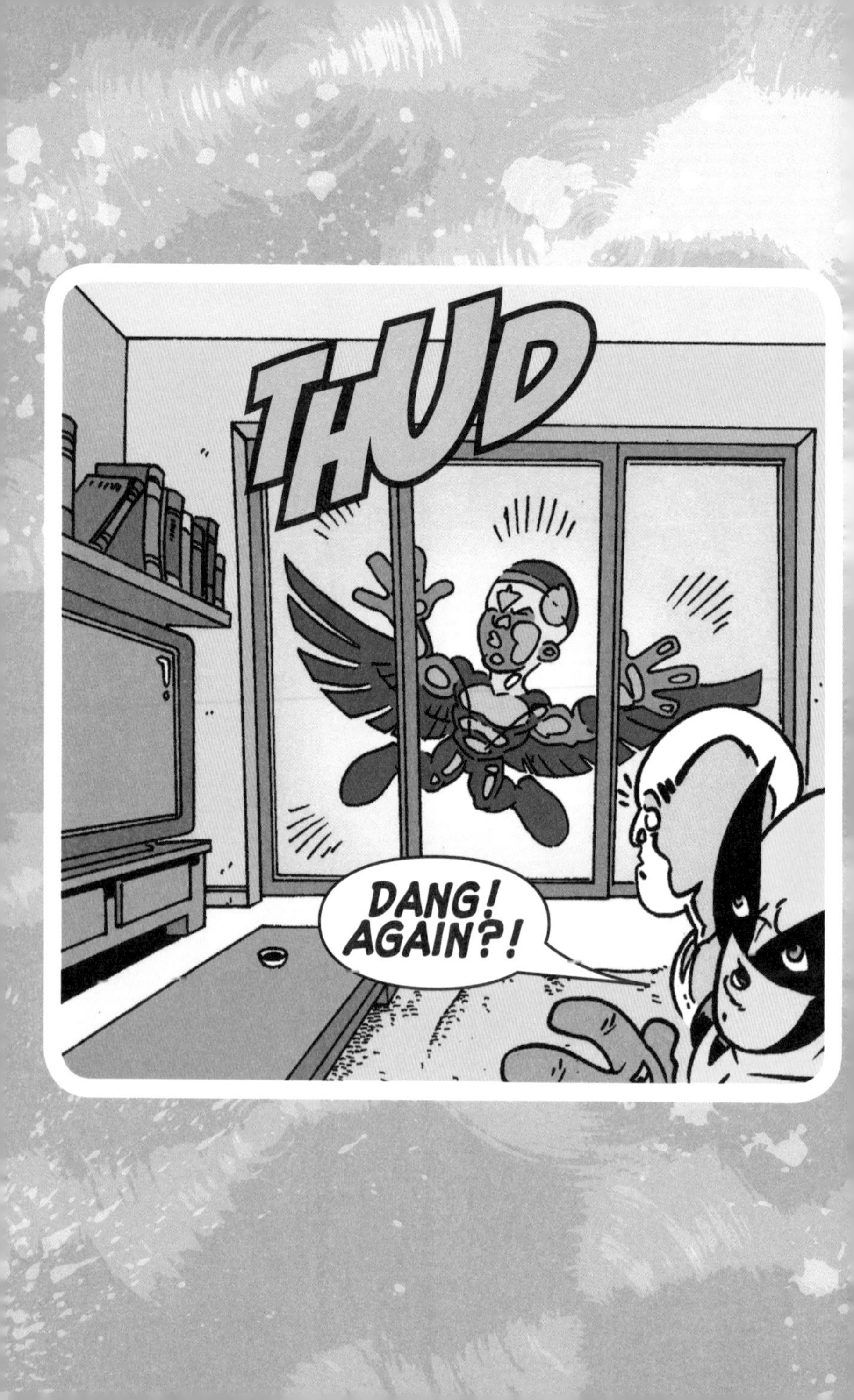
THUD
DANG! AGAIN?!

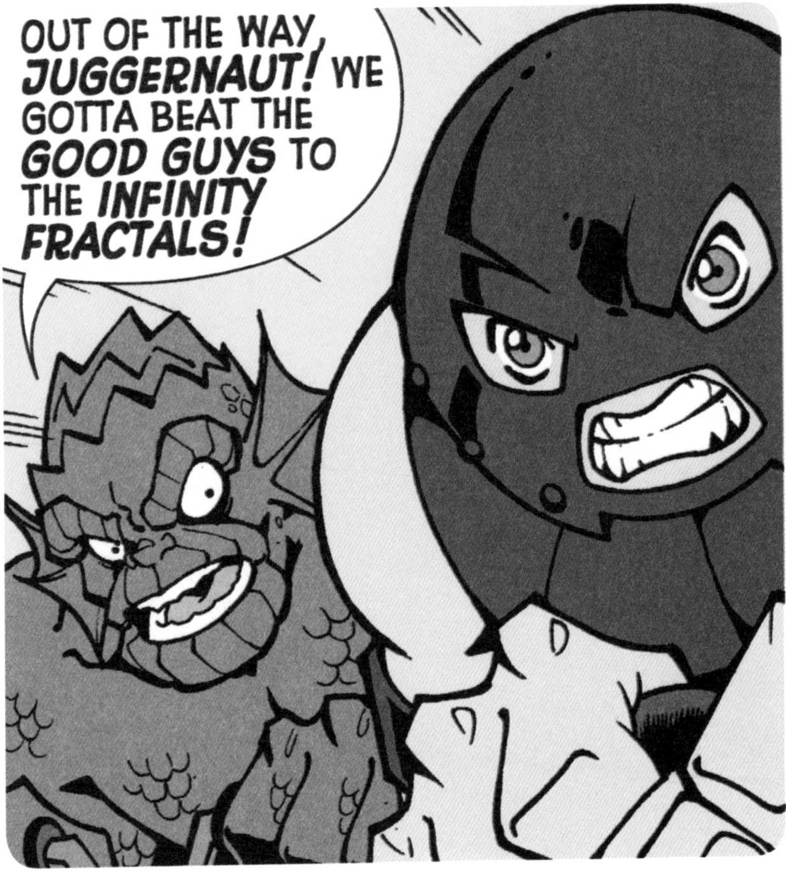
OUT OF THE WAY, JUGGERNAUT! WE GOTTA BEAT THE GOOD GUYS TO THE INFINITY FRACTALS!

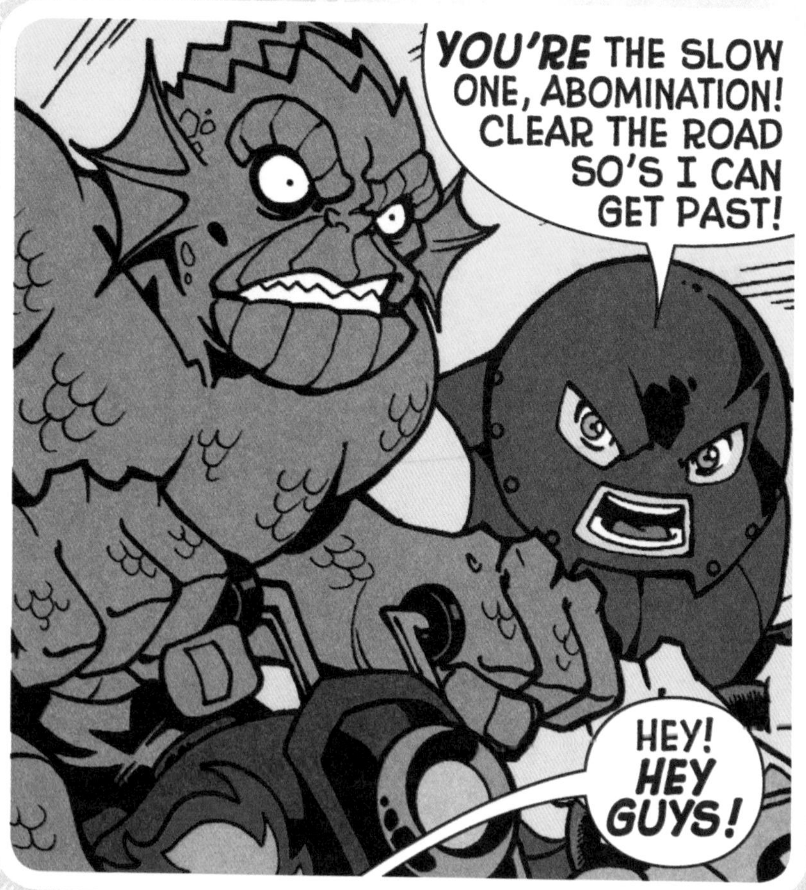
YOU'RE THE SLOW ONE, ABOMINATION! CLEAR THE ROAD SO'S I CAN GET PAST!
HEY! HEY GUYS!

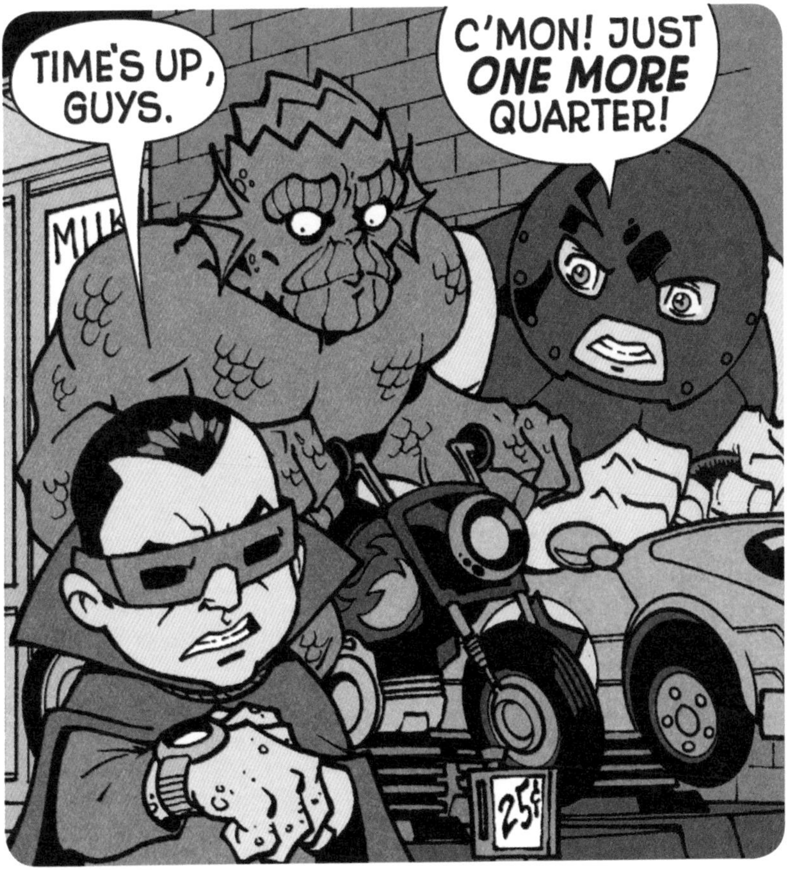
TIME'S UP, GUYS.
C'MON! JUST ONE MORE QUARTER!
MILK
25¢

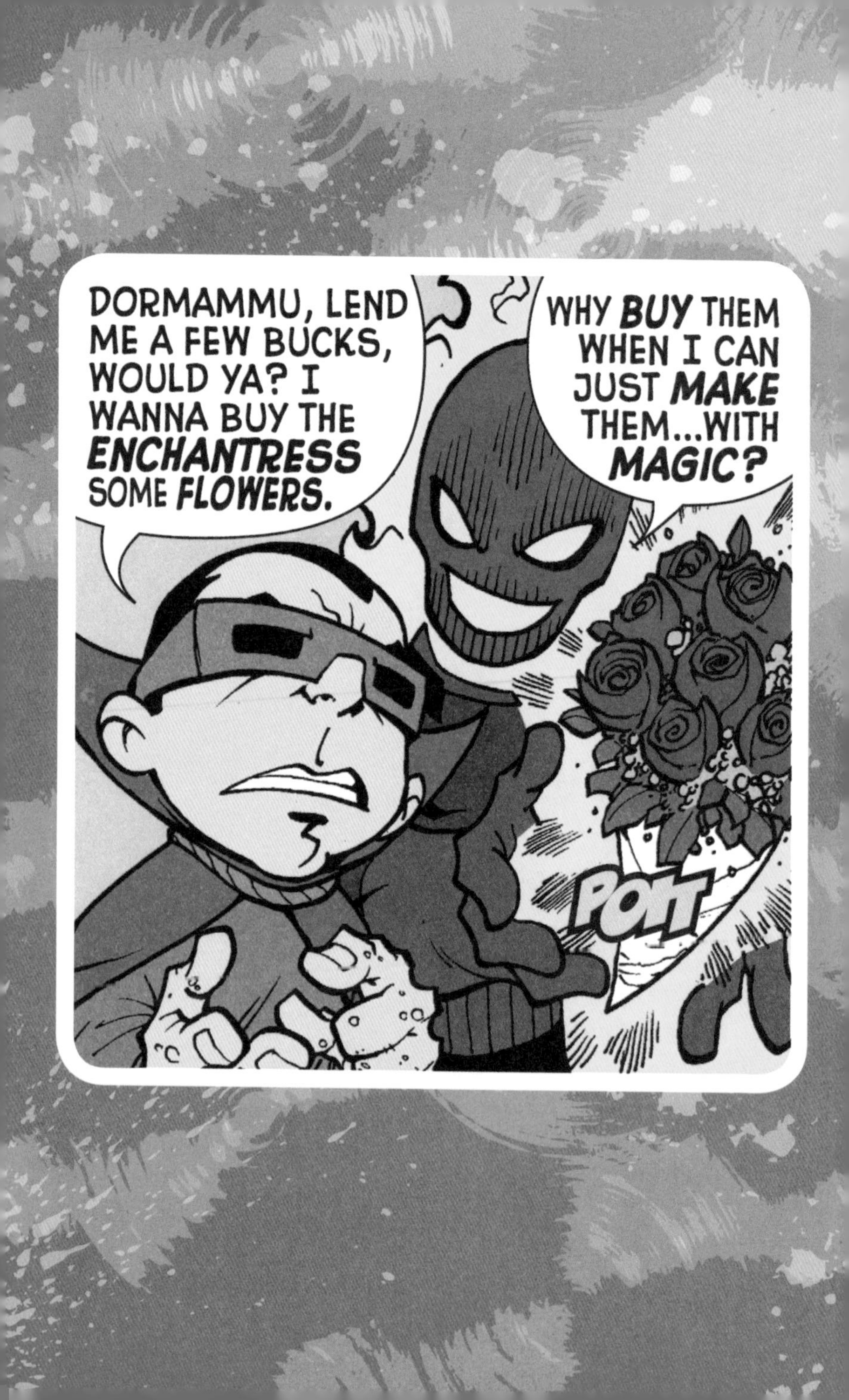
DORMAMMU, LEND ME A FEW BUCKS, WOULD YA? I WANNA BUY THE ENCHANTRESS SOME FLOWERS.
WHY BUY THEM WHEN I CAN JUST MAKE THEM...WITH MAGIC?
POIT

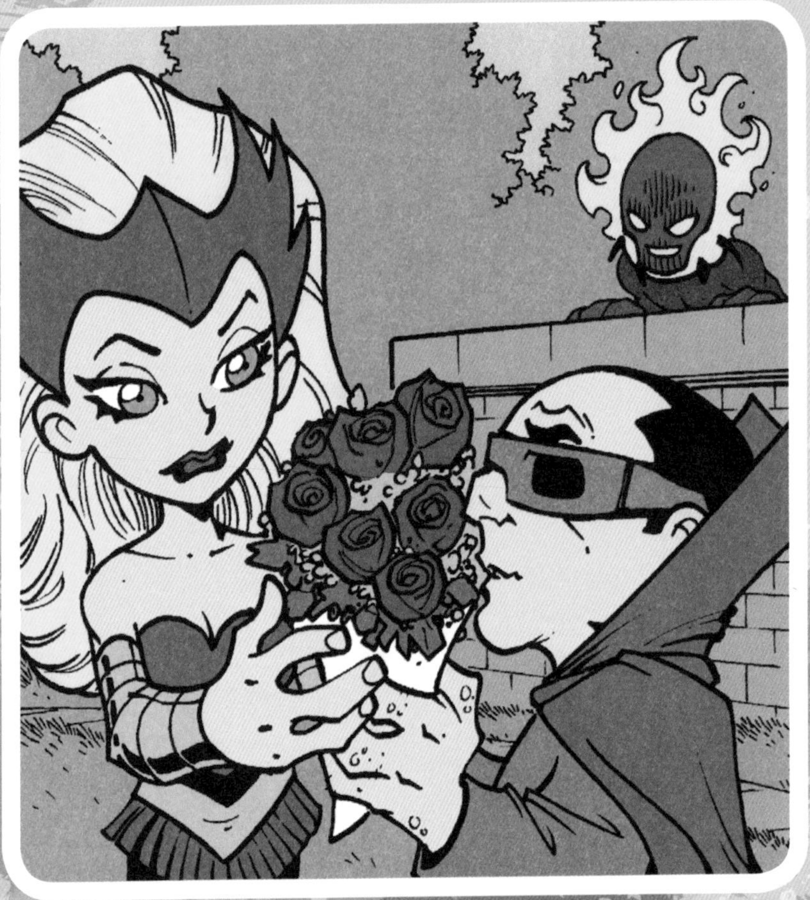

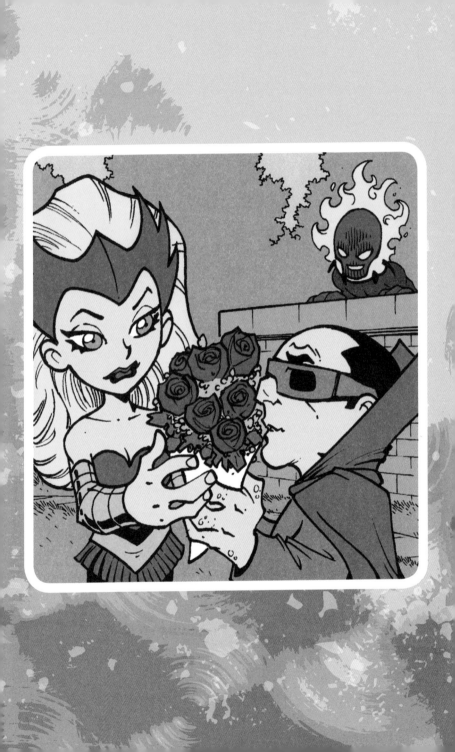

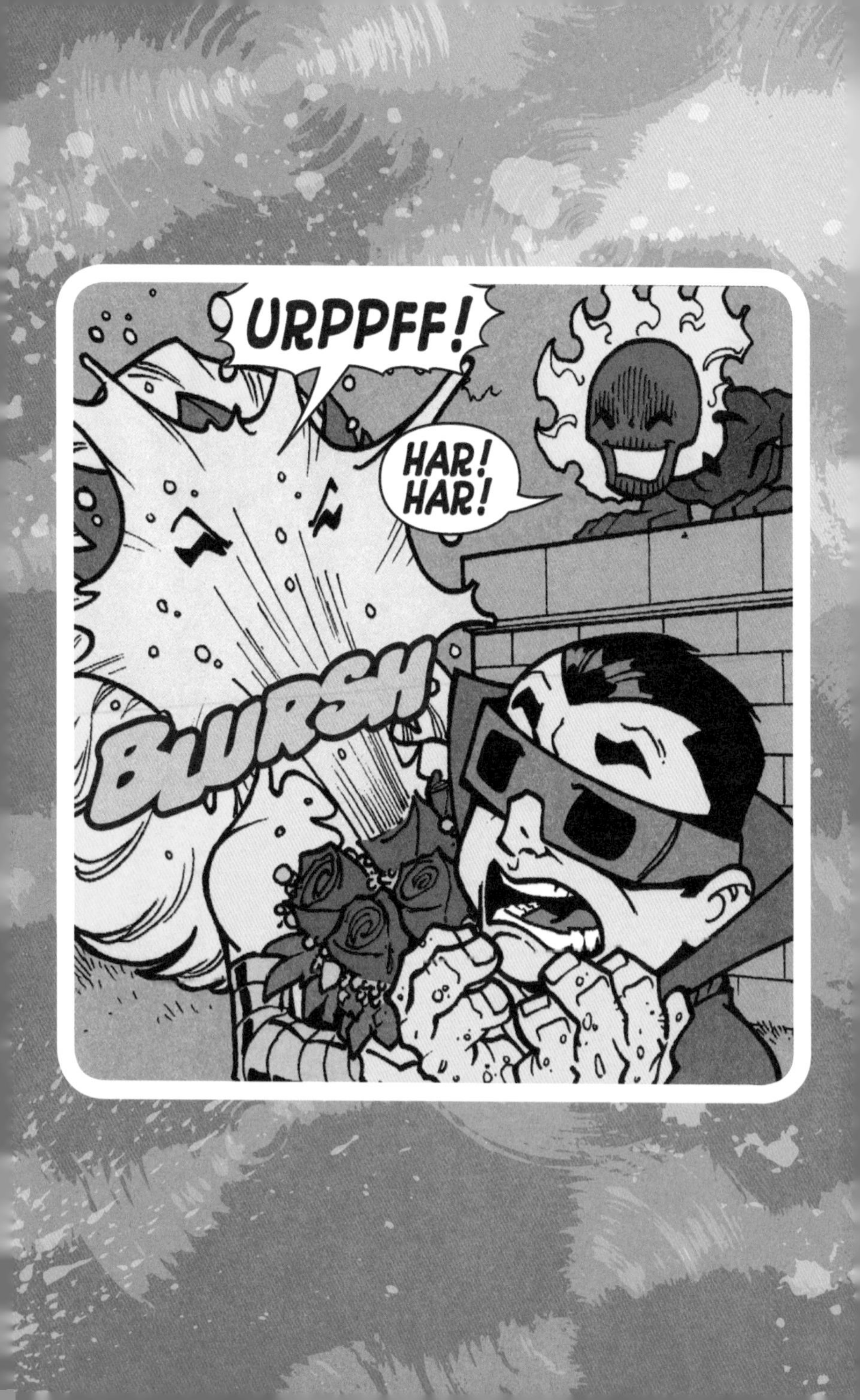
URPPFF!
HAR! HAR!
BLURSH

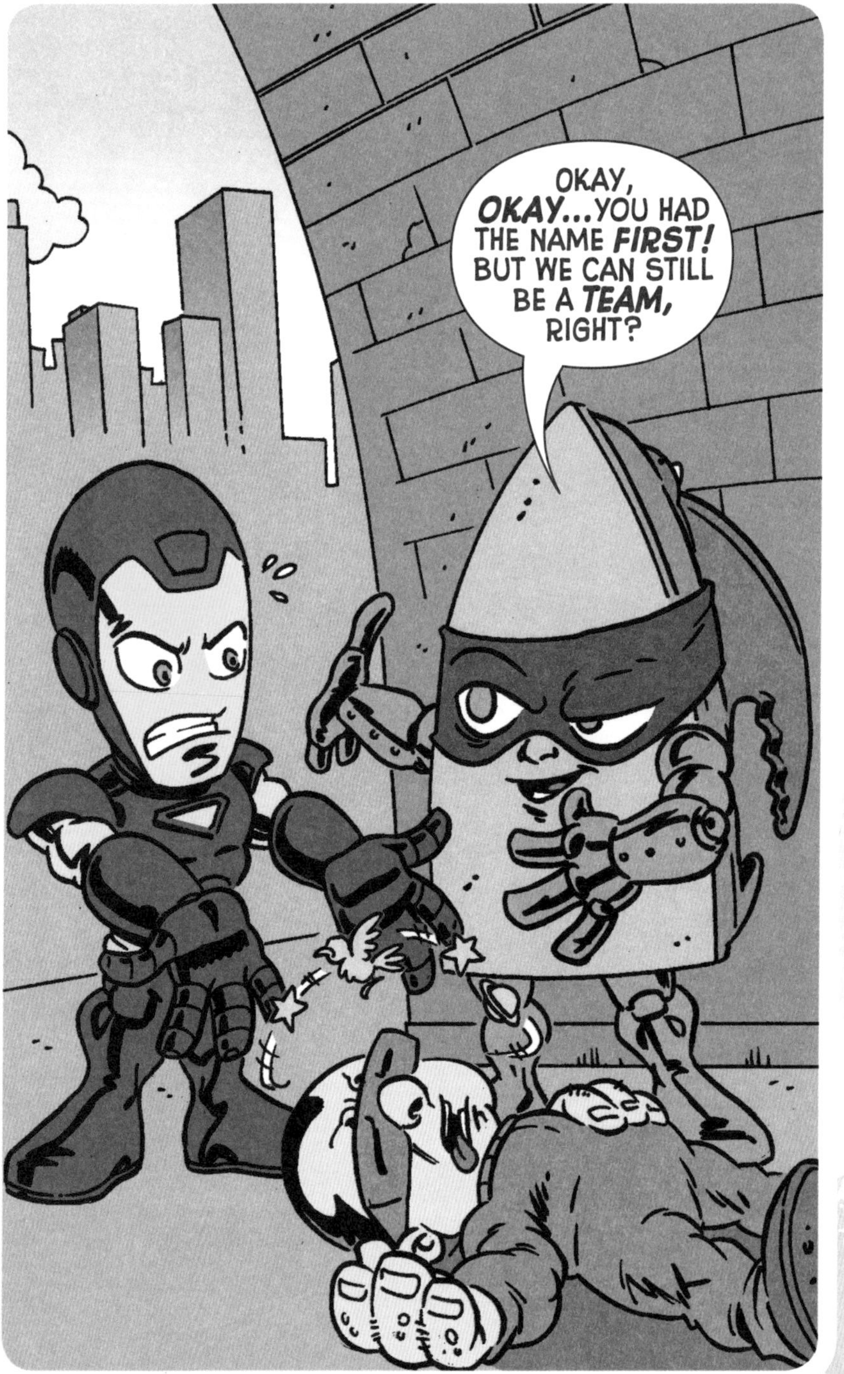
OKAY, OKAY...YOU HAD THE NAME FIRST! BUT WE CAN STILL BE A TEAM, RIGHT?

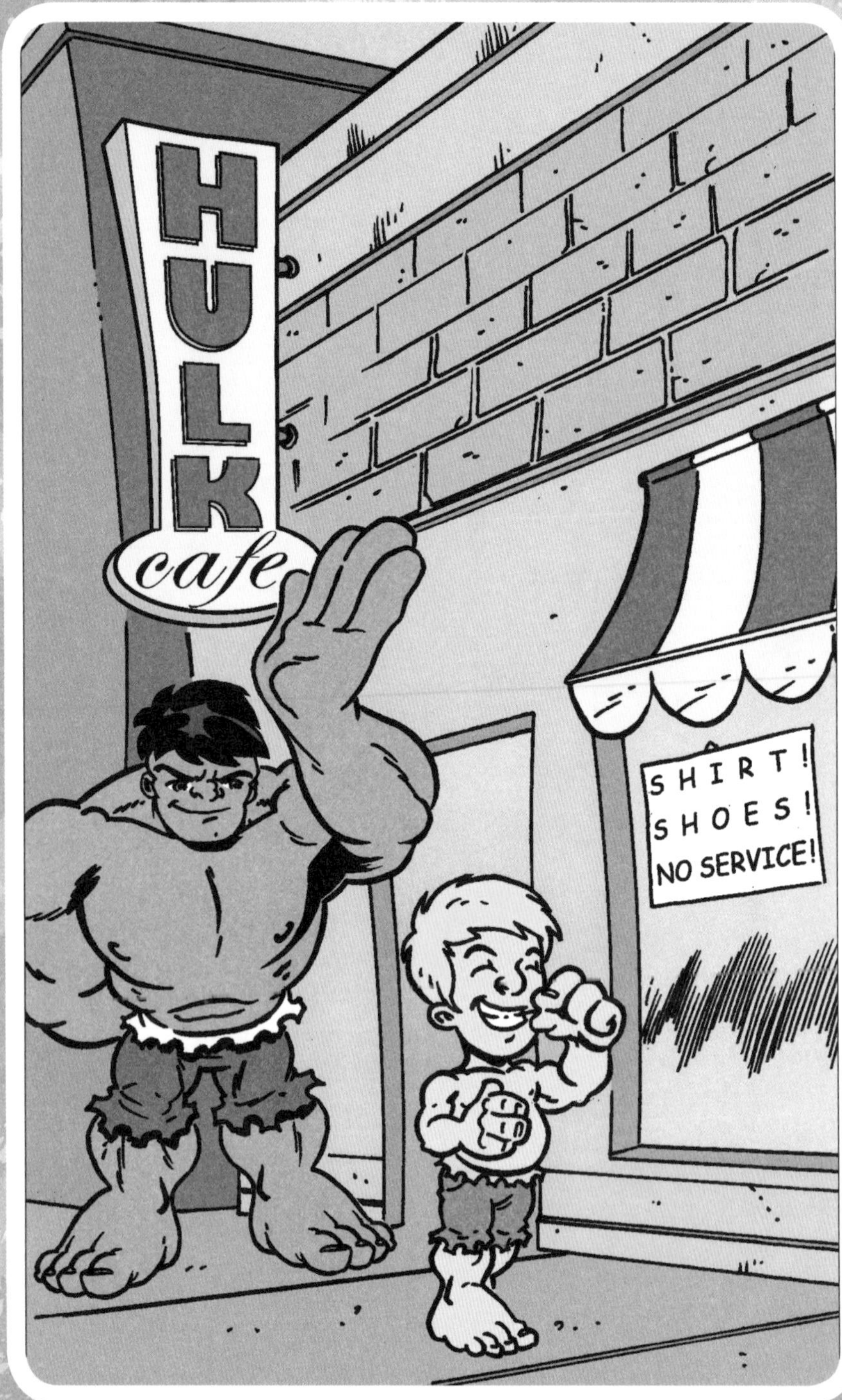
HULK
cafe
SHIRT!
SHOES!
NO SERVICE!

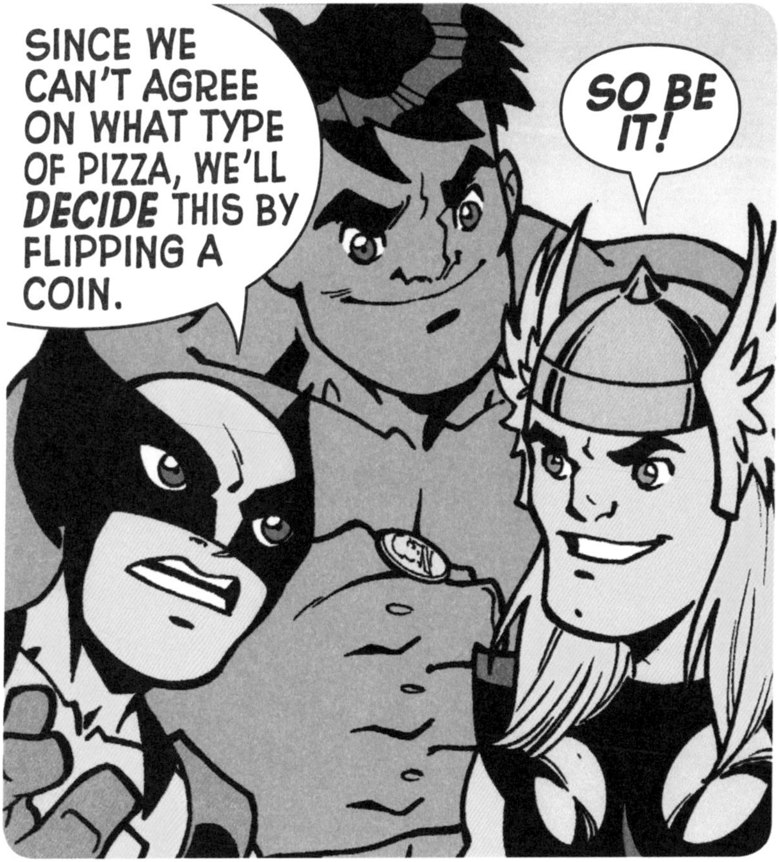
SINCE WE CAN'T AGREE ON WHAT TYPE OF PIZZA, WE'LL *DECIDE* THIS BY FLIPPING A COIN.
SO BE IT!

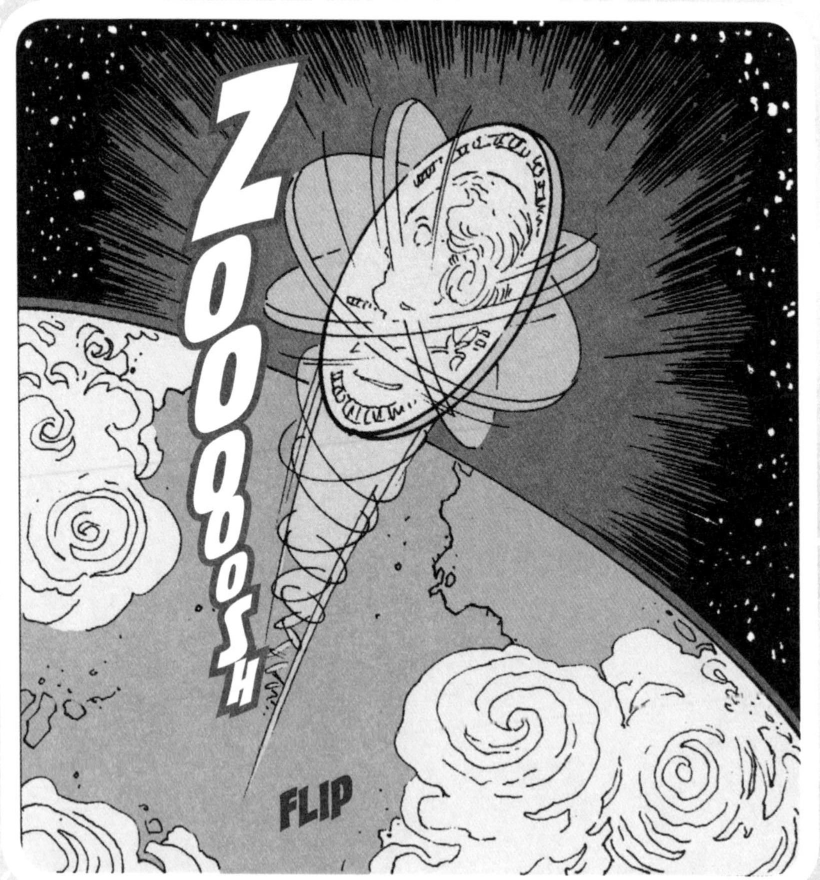
ZOOOOOSH
FLIP

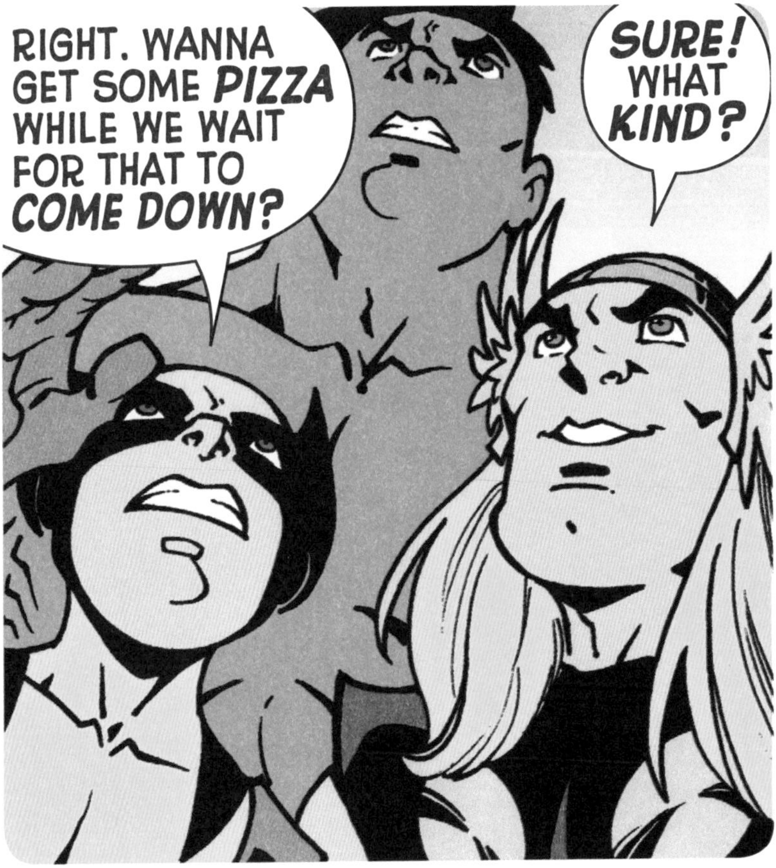
RIGHT. WANNA GET SOME PIZZA WHILE WE WAIT FOR THAT TO COME DOWN?
SURE! WHAT KIND?

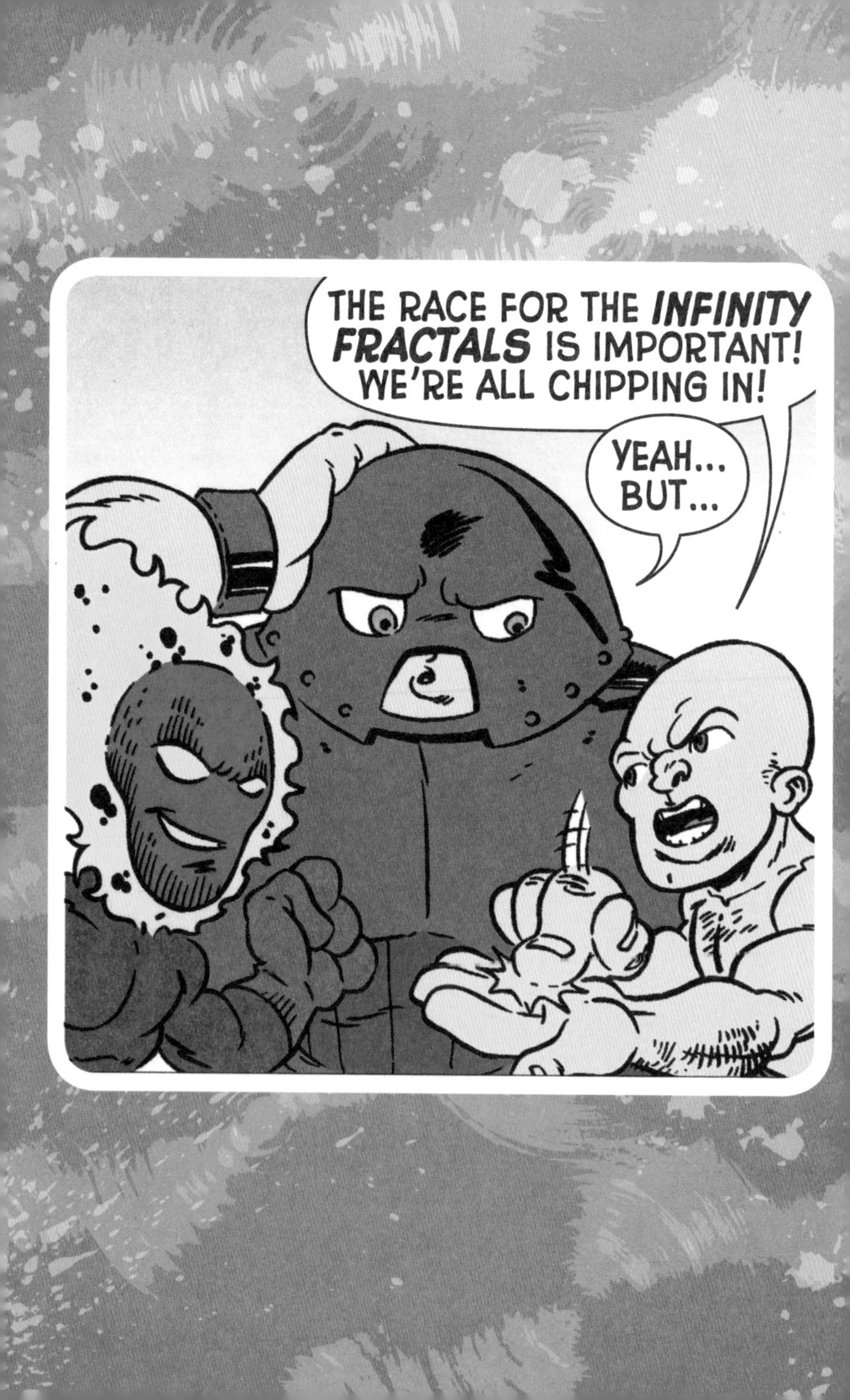
THE RACE FOR THE *INFINITY FRACTALS* IS IMPORTANT! WE'RE ALL CHIPPING IN!
YEAH... BUT...

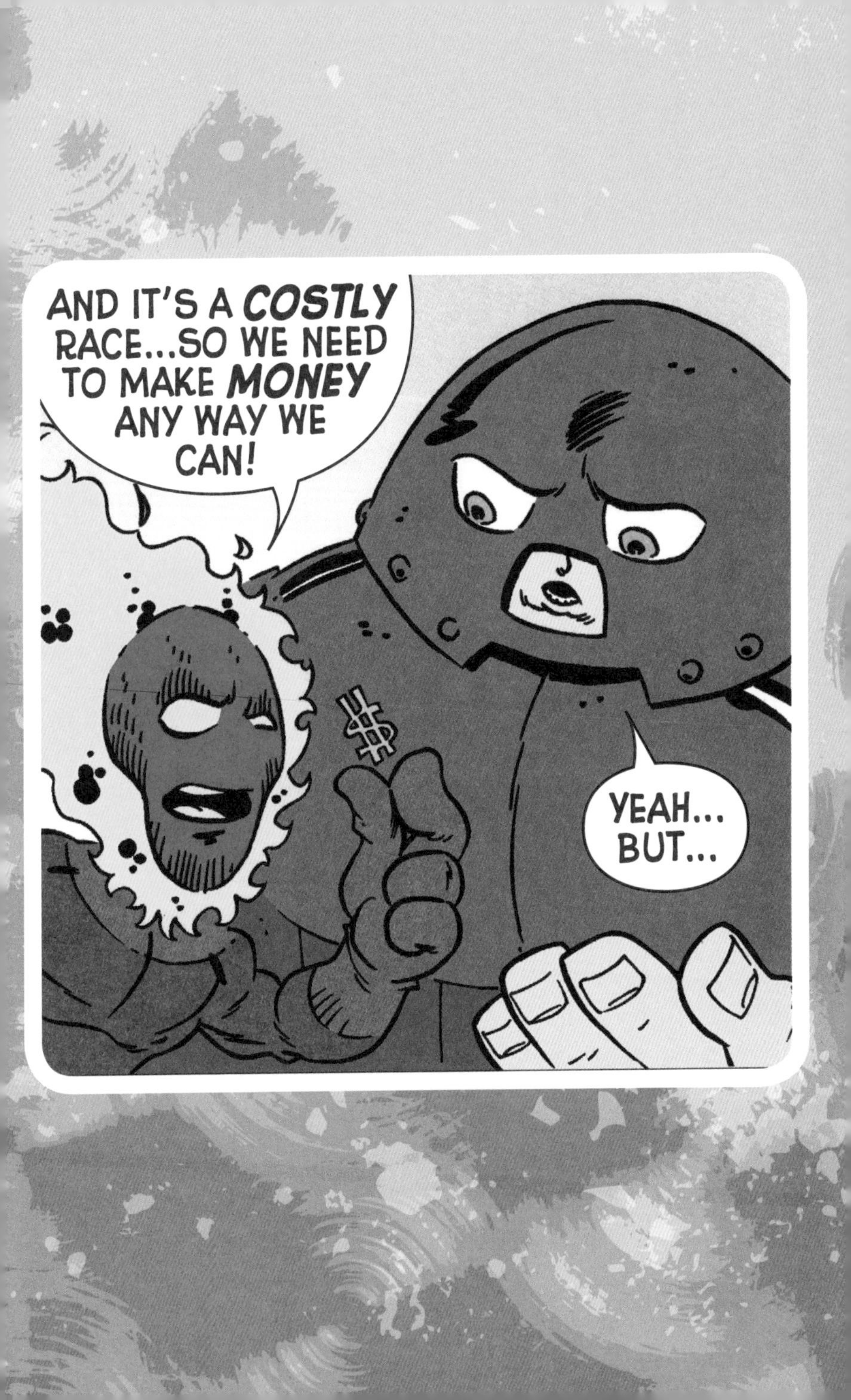
AND IT'S A COSTLY RACE...SO WE NEED TO MAKE MONEY ANY WAY WE CAN!
YEAH... BUT...

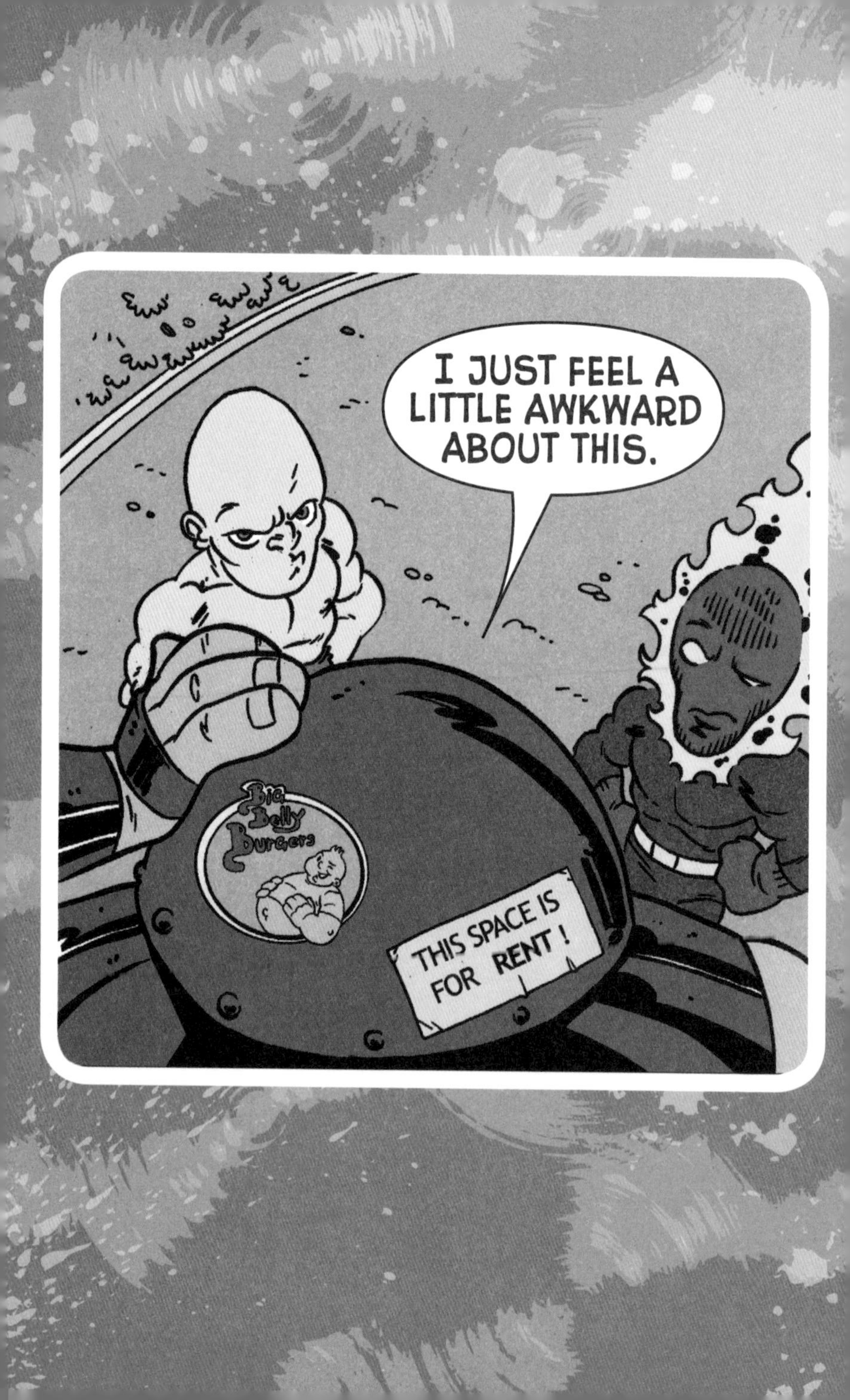
I JUST FEEL A LITTLE AWKWARD ABOUT THIS.
Big Belly Burgers
THIS SPACE IS FOR RENT!

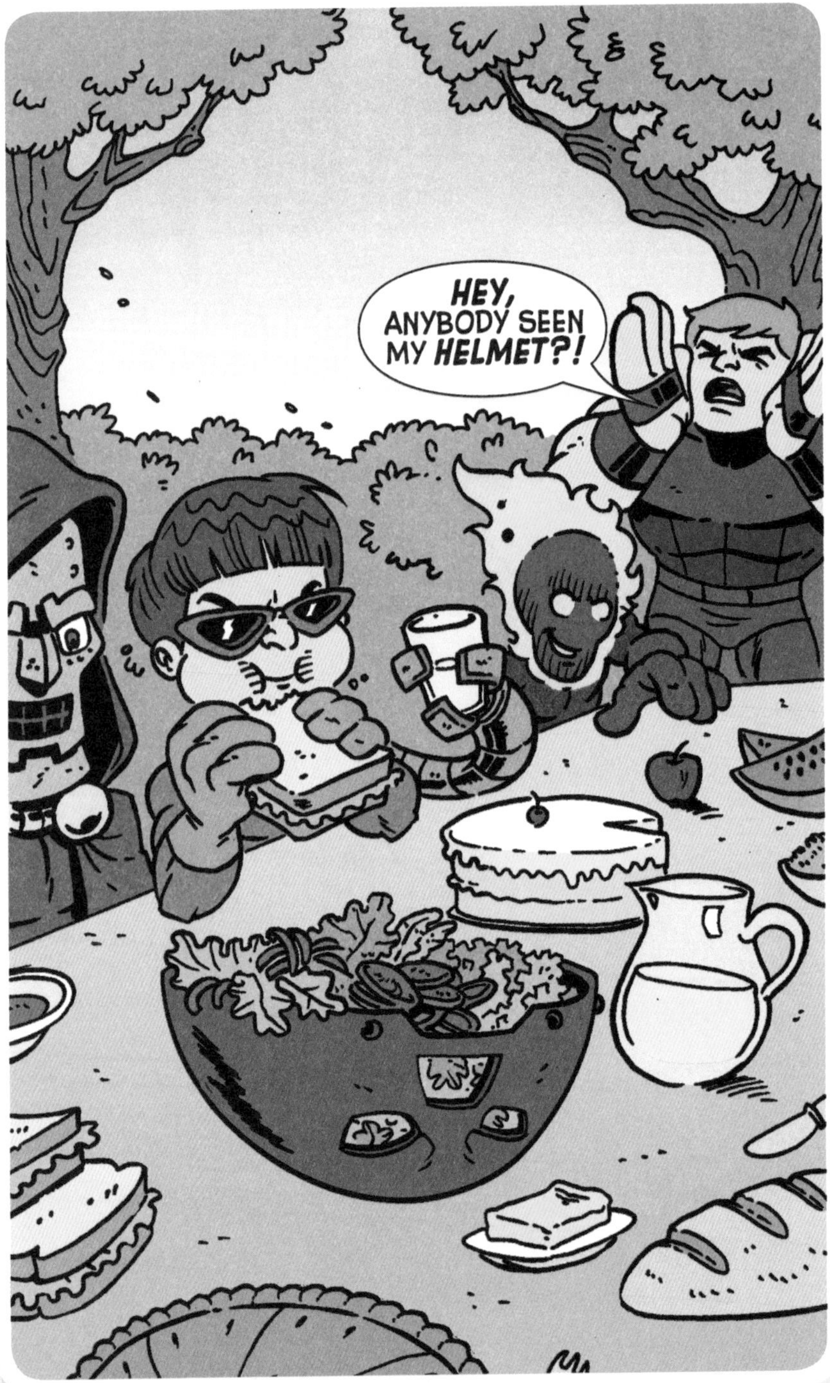
HEY, ANYBODY SEEN MY HELMET?!

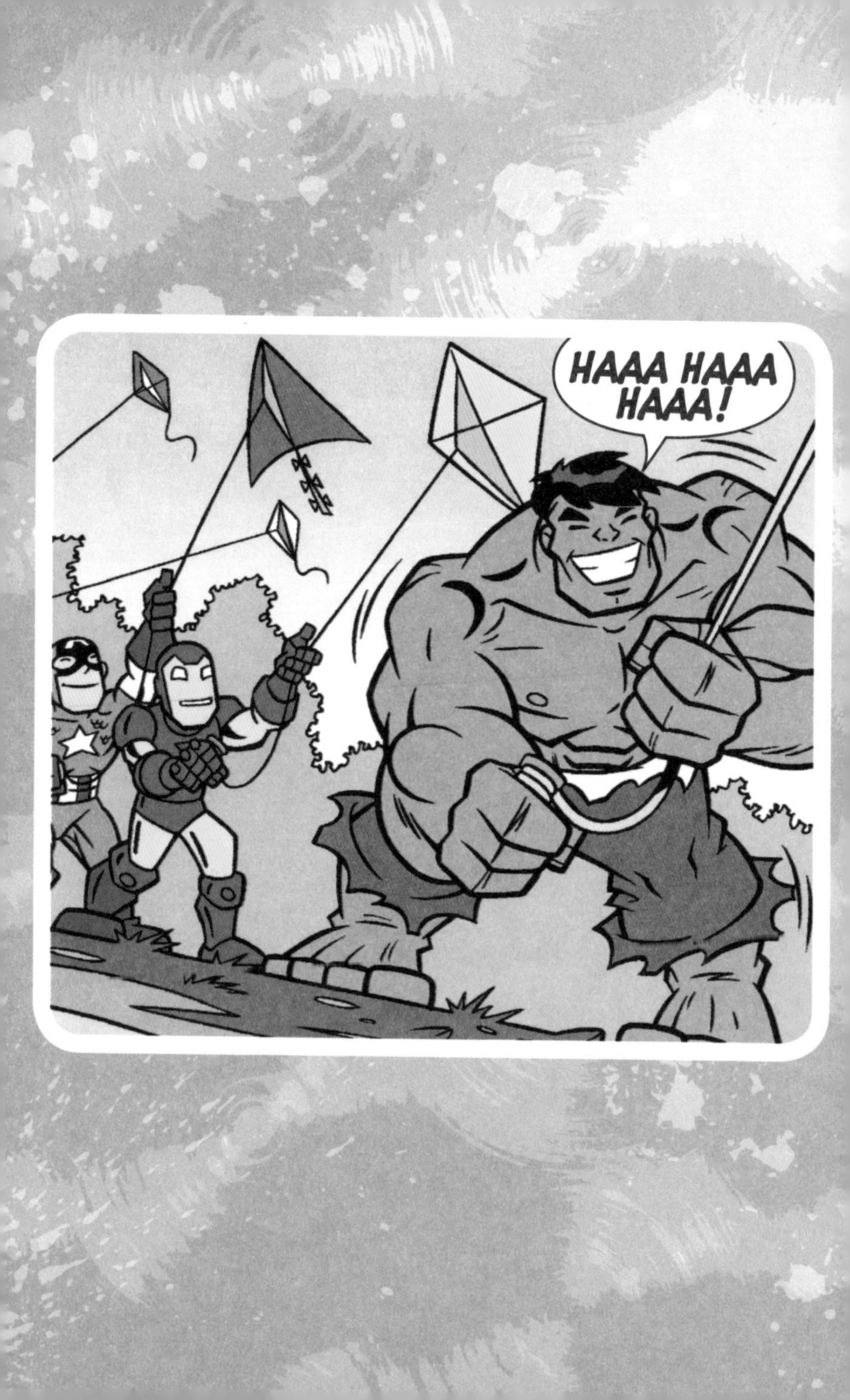
HAAA HAAA HAAA!

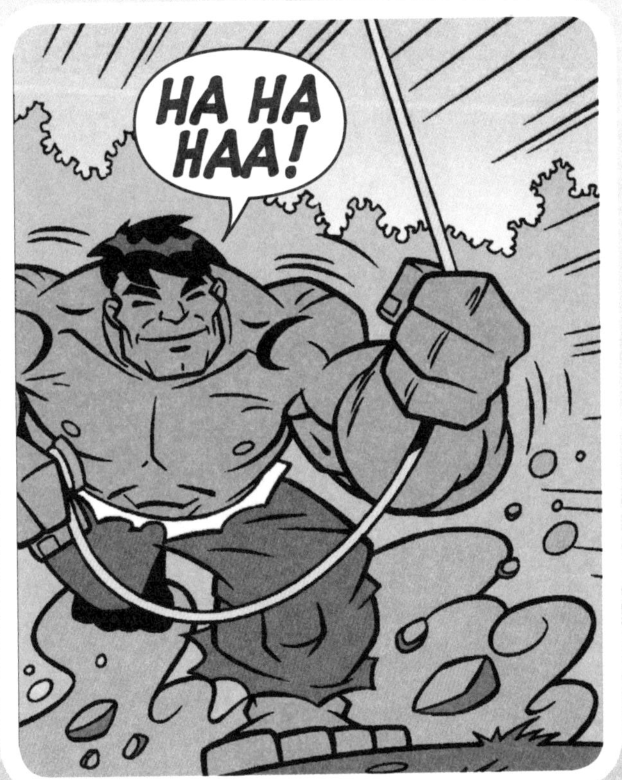
HA HA HAA!

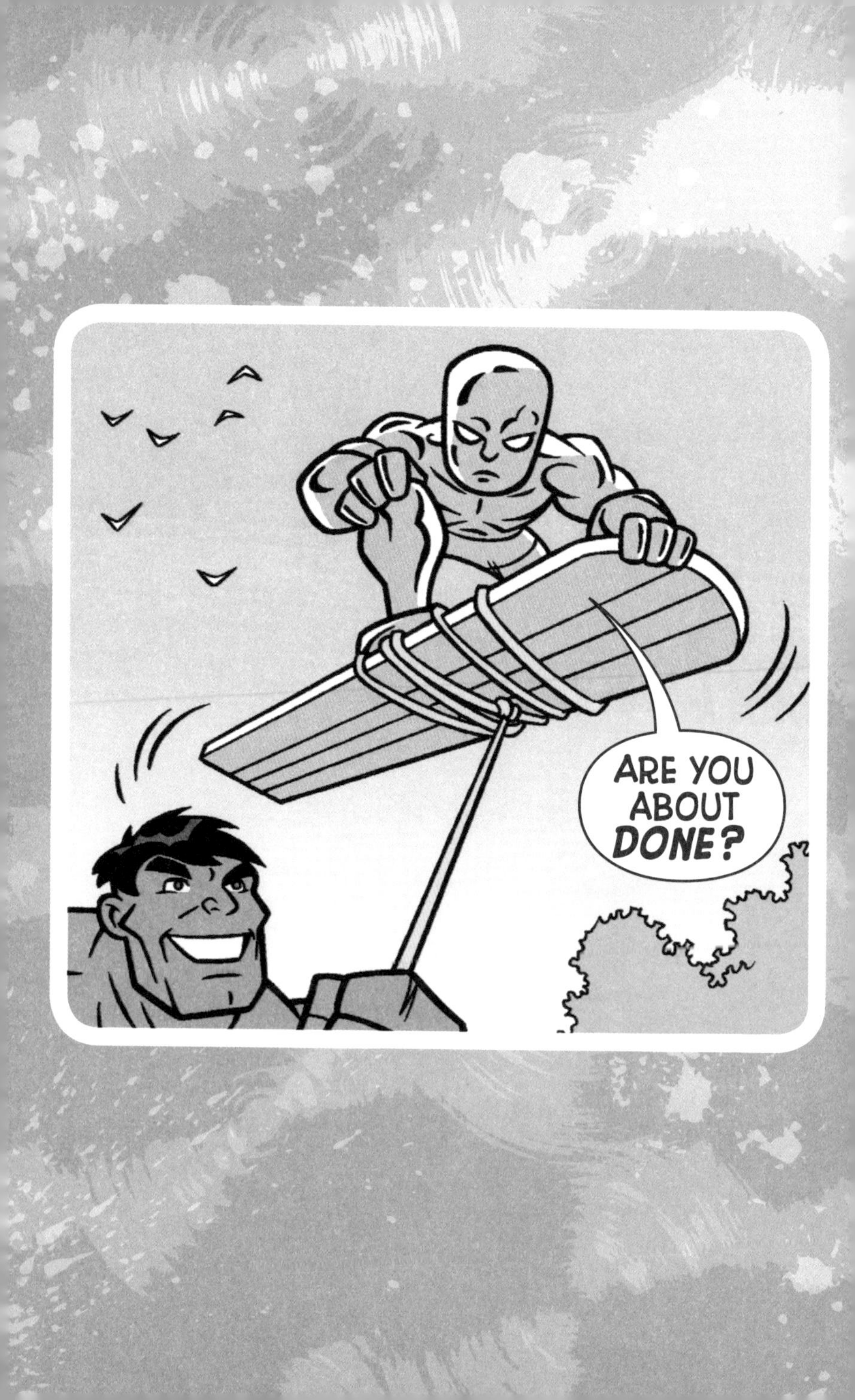
ARE YOU ABOUT DONE?

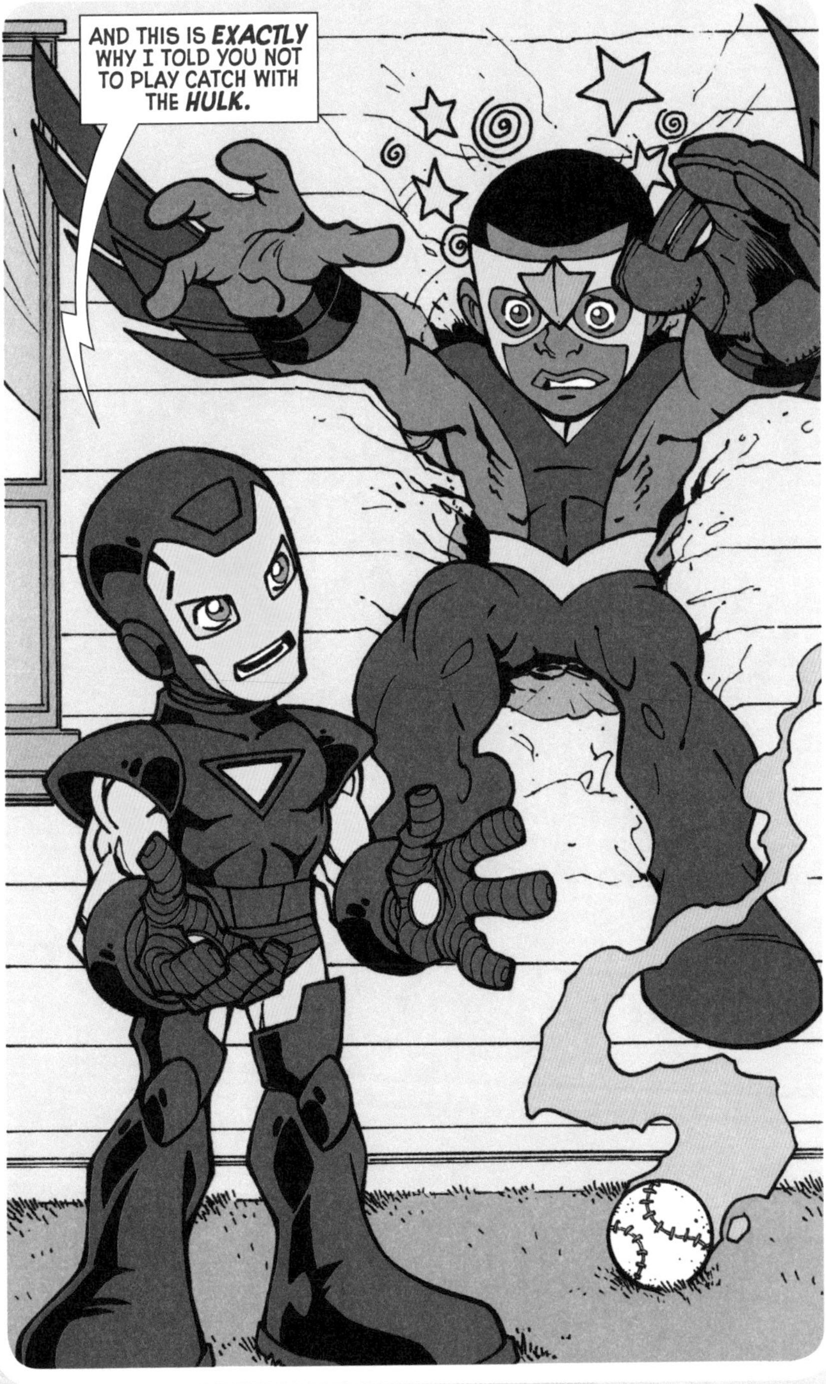
AND THIS IS EXACTLY WHY I TOLD YOU NOT TO PLAY CATCH WITH THE HULK.

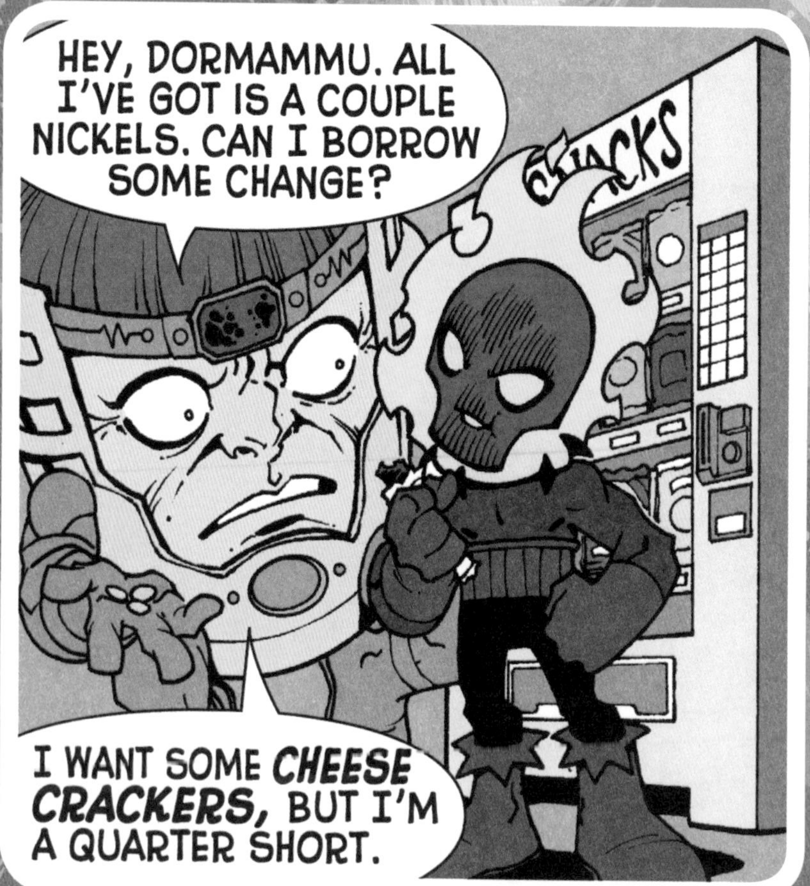
HEY, DORMAMMU. ALL I'VE GOT IS A COUPLE NICKELS. CAN I BORROW SOME CHANGE?
I WANT SOME CHEESE CRACKERS, BUT I'M A QUARTER SHORT.

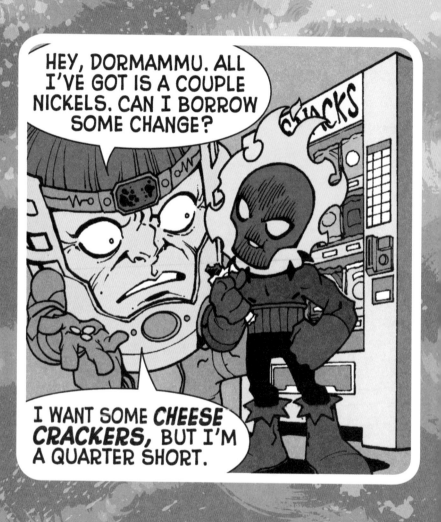

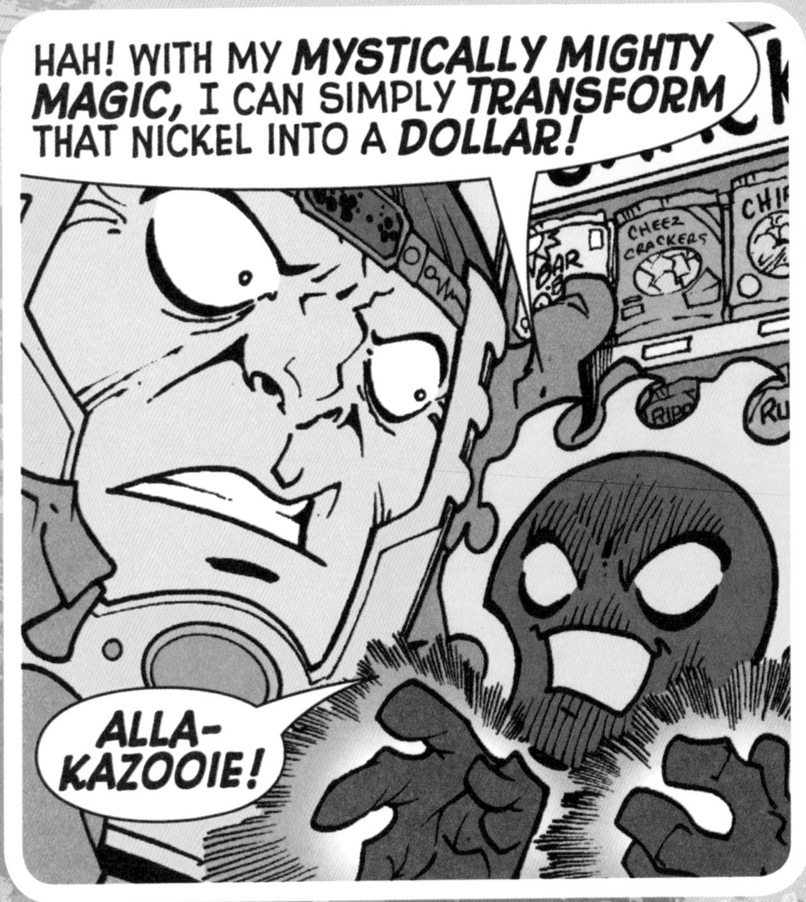
HAH! WITH MY MYSTICALLY MIGHTY MAGIC, I CAN SIMPLY TRANSFORM THAT NICKEL INTO A DOLLAR!
CHEEZ CRACKERS
ALLA-KAZOOIE!

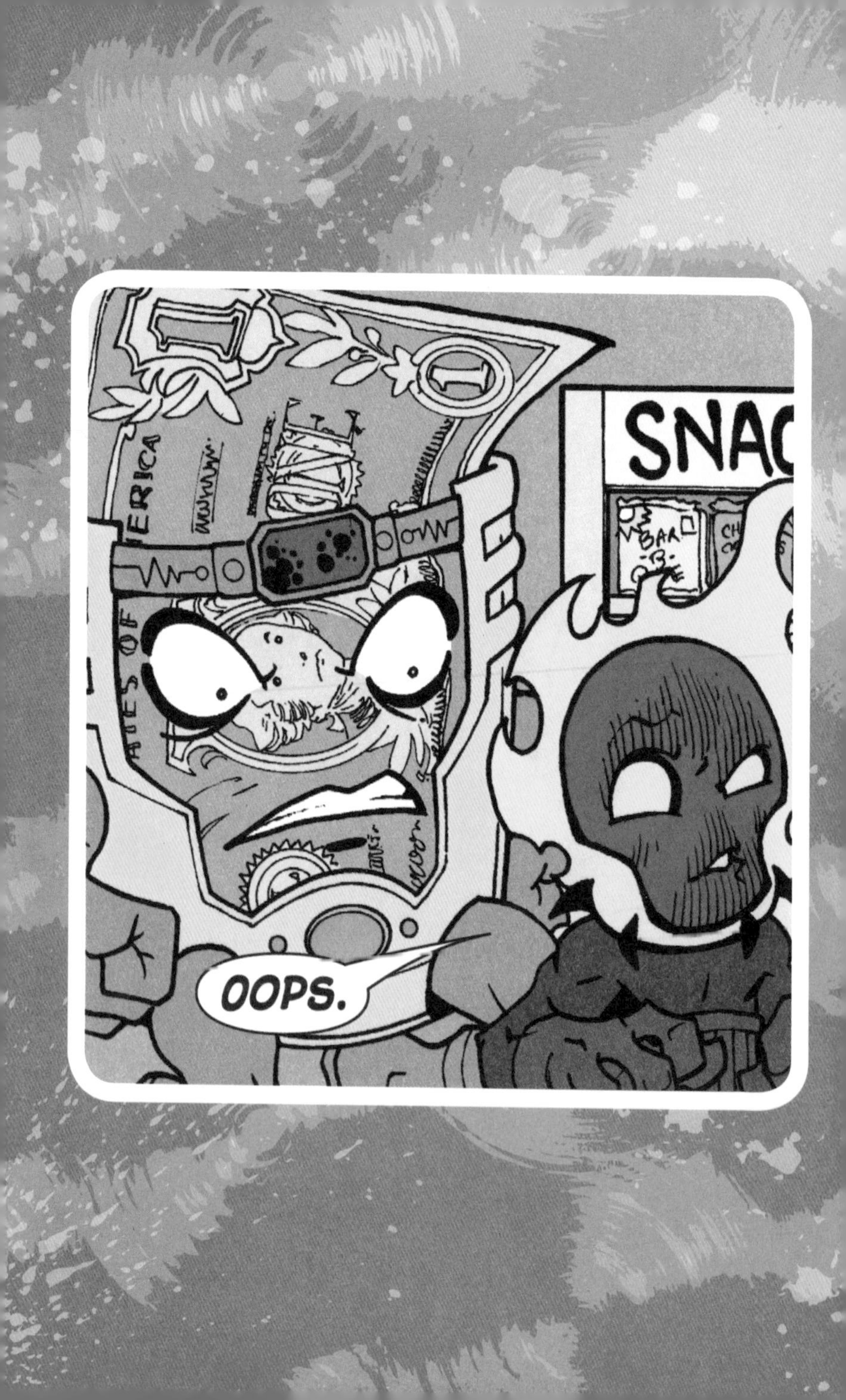
OOPS.

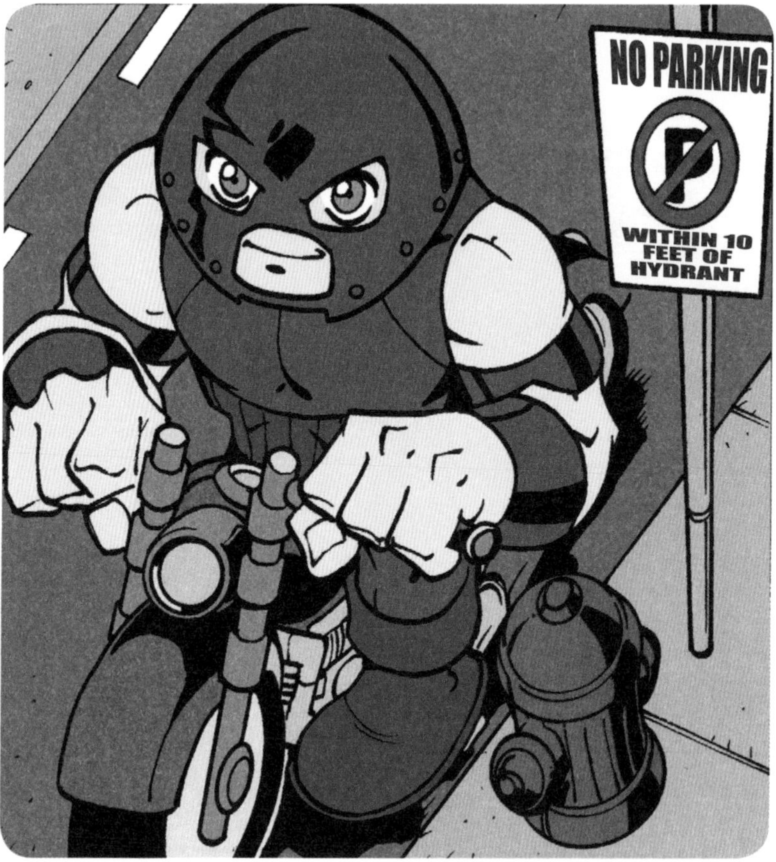
NO PARKING
P
WITHIN 10
FEET OF
HYDRANT

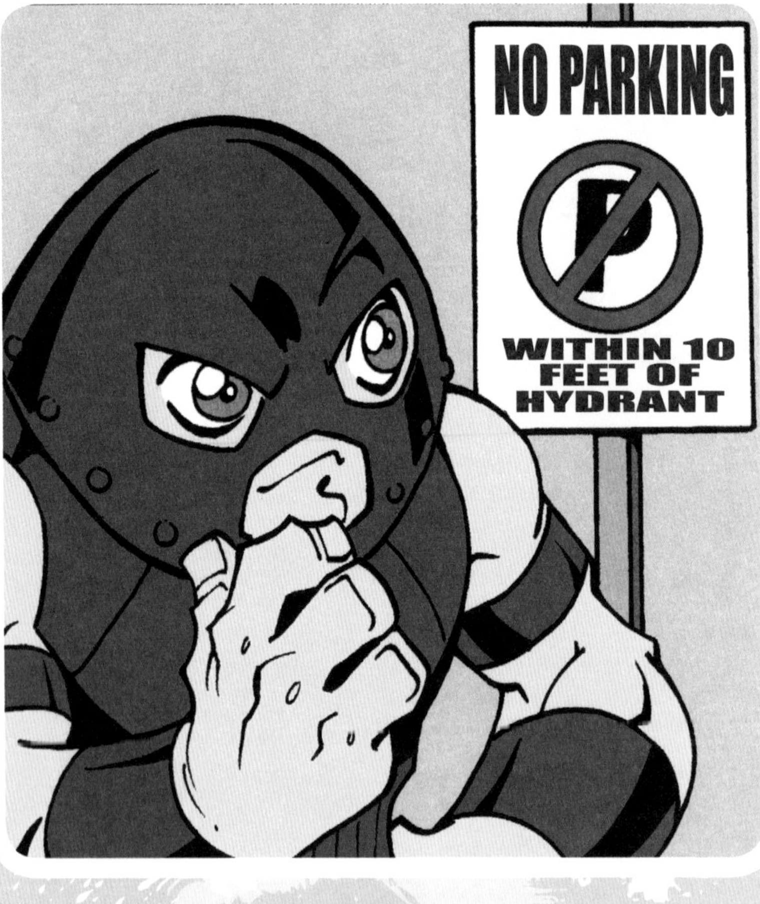
NO PARKING
WITHIN 10
FEET OF
HYDRANT

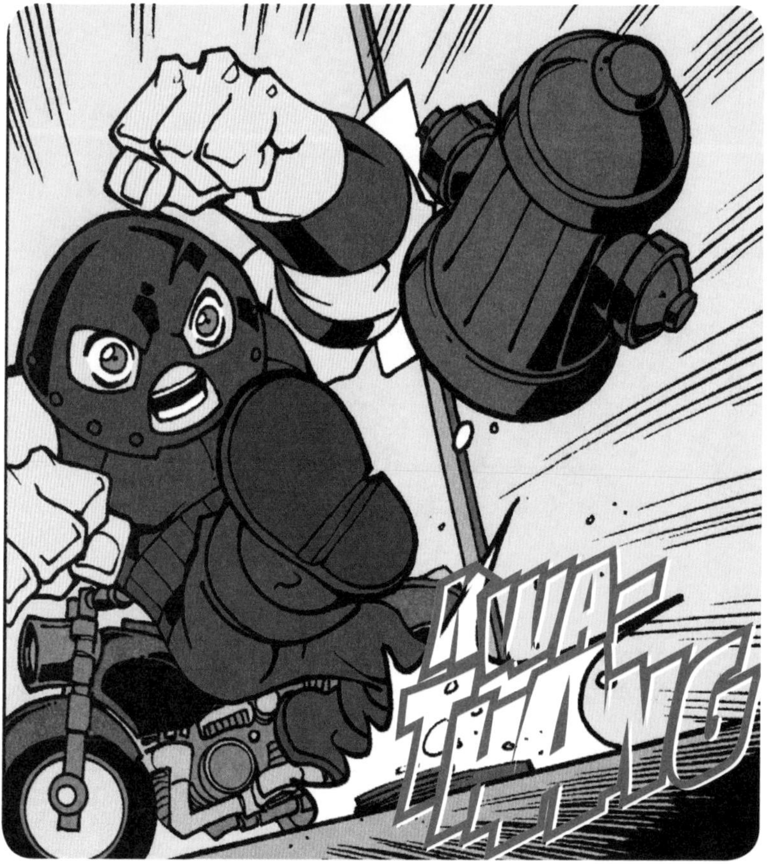
KWA-
THANG

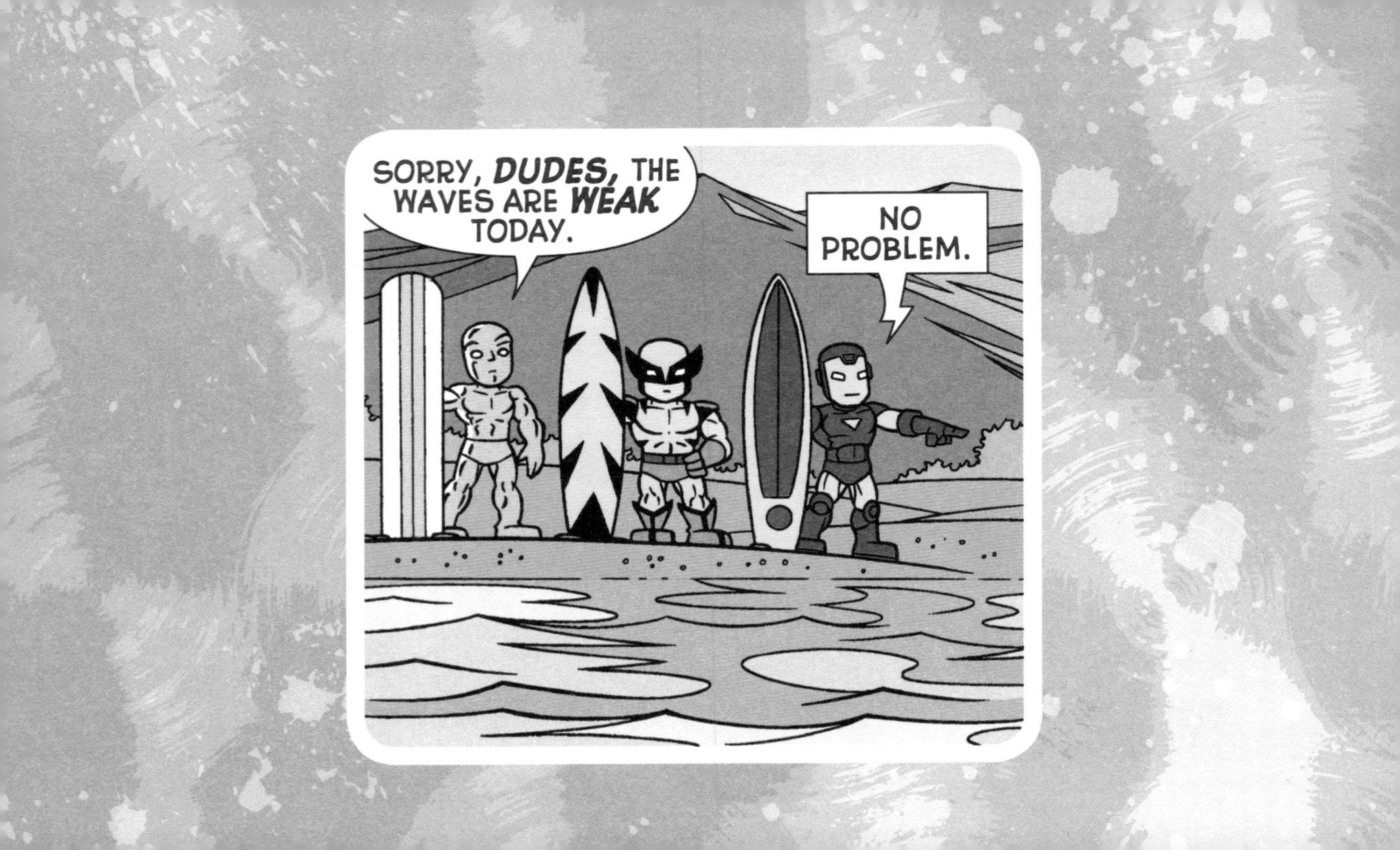
SORRY, DUDES, THE WAVES ARE WEAK TODAY.
NO PROBLEM.

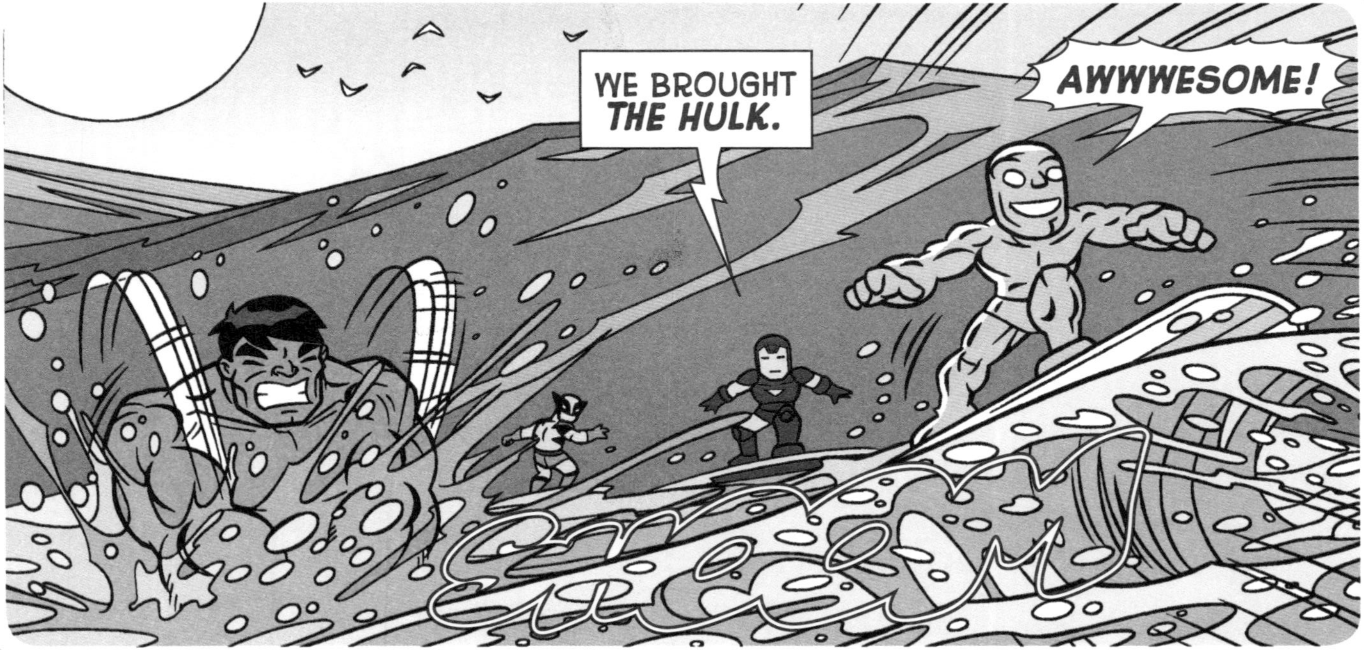
WE BROUGHT THE HULK.
AWWWESOME!

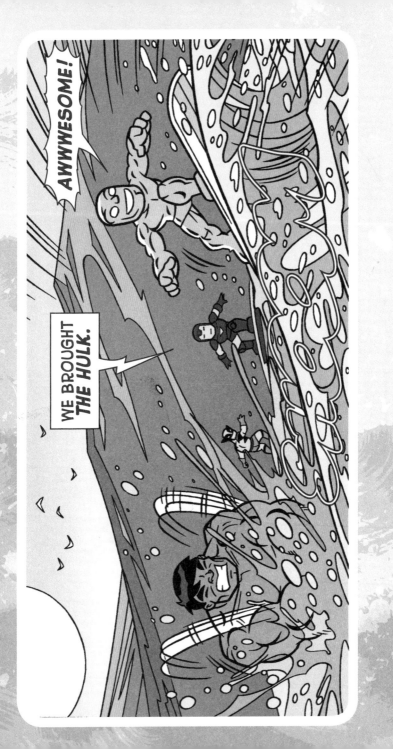

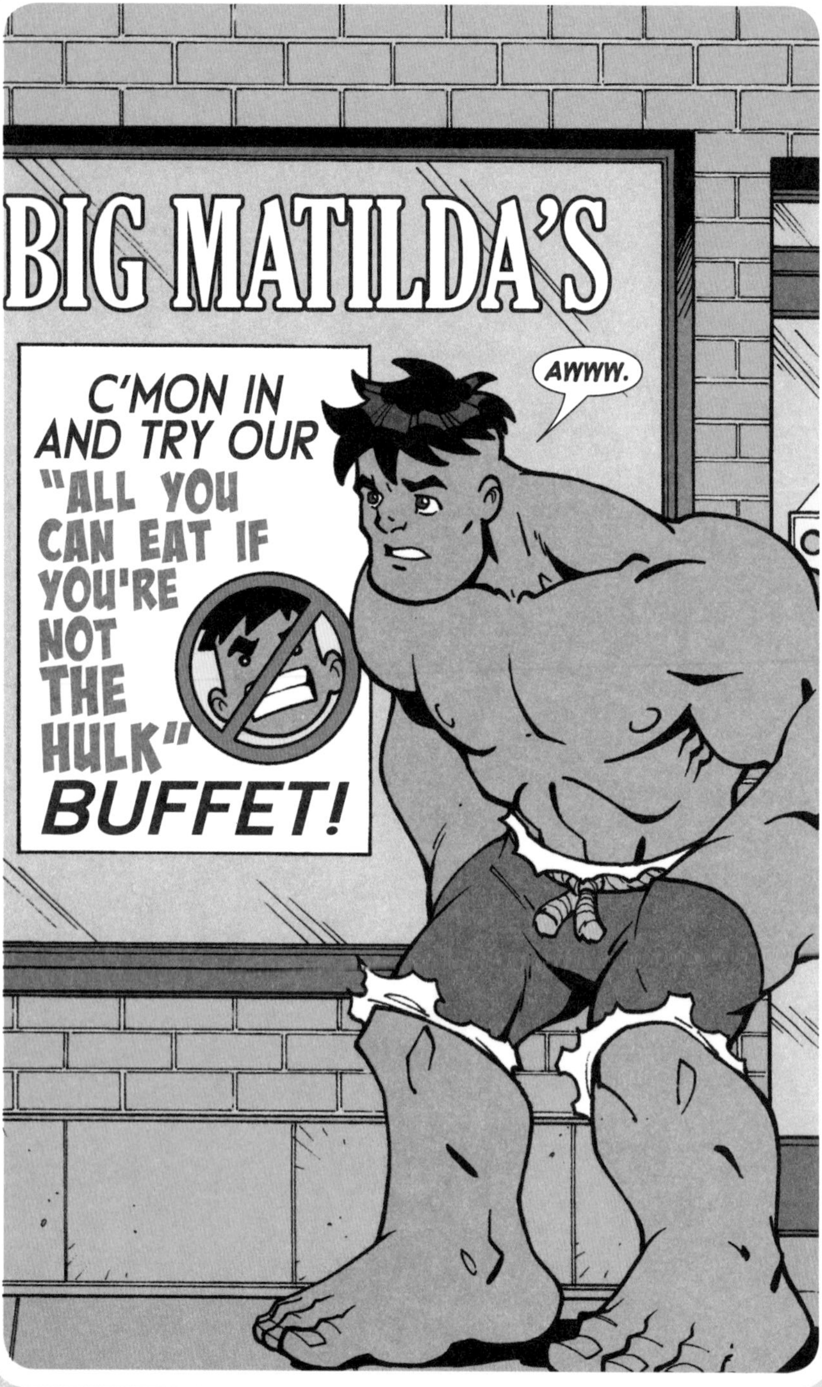
BIG MATILDA'S
C'MON IN AND TRY OUR "ALL YOU CAN EAT IF YOU'RE NOT THE HULK" BUFFET!
AWWW.

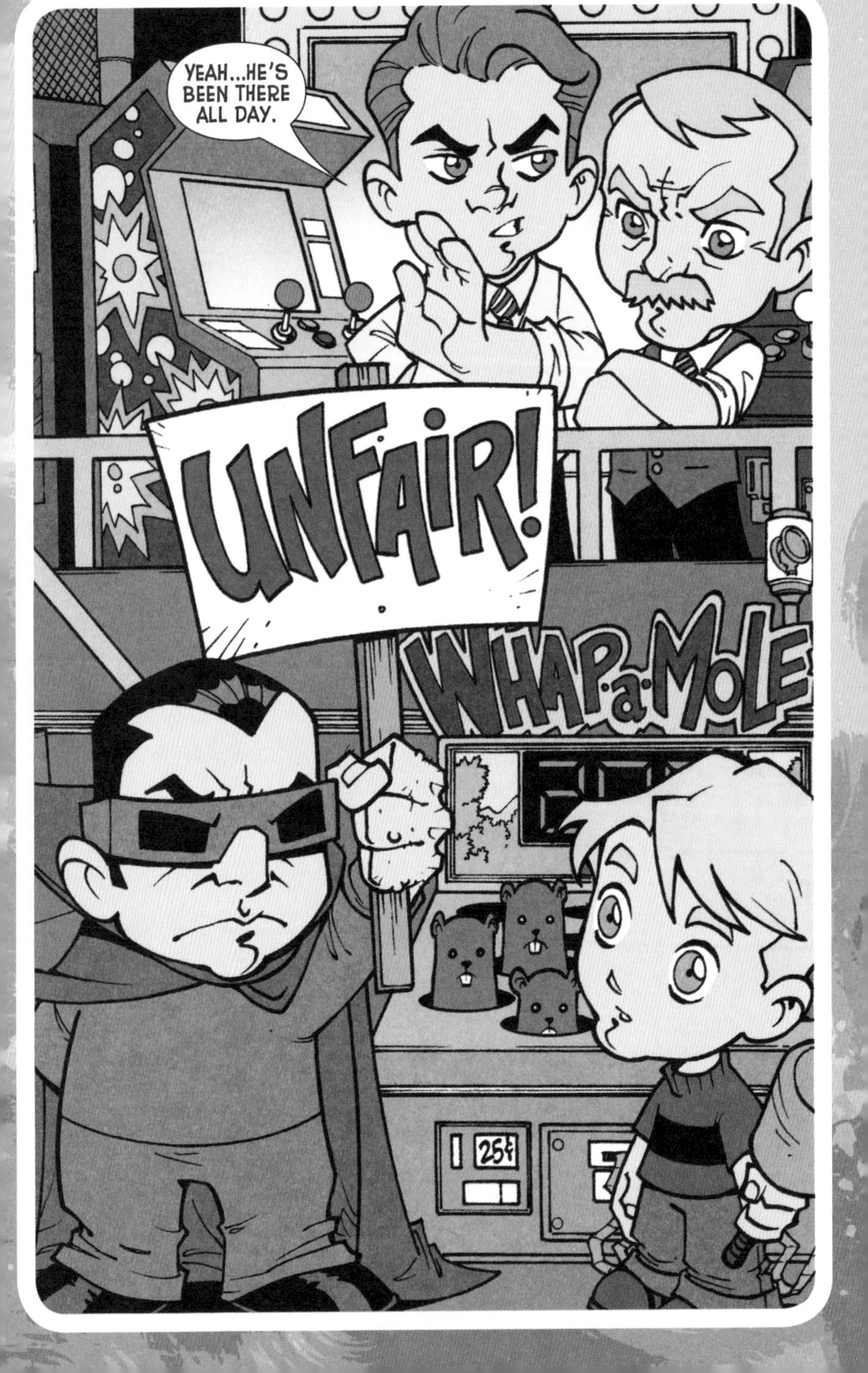
YEAH...HE'S BEEN THERE ALL DAY.
UNFAIR!
WHAP-a-MOLE
25¢

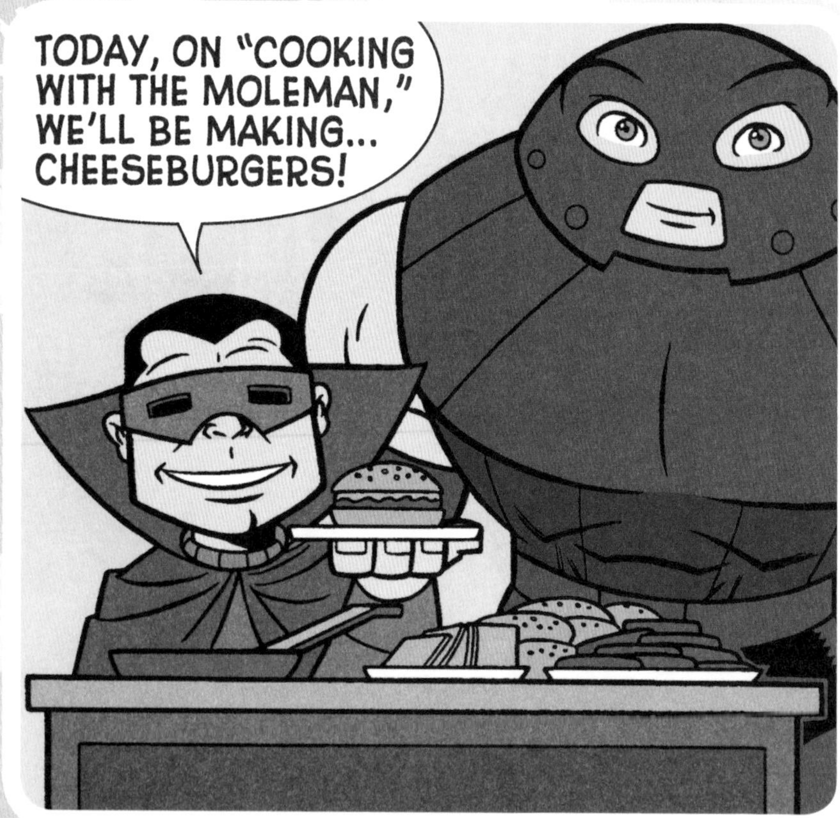
TODAY, ON "COOKING WITH THE MOLEMAN," WE'LL BE MAKING... CHEESEBURGERS!

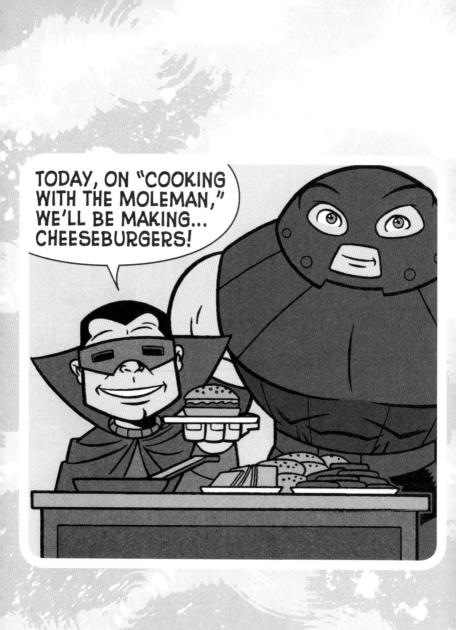

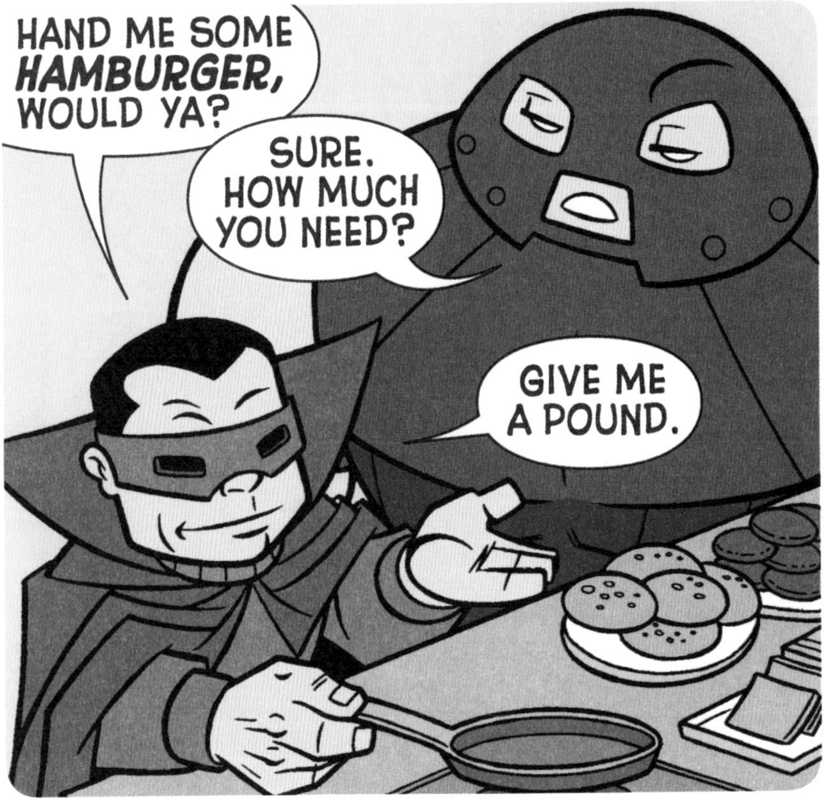
HAND ME SOME *HAMBURGER,* WOULD YA?
SURE. HOW MUCH YOU NEED?
GIVE ME A POUND.

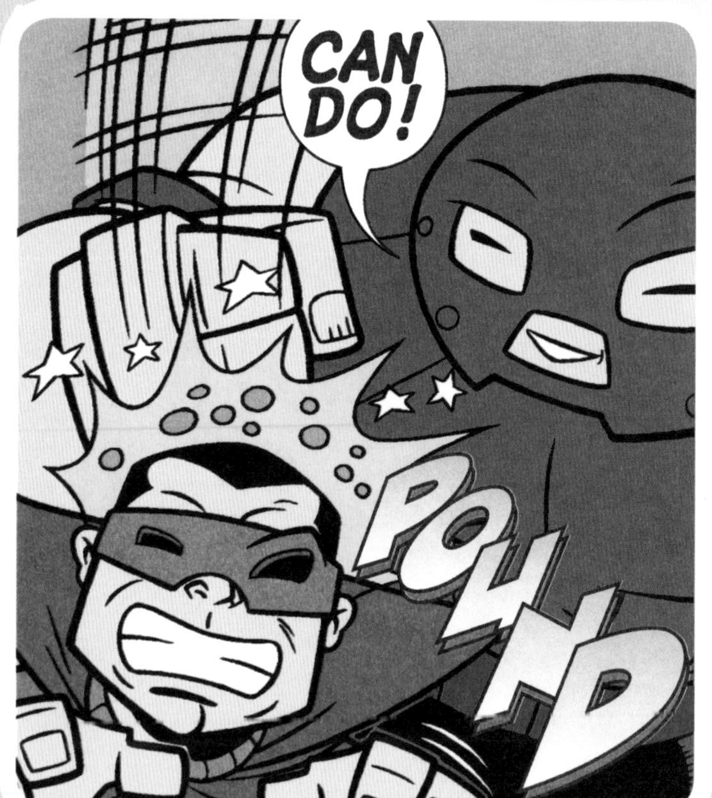
CAN DO!
POUND

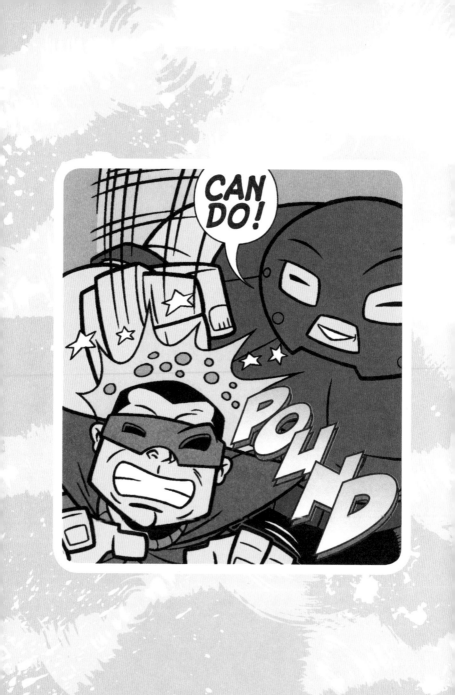

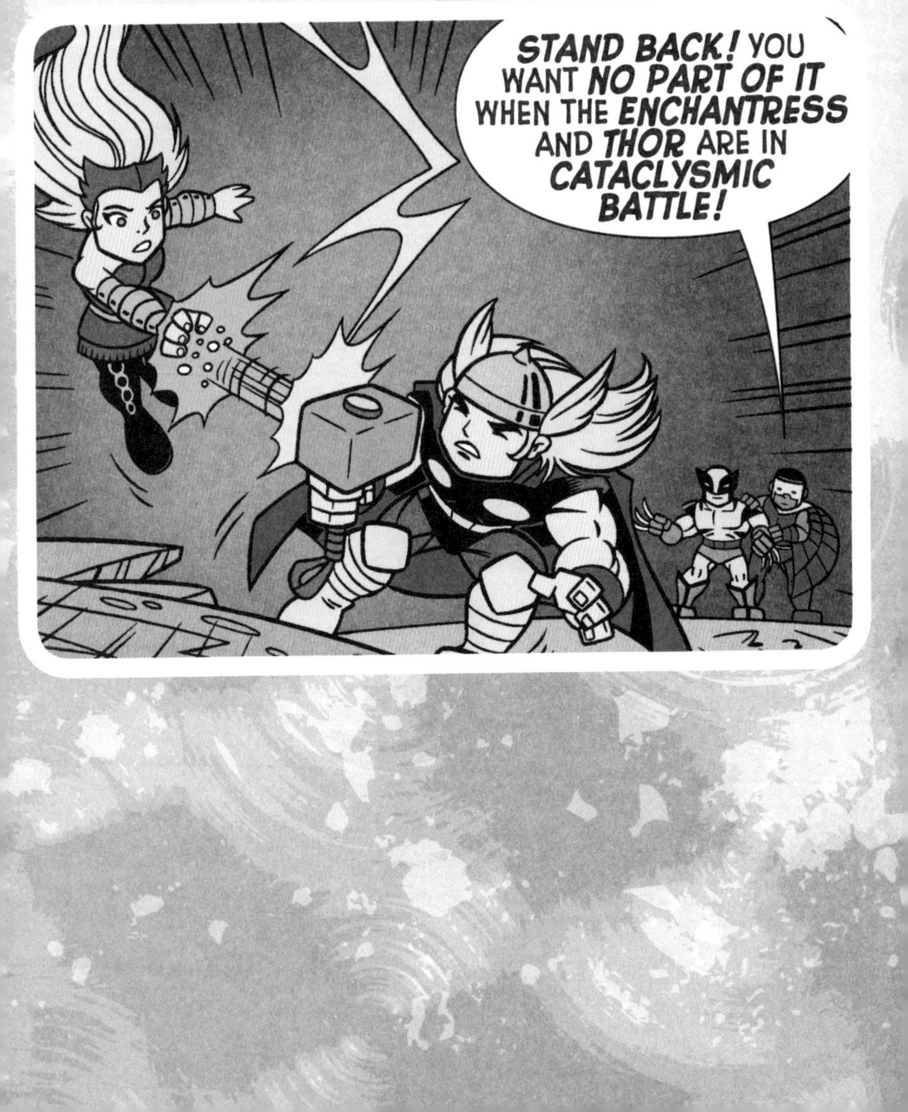
STAND BACK! YOU WANT NO PART OF IT WHEN THE ENCHANTRESS AND THOR ARE IN CATACLYSMIC BATTLE!

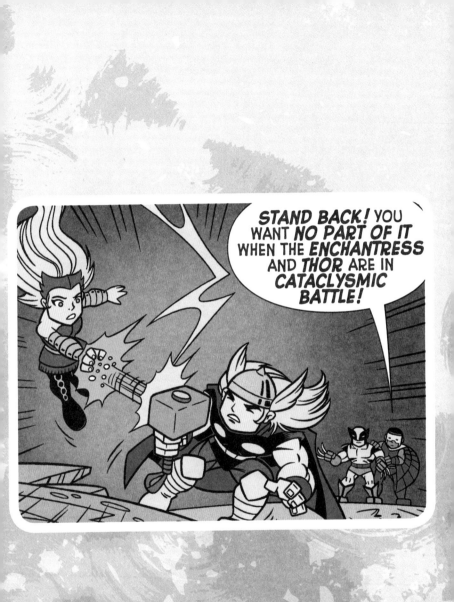

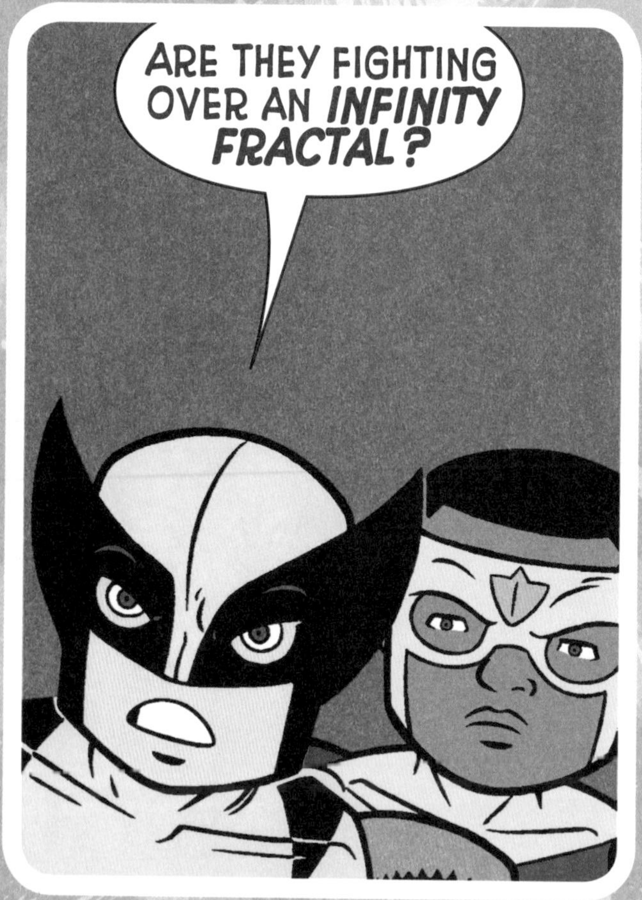
ARE THEY FIGHTING OVER AN *INFINITY FRACTAL*?

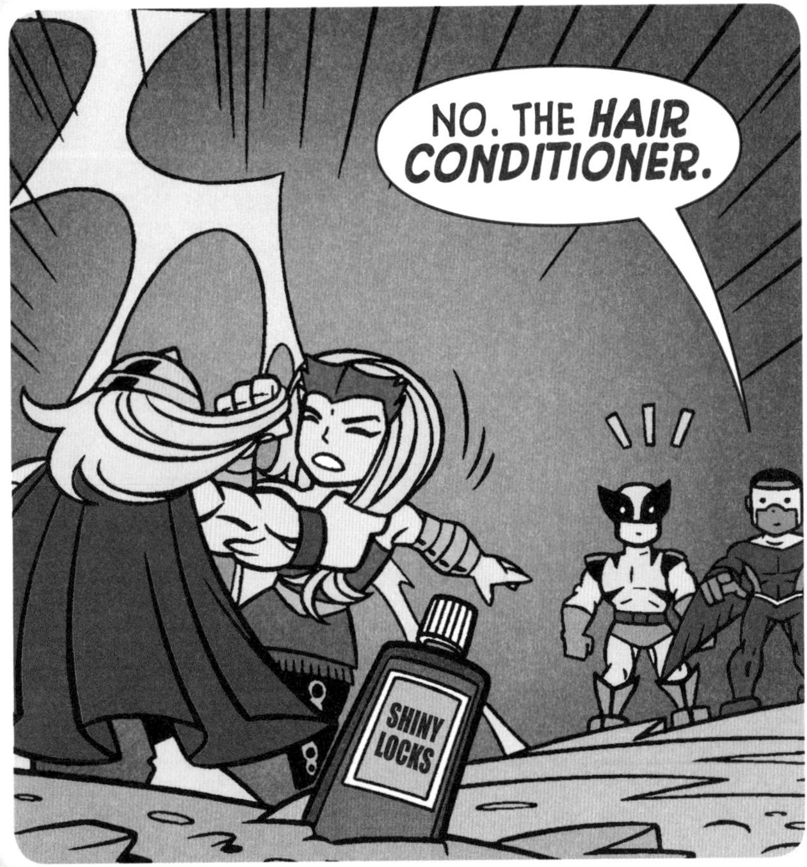
NO. THE HAIR CONDITIONER.
SHINY LOCKS

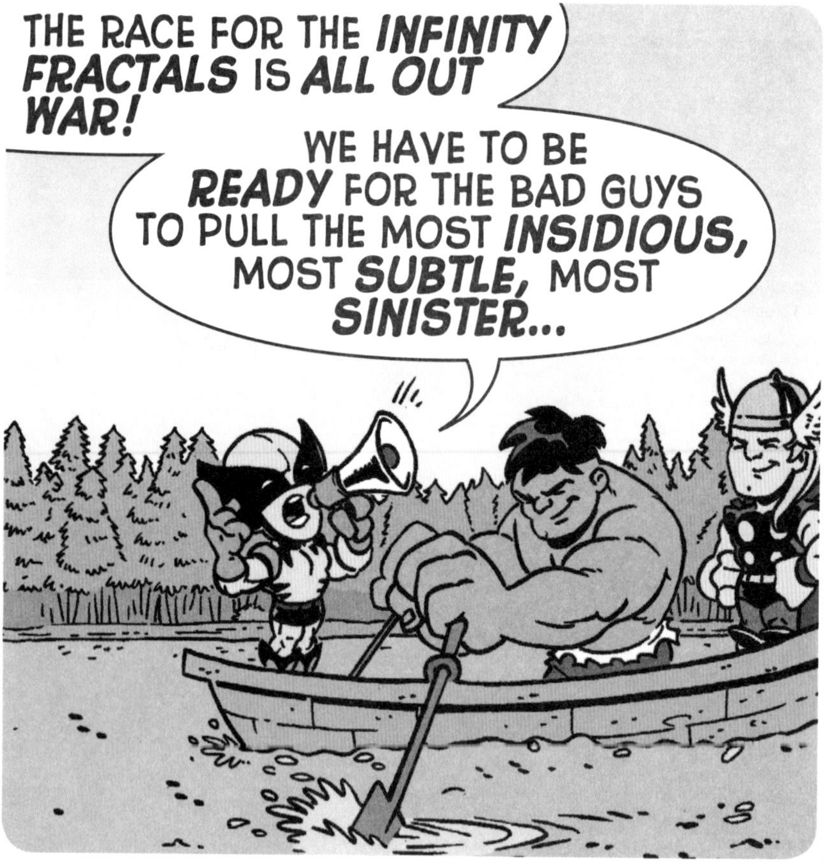
THE RACE FOR THE INFINITY FRACTALS IS ALL OUT WAR!
WE HAVE TO BE READY FOR THE BAD GUYS TO PULL THE MOST INSIDIOUS, MOST SUBTLE, MOST SINISTER...

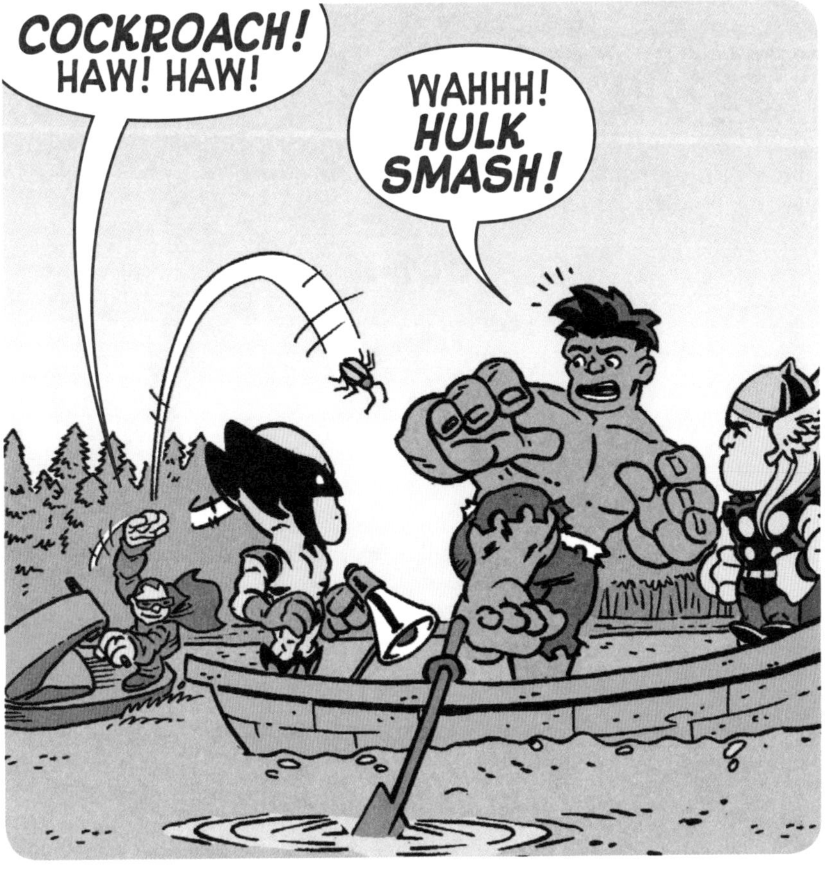
COCKROACH! HAW! HAW!
WAHHH! HULK SMASH!

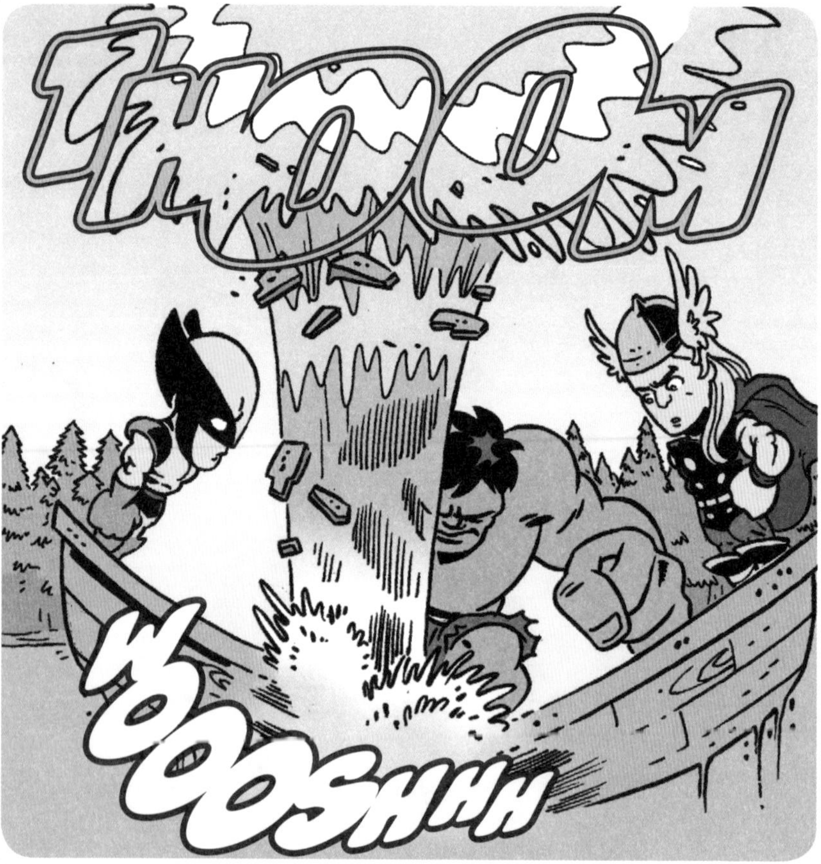
THOOM
WOOOSHHH

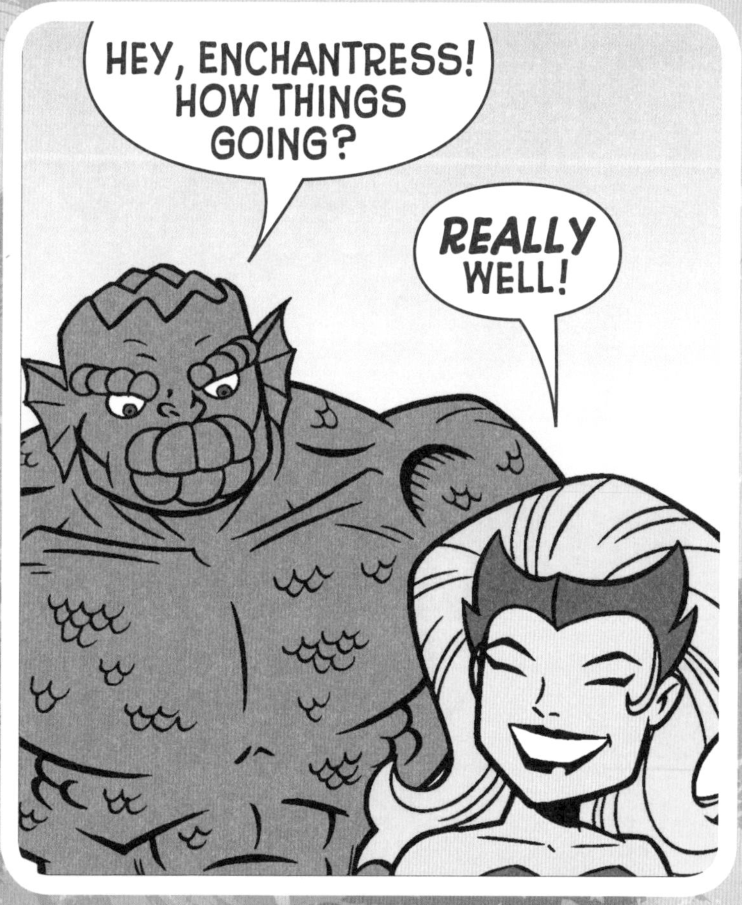
HEY, ENCHANTRESS! HOW THINGS GOING?
REALLY WELL!

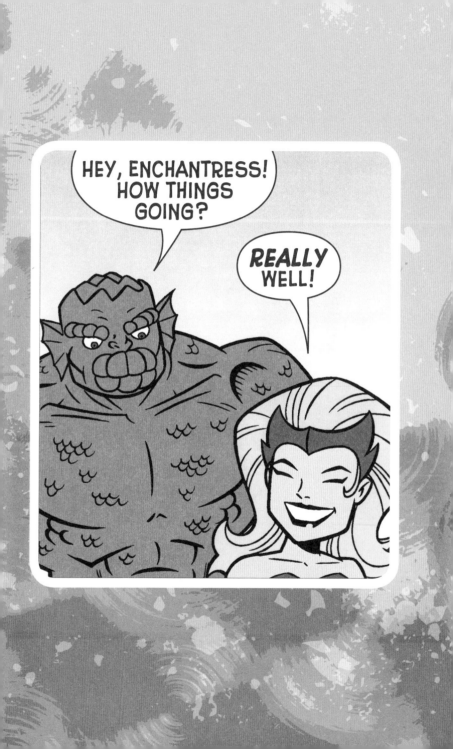

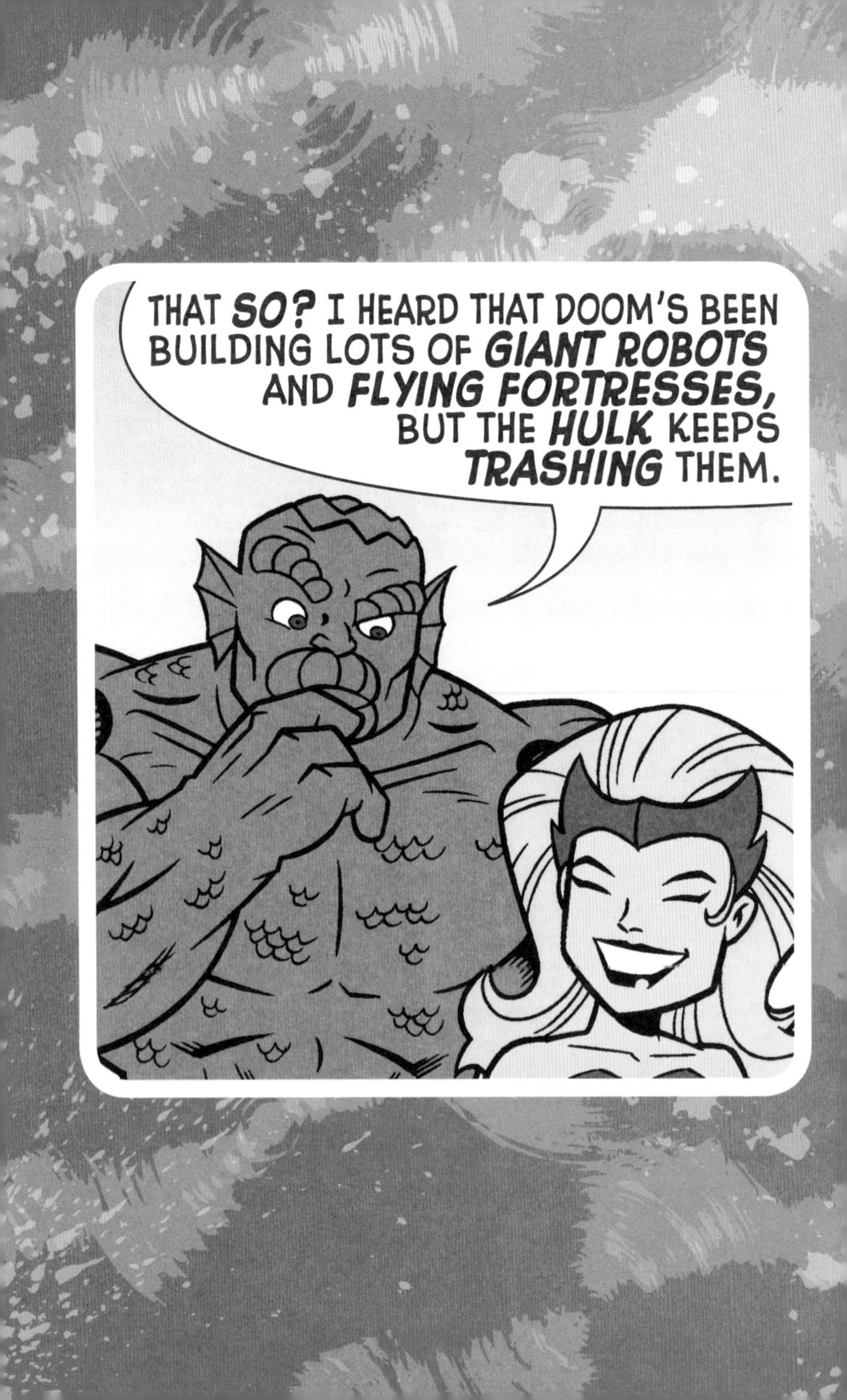
THAT SO? I HEARD THAT DOOM'S BEEN BUILDING LOTS OF GIANT ROBOTS AND FLYING FORTRESSES, BUT THE HULK KEEPS TRASHING THEM.

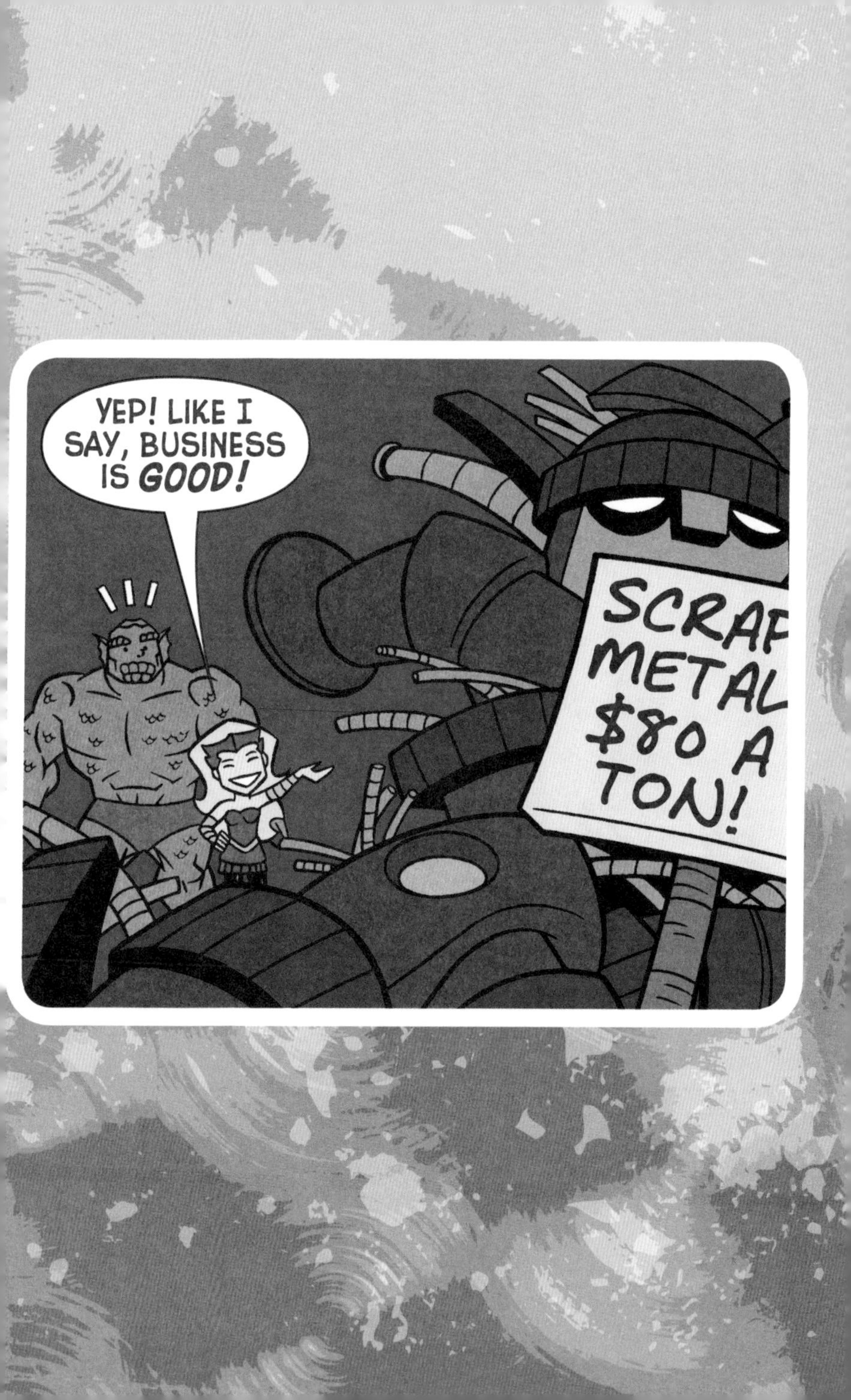
YEP! LIKE I SAY, BUSINESS IS GOOD!
SCRAP METAL $80 A TON!

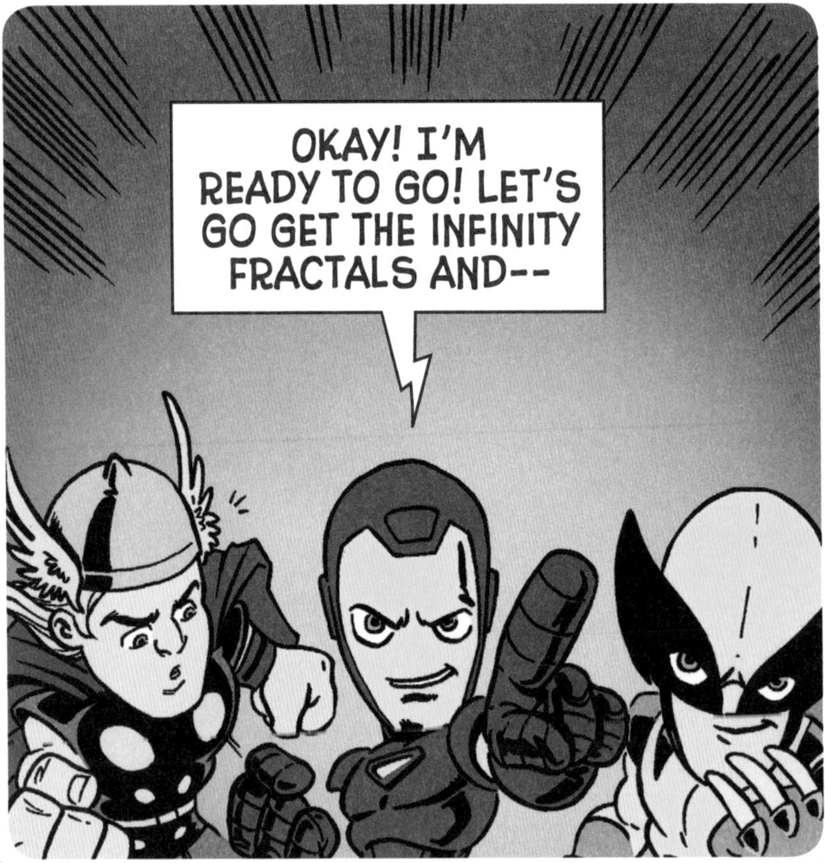
OKAY! I'M READY TO GO! LET'S GO GET THE INFINITY FRACTALS AND--

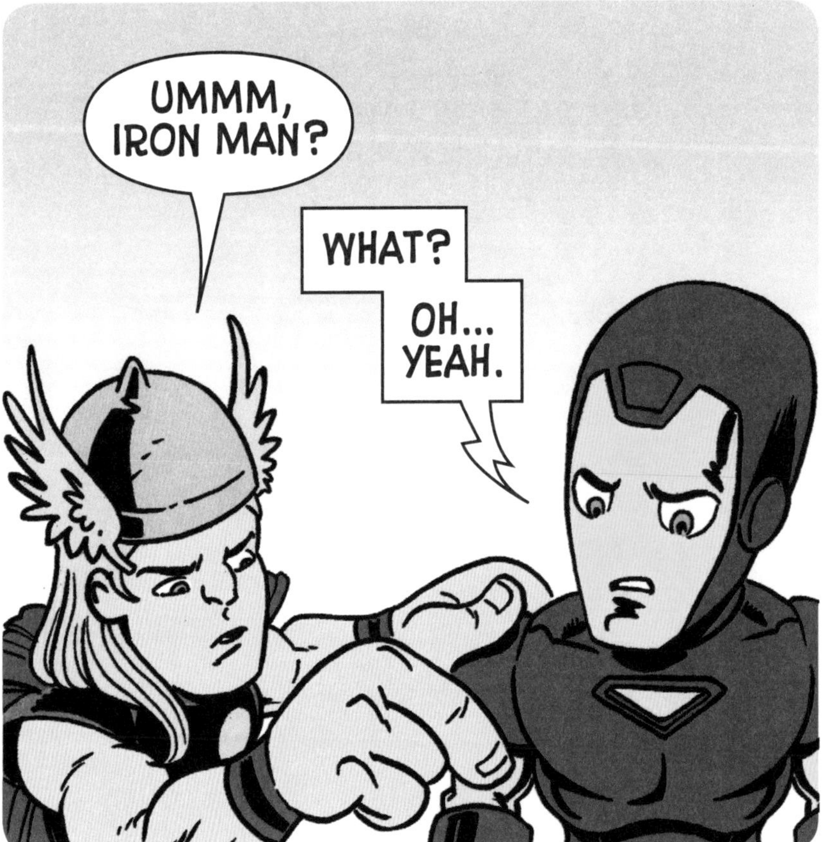
UMMM, IRON MAN?
WHAT?
OH... YEAH.

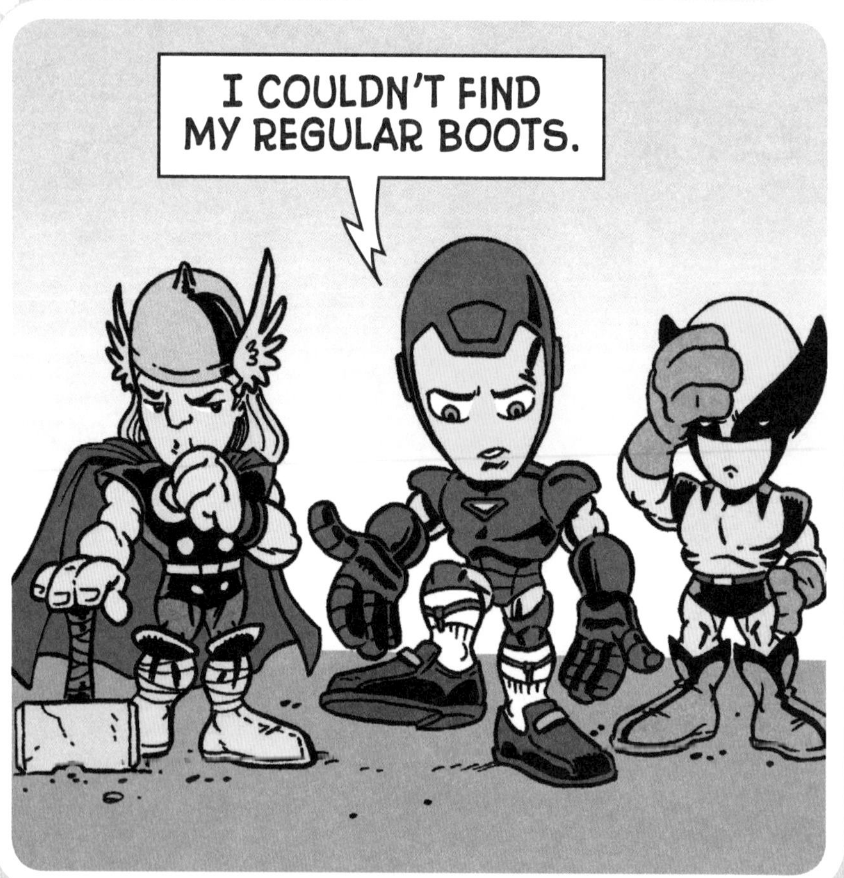
I COULDN'T FIND
MY REGULAR BOOTS.

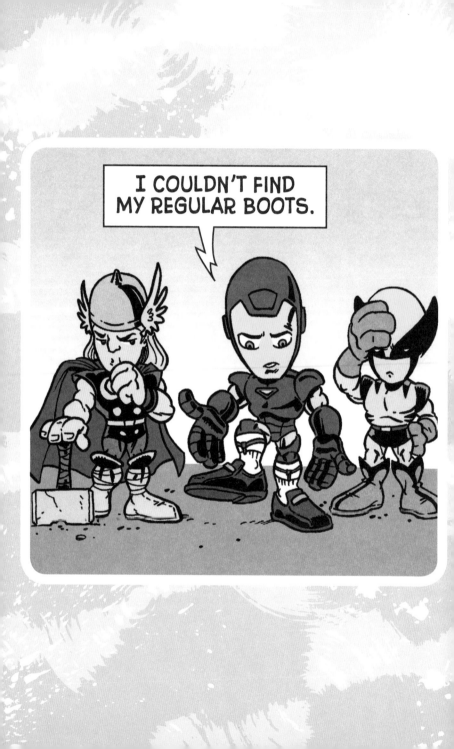

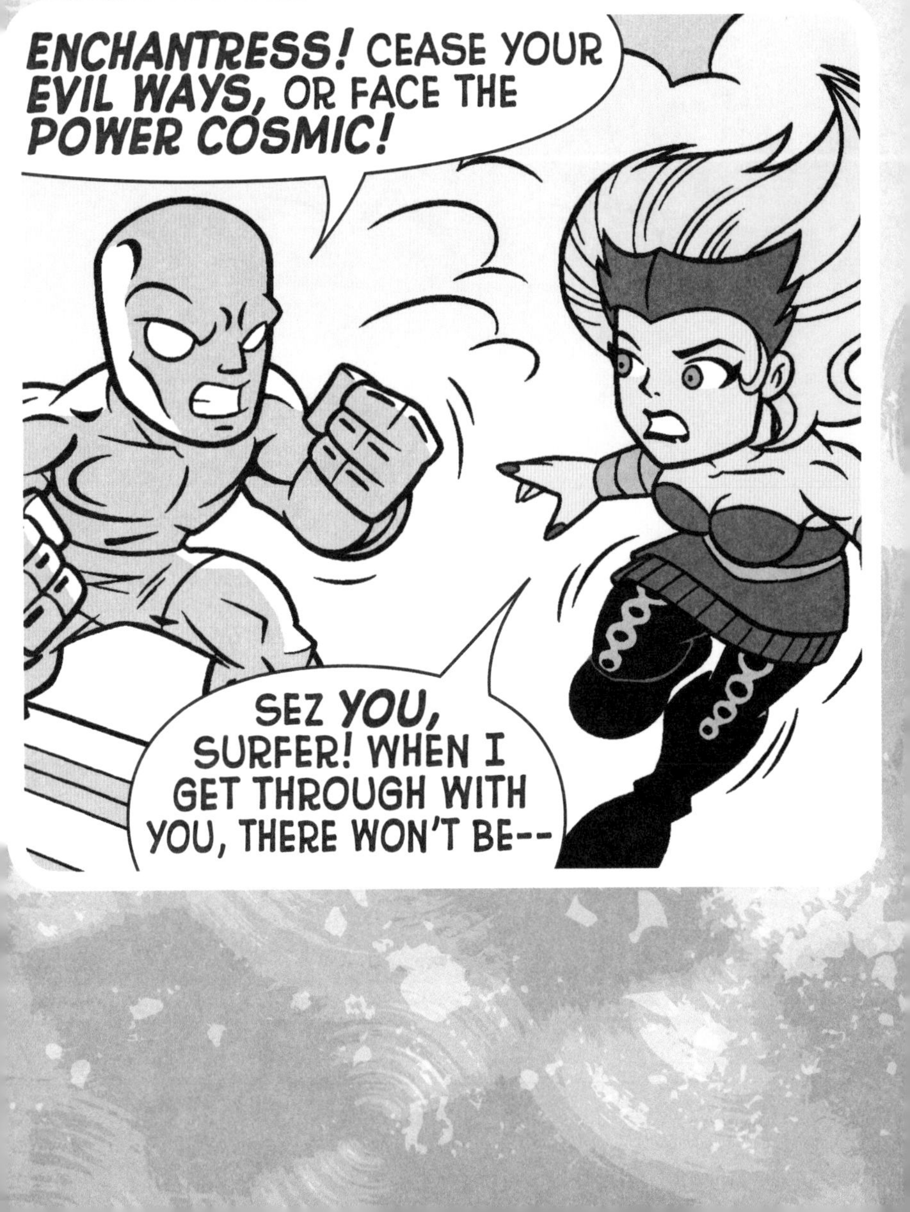
ENCHANTRESS! CEASE YOUR EVIL WAYS, OR FACE THE POWER COSMIC!
SEZ YOU, SURFER! WHEN I GET THROUGH WITH YOU, THERE WON'T BE--

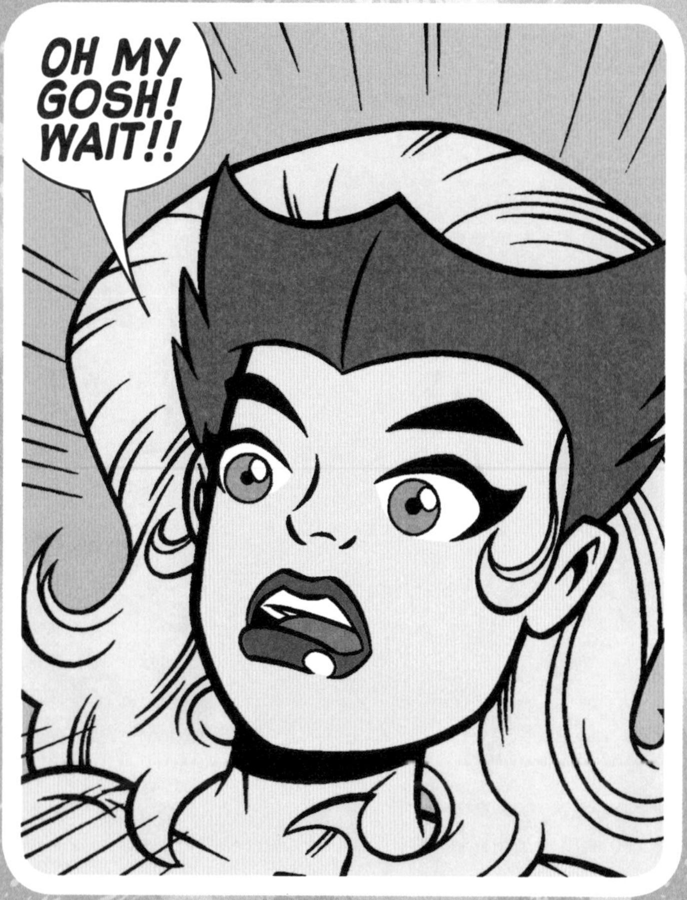
OH MY GOSH! WAIT!!

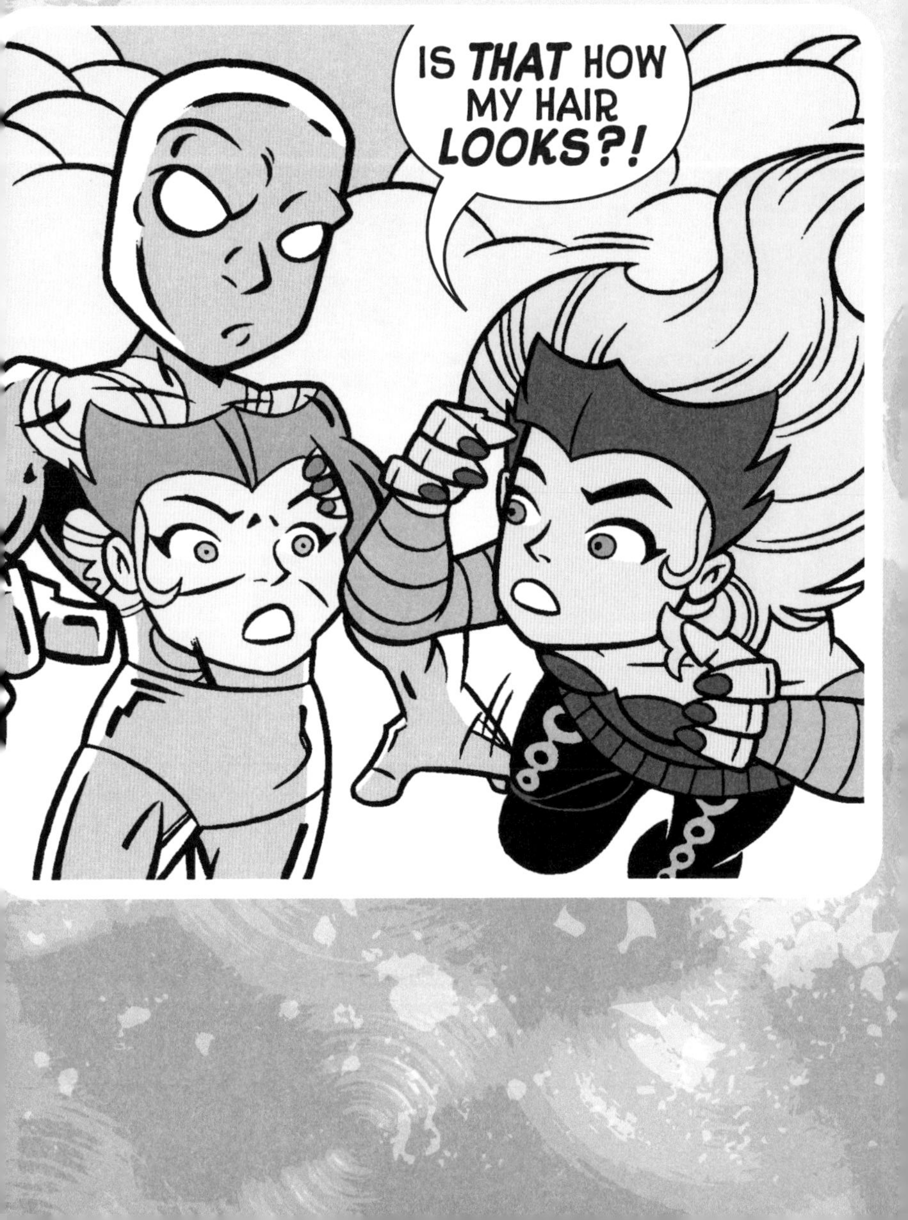
IS THAT HOW MY HAIR LOOKS?!

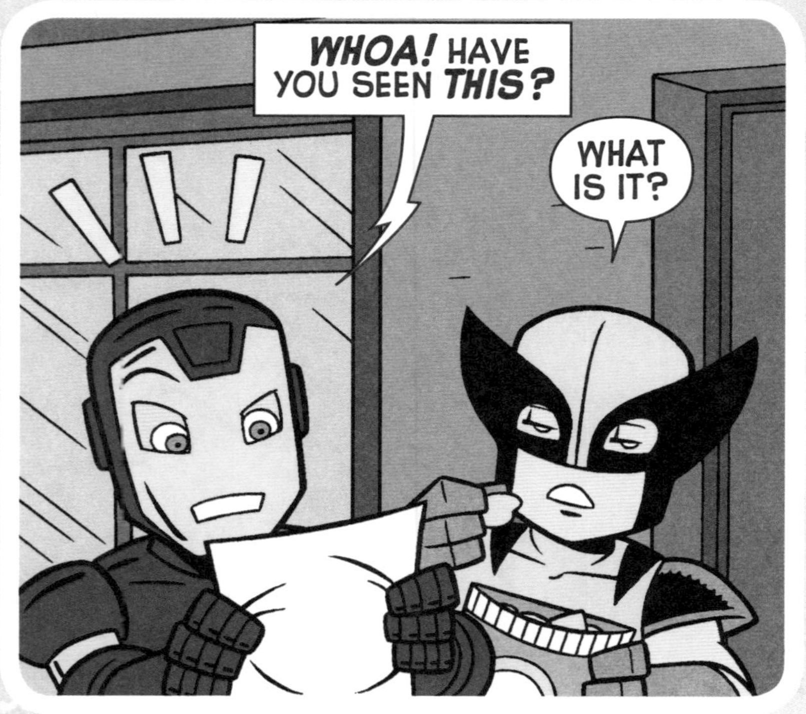
WHOA! HAVE YOU SEEN THIS?
WHAT IS IT?

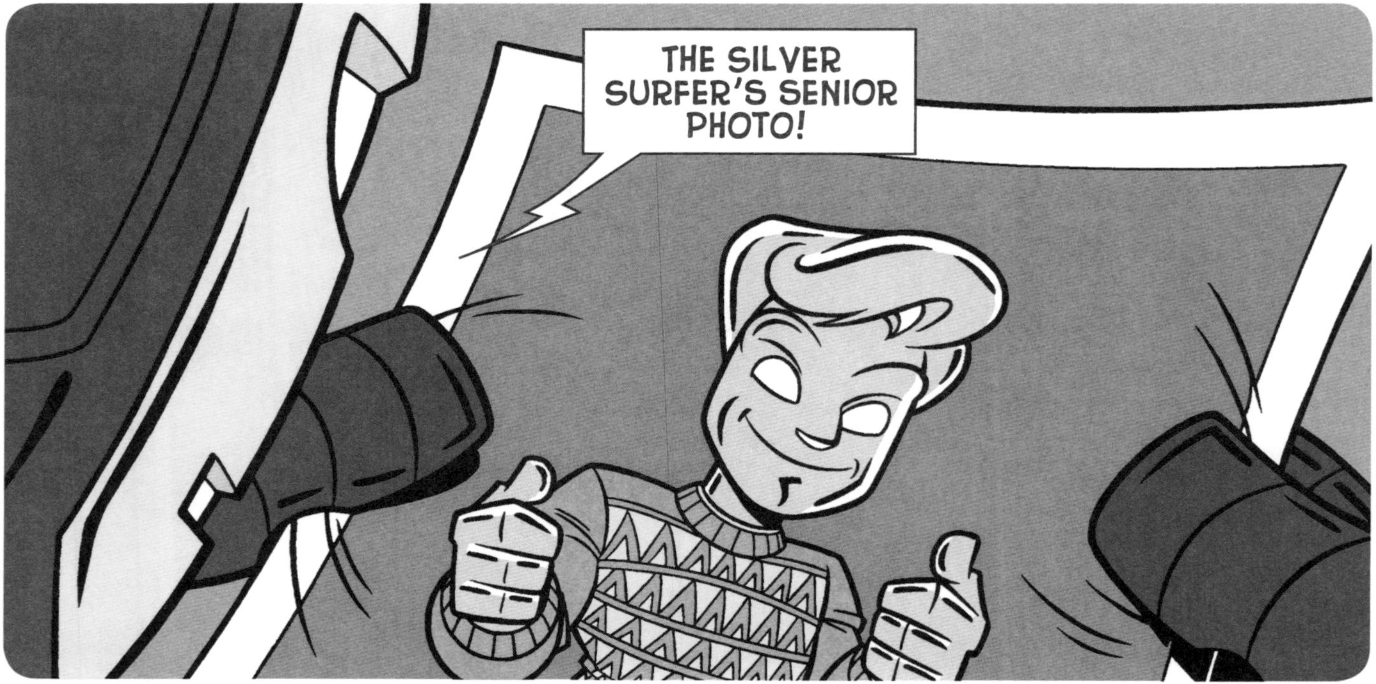
THE SILVER SURFER'S SENIOR PHOTO!

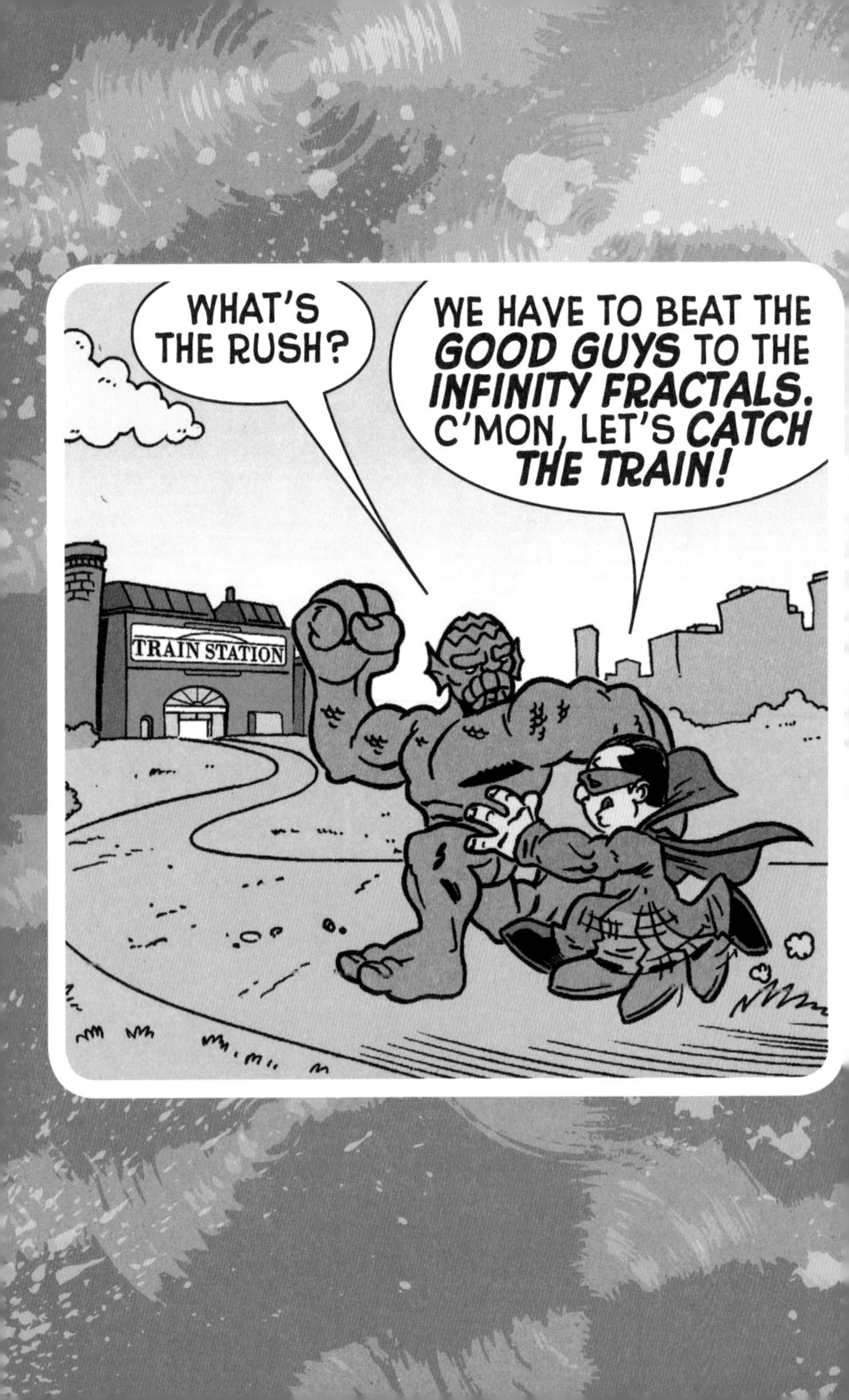
WHAT'S THE RUSH?
WE HAVE TO BEAT THE GOOD GUYS TO THE INFINITY FRACTALS. C'MON, LET'S CATCH THE TRAIN!
TRAIN STATION

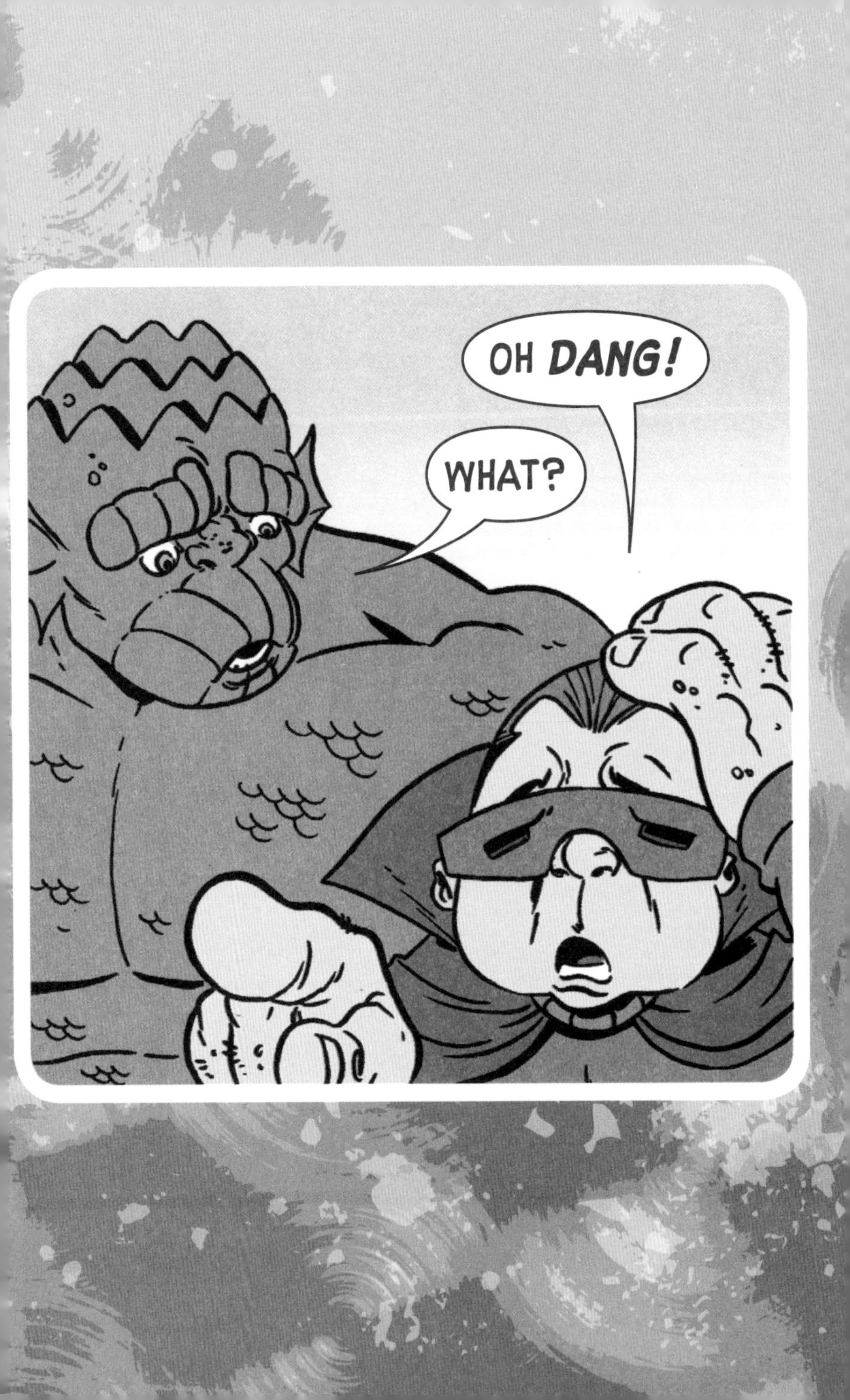
OH DANG!
WHAT?

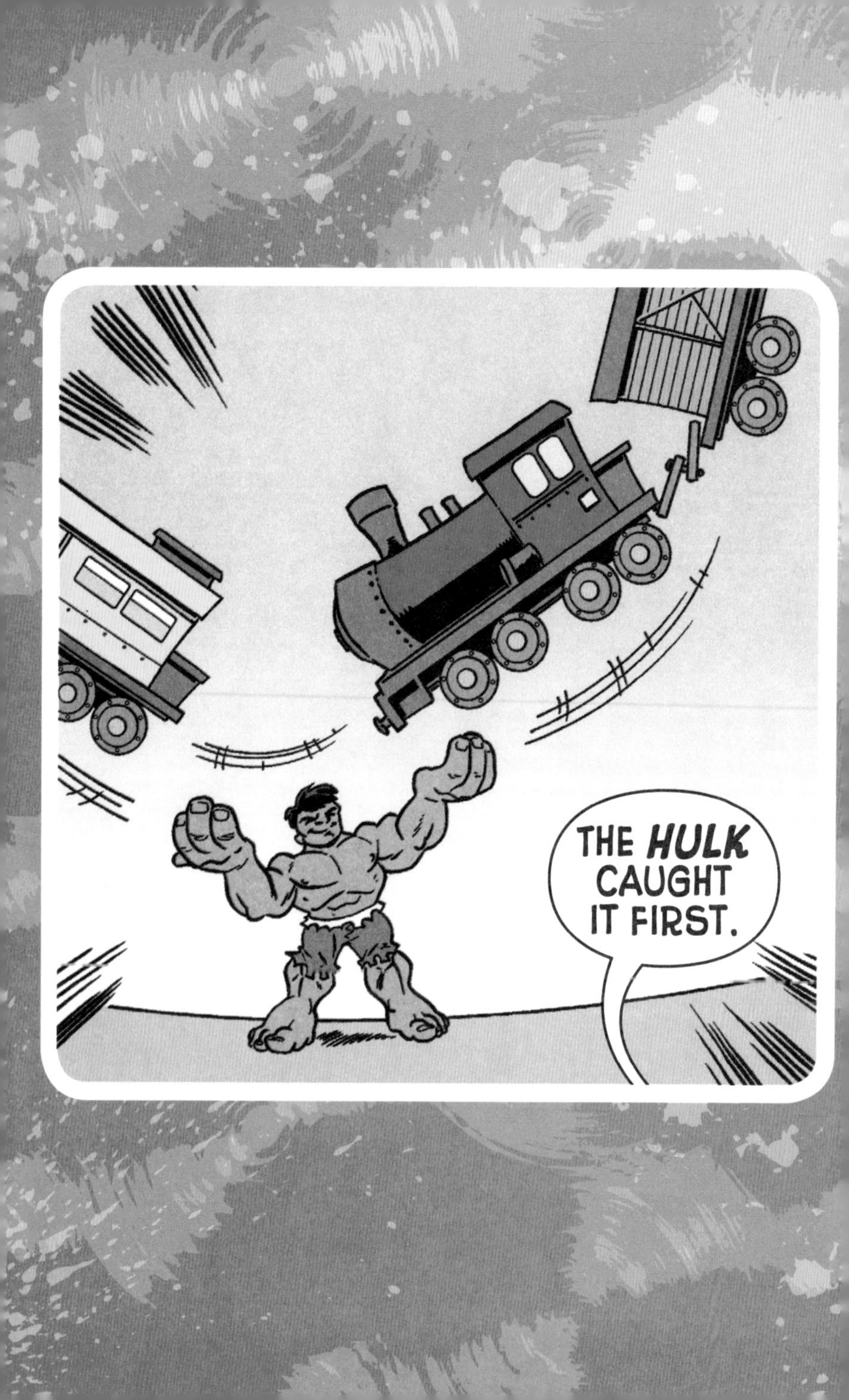
THE HULK CAUGHT IT FIRST.

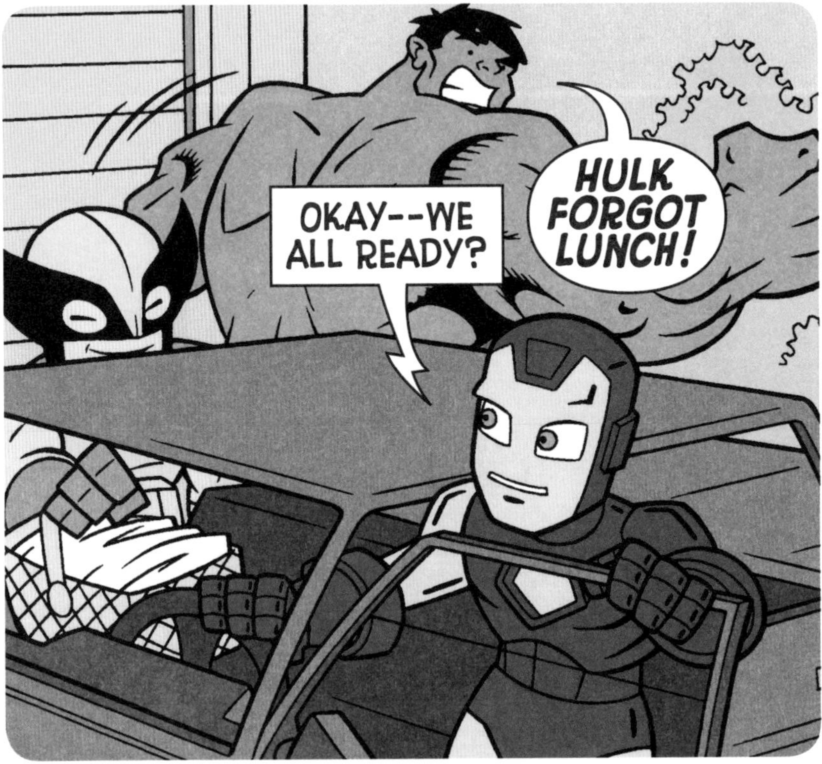
OKAY--WE ALL READY?
HULK FORGOT LUNCH!

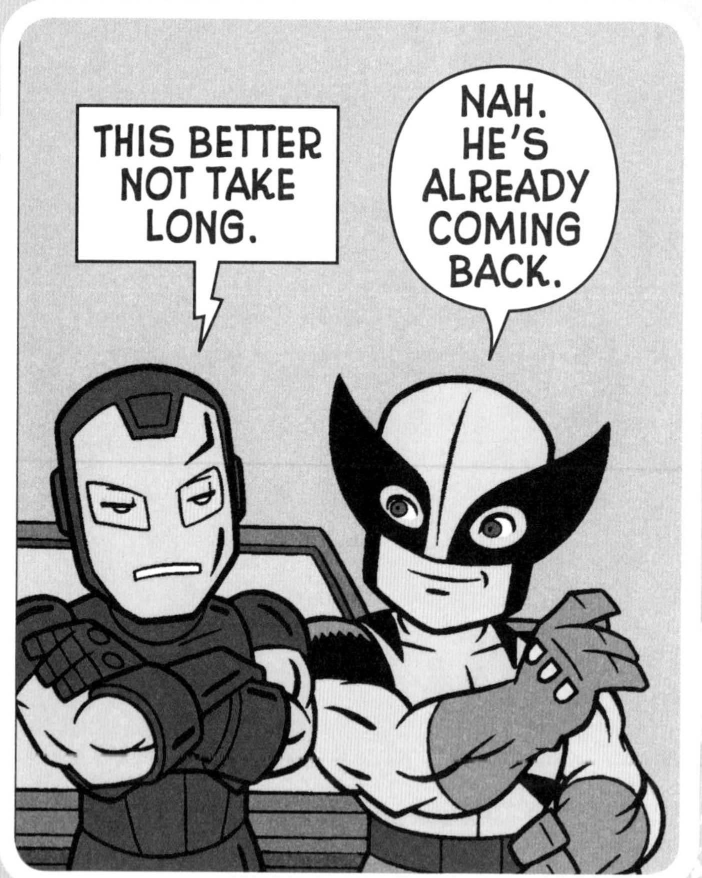
THIS BETTER NOT TAKE LONG.
NAH. HE'S ALREADY COMING BACK.

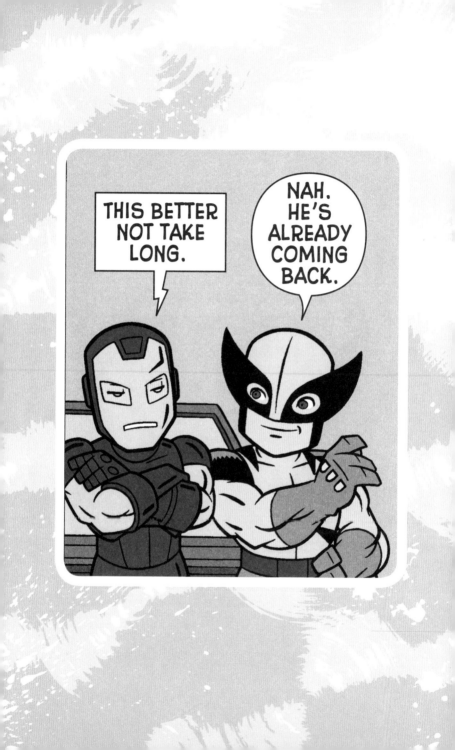

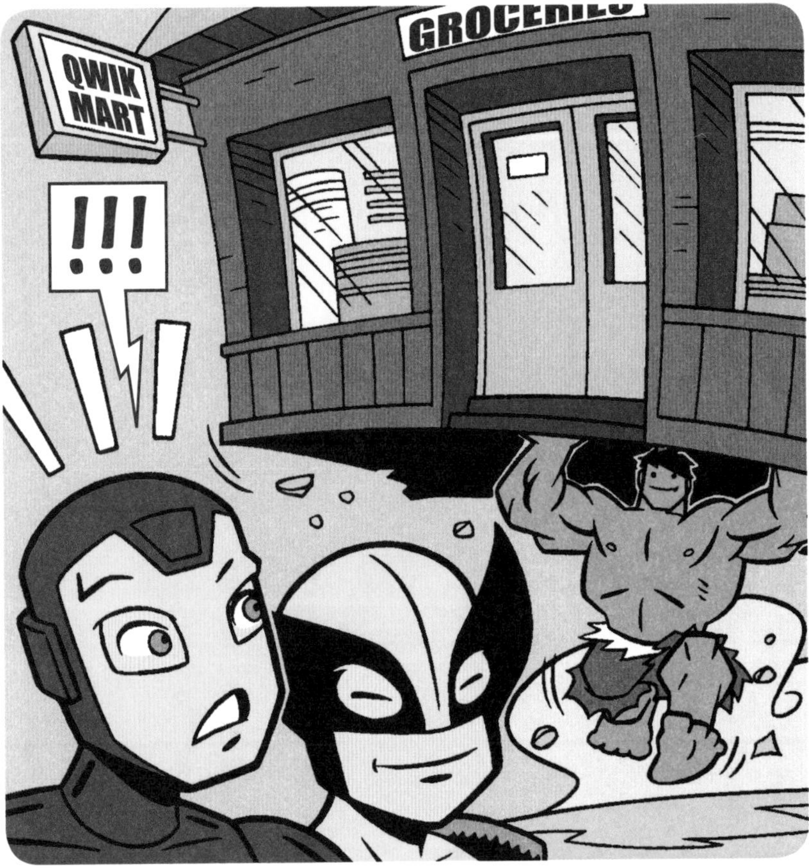
GROCERIES
QWIK MART
!!!

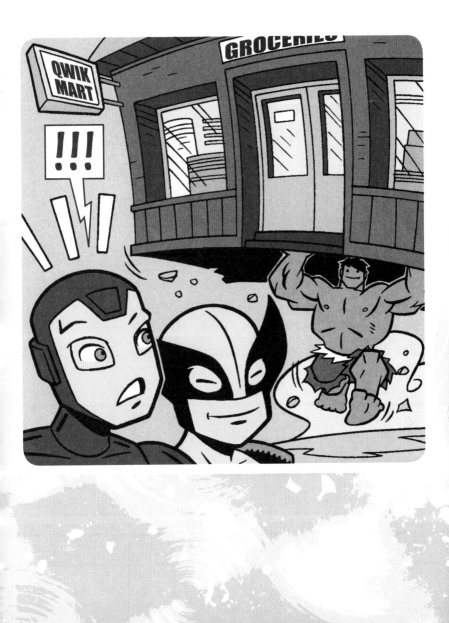

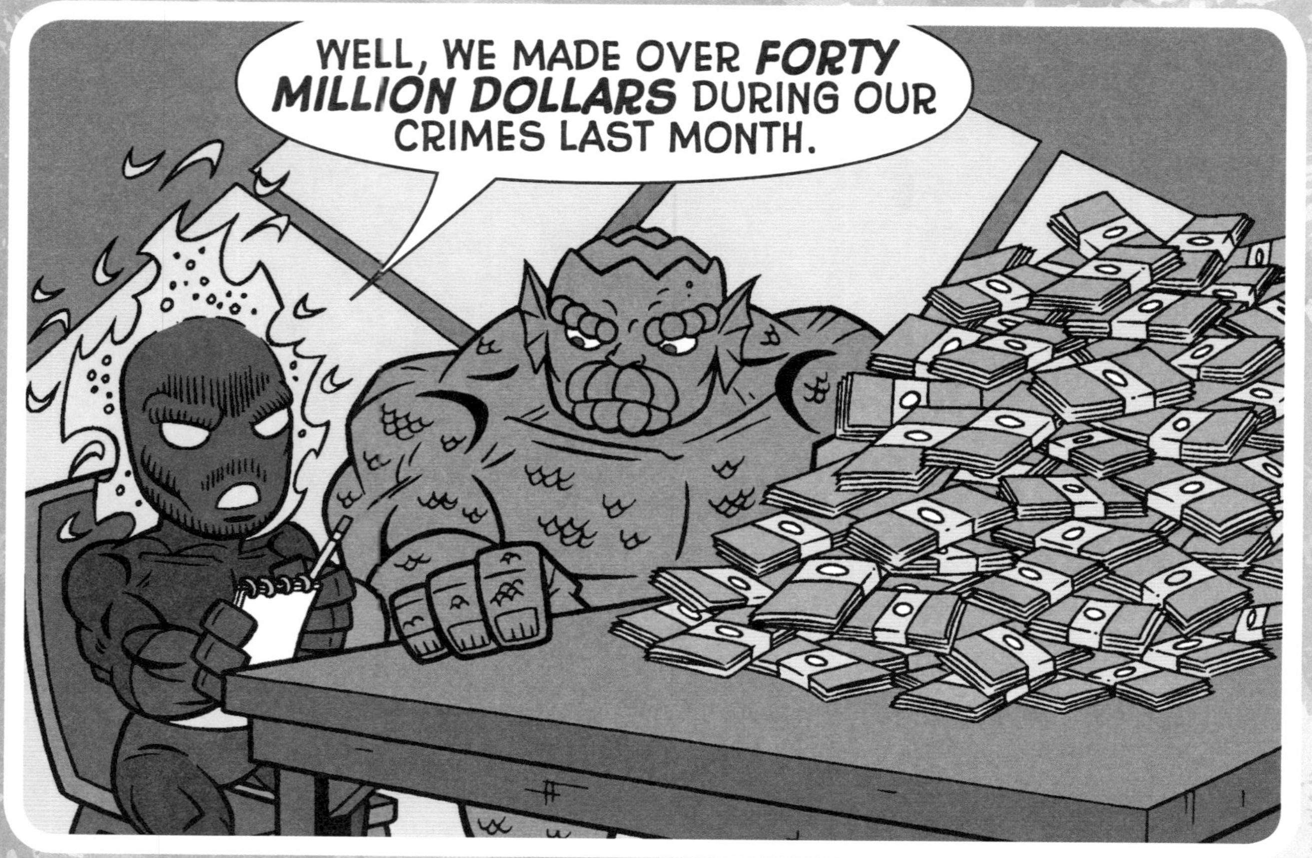
WELL, WE MADE OVER FORTY MILLION DOLLARS DURING OUR CRIMES LAST MONTH.

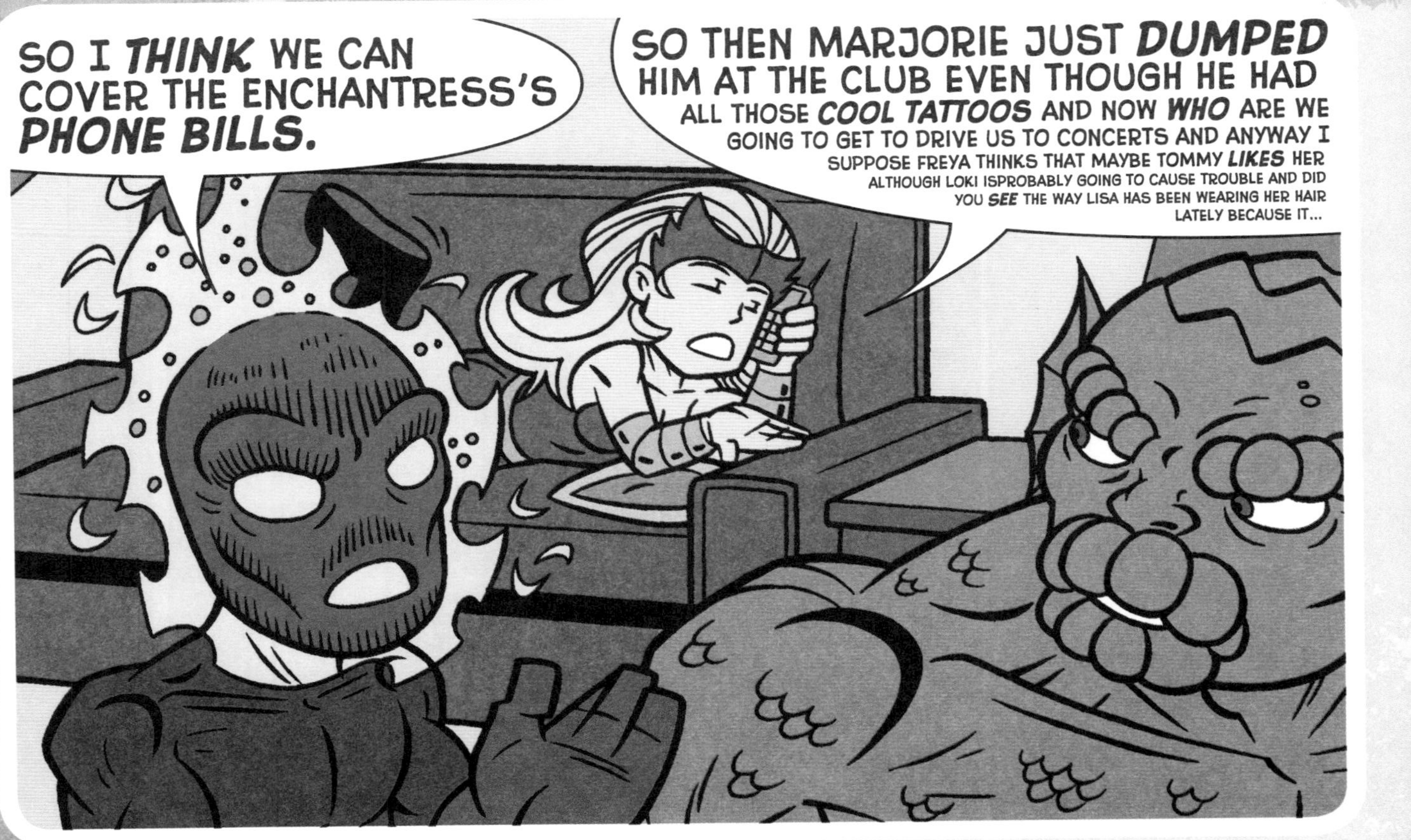
SO I THINK WE CAN COVER THE ENCHANTRESS'S PHONE BILLS.
SO THEN MARJORIE JUST DUMPED HIM AT THE CLUB EVEN THOUGH HE HAD ALL THOSE COOL TATTOOS AND NOW WHO ARE WE GOING TO GET TO DRIVE US TO CONCERTS AND ANYWAY I SUPPOSE FREYA THINKS THAT MAYBE TOMMY LIKES HER ALTHOUGH LOKI ISPROBABLY GOING TO CAUSE TROUBLE AND DID YOU SEE THE WAY LISA HAS BEEN WEARING HER HAIR LATELY BECAUSE IT...

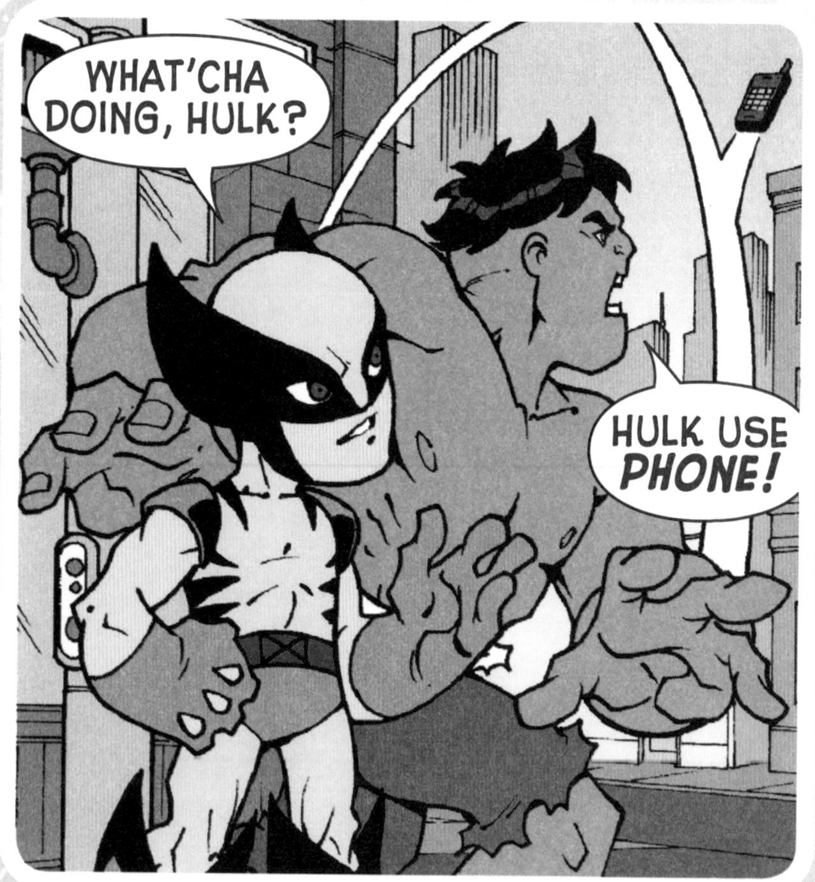
WHAT'CHA DOING, HULK?
HULK USE PHONE!

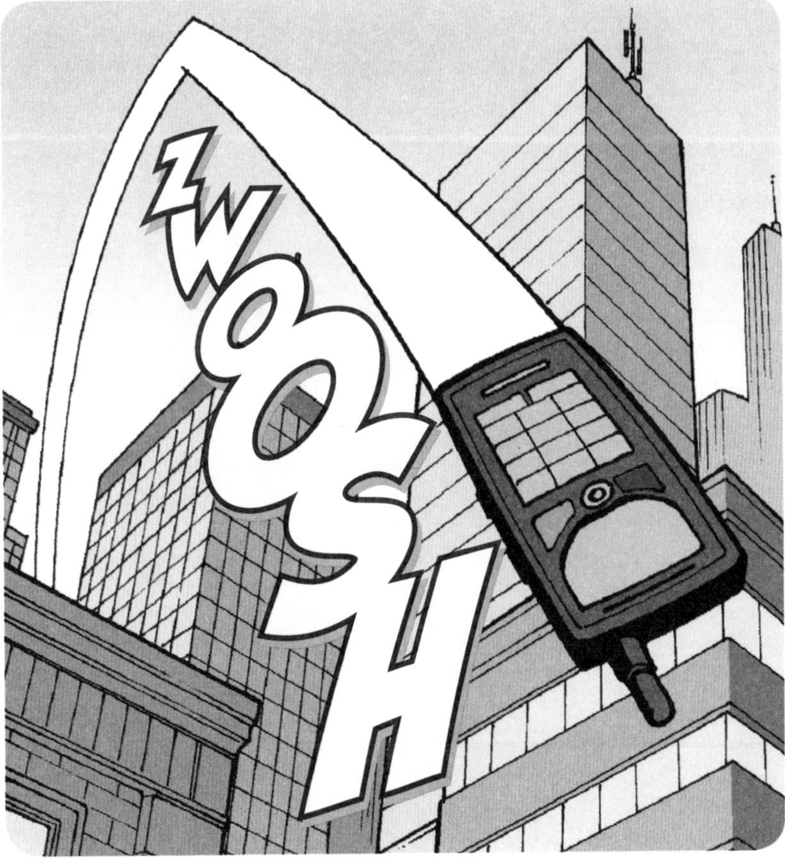
ZWOOSH

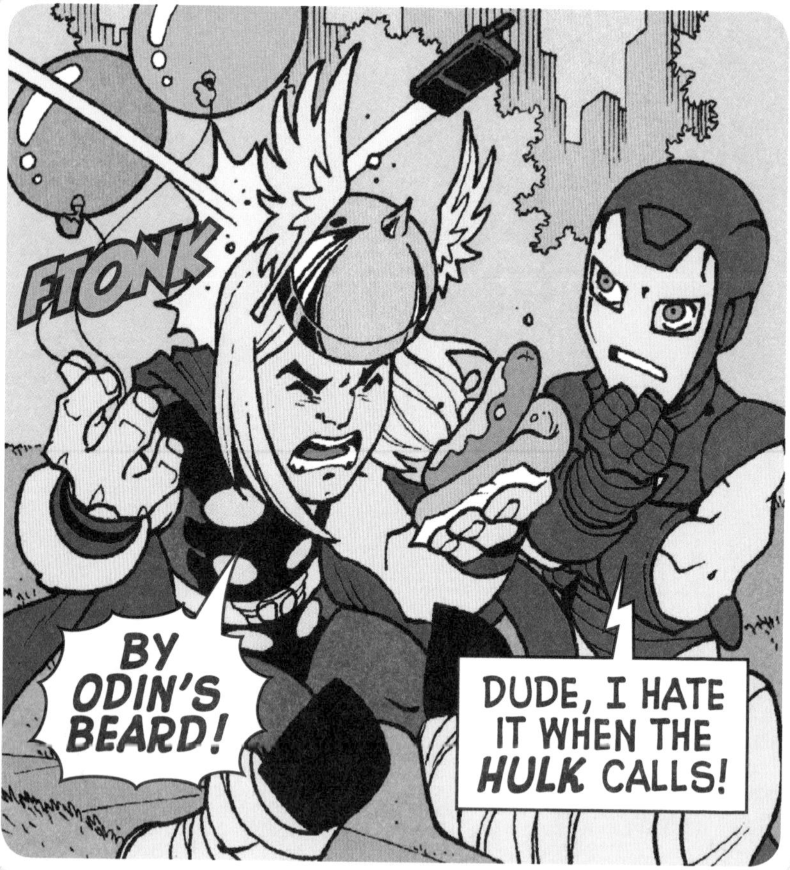
FTONK
BY ODIN'S BEARD!
DUDE, I HATE IT WHEN THE HULK CALLS!

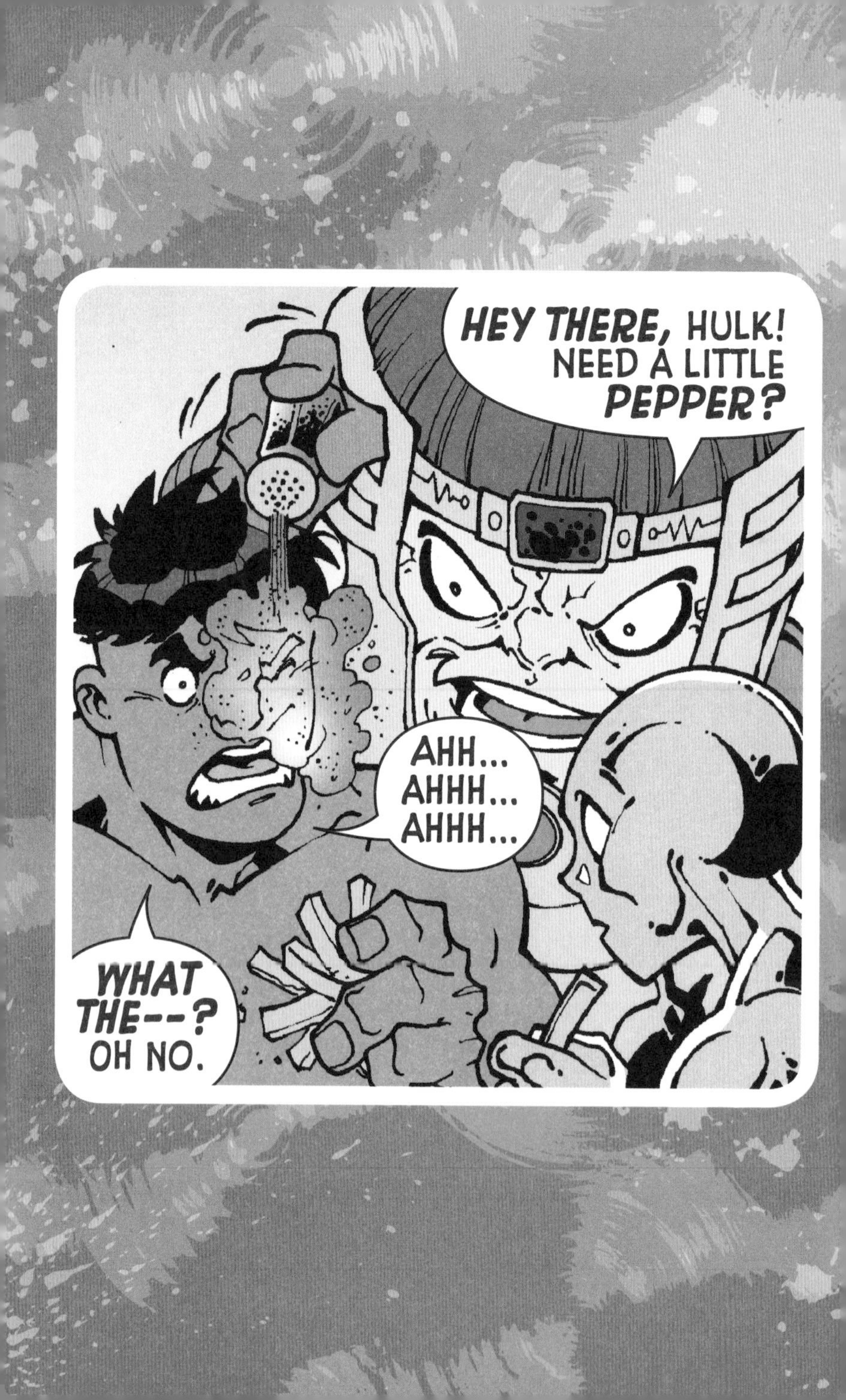
HEY THERE, HULK! NEED A LITTLE PEPPER?
AHH... AHHH... AHHH...
WHAT THE--? OH NO.

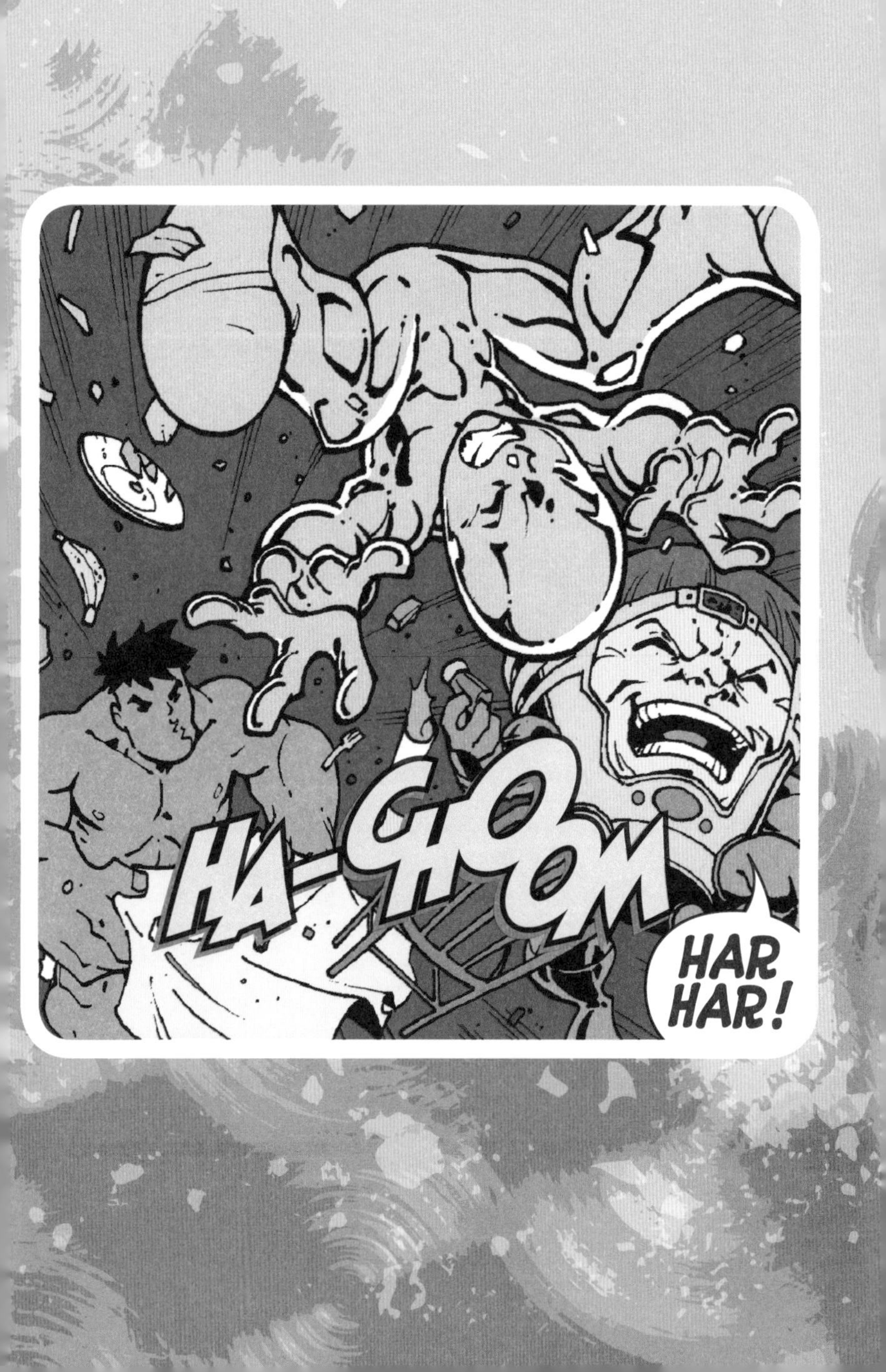
HA-CHOOM
HAR HAR!

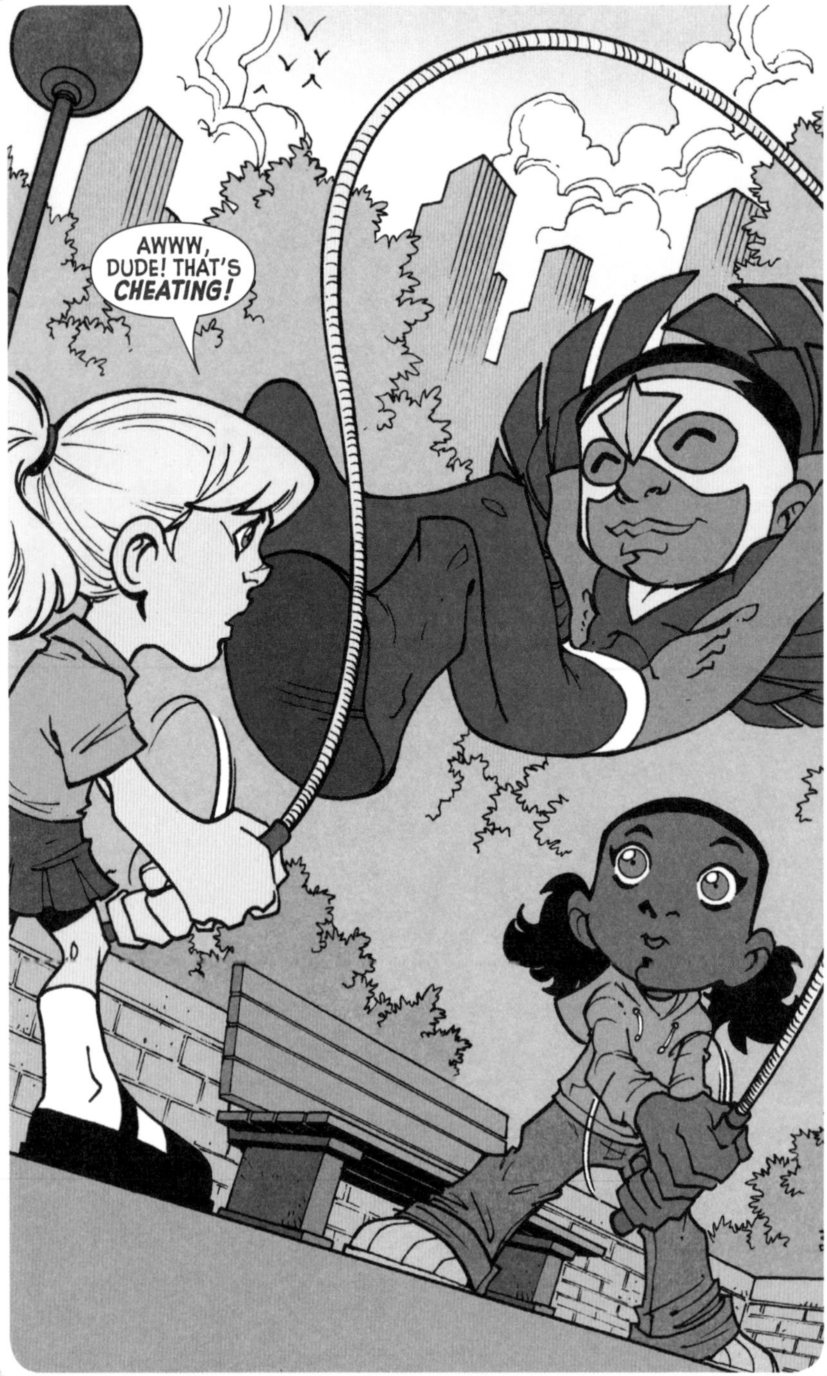
AWWW, DUDE! THAT'S CHEATING!